Mrs. Claus and the Trouble with Turkeys

Liz Ireland

Kensington Publishing Corp.
www.kensingtonbooks.com

Books by Liz Ireland

MRS. CLAUS AND THE SANTALAND SLAYINGS

MRS. CLAUS AND THE HALLOWEEN HOMICIDE

MRS. CLAUS AND THE EVIL ELVES

MRS. CLAUS AND THE TROUBLE WITH TURKEYS

HALLOWEEN CUPCAKE MURDER
(with Carlene O'Connor and Carol J. Perry)

Published by Kensington Publishing Corp.

Mrs. Claus and the Trouble with Turkeys

Chapter 1

Gobbles had vanished.

When I looked inside the fancy turkey cage Salty the groundskeeper had built just outside Castle Kringle, the wrong bird stared back at me.

"Grimstock."

The vulture was the result of a mix-up that had occurred when Butterbean the elf, in anticipation of Santaland's first Thanksgiving, sent off for a live bird from a scam turkey-by-mail company. Eventually an actual live turkey had been procured and installed in the cage to be fattened up for the big day, but due to a strict no-returns policy Grimstock remained stuck in Santaland. Now it looked as if, like a cuckoo, he had managed to push the turkey out of its cushy nest. Gobbles wasn't there.

"Someone's stolen Gobbles," Salty and Jingles blurted at me in unison.

Their words landed in my ears like a Greek chorus of Thanksgiving doom. One thing I'd learned in my first years as Mrs. Claus was that even the most festive holiday was bound to have a few troubling hiccups, and turkey theft—if Gobbles truly had been stolen—was a bad omen for Santaland's first-ever Thanksgiving celebration.

"Stolen him?" I asked. "Why would you say that?"

Both elves sounded upset, but by far the most visibly distraught was Salty, who stood red-eyed, twisting his cap in his hands. Even his large ears seemed to droop. "What else could have happened?" he asked. "The cage was locked."

More caustically, Jingles added, "The bird didn't just decide to let himself out and go for a stroll." Castle Kringle's steward was Salty's opposite, fastidious in his castle uniform of red tunic and green piping, with a matching cap.

I nodded toward the buzzard, who stared at us defiantly. "If the cage was locked, how did Grimstock get in?"

"We let him stay in the cage if he wants to," Salty said. "He's good company for Gobbles."

It was hard to imagine Grimstock being good company. The red-headed buzzard with his feathery cowl and long, white-tipped beak resembled a turkey's evil cousin. "Do they really get along?"

"Oh sure," Salty said. "Well, about as well as Grimstock gets along with anybody. He's not the friendliest of birds." In a lower voice, he added, "He doesn't have Gobbles's pleasing personality."

Grimstock might like Gobbles, but he obviously hadn't been inclined to follow his wattled buddy to freedom, or to a different captivity, or wherever Gobbles had gone to.

The other elf present with us out in the cold by the fowl house—Felice, the castle cook—had been annoyed since the Thanksgiving scheme had been floated. It had taken some persuasion to get her on board with roasting a kind of giant bird she'd never laid eyes on, but now she was irritated that her careful meal planning might be thrown for a loop. "It was bad enough having to figure out how to cook all the things on the ridiculous menu Butterbean gave me. *Now* what am I supposed to do?"

With tears in his eyes, Salty rounded on her. "How can you be so heartless? Gobbles is *missing*."

She planted her hands on her ample hips. "He's a bird— and a bird marked for death, at that."

A tear trickled down Salty's cheek, which gave me pause. Gobbles had only been on the castle grounds for a few weeks, but during that brief time the bird and his elf keeper had apparently developed a close bond. The thought crossed my mind that Salty might have him cached away somewhere until after Thanksgiving dinner . . . except the elf seemed genuinely upset about not knowing his charge's whereabouts.

"Now, let's not talk about death." Jingles's white-gloved fingers drummed on the soft pot belly against his livery tunic. "Thanksgiving is about gratitude and joy, not death."

"You should ask this turkey everyone's so fond of about that," the cook grumbled. "How much joy will he feel when his neck's on the chopping block?"

"Felice, please." I nodded toward an increasingly upset Salty. The words *chopping block* nearly caused him to swoon.

"I just want to know what I'm supposed to do with all the turkey fixings and no turkey," the cook huffed in frustration. "I've spent two weeks hunting down recipes. We were going to have turducken. Now what am I supposed to do? Goose-ducken?"

"A nice walrus steak is always my family's go-to for special occasions," Salty suggested.

"Wal-ducken?" That sounded less than appetizing to me.

Felice glowered at us. "I've got ten pounds of cranberries ready to sauce. I can't see eating cranberry sauce with walrus, can you?"

"No," I said, happy to put the notion of a holiday meal of walrus to rest.

Her face contorted in thought. "I suppose there's always musk ox roast."

My heart sank. Musk ox *again*?

A feast is about more than food. And of course, Felice was a fantastic cook, and her musk ox roast was to die for—but my taste buds were primed for a traditional turkey dinner, like the ones I'd grown up eating in the United States. Turkey, stuffing, sweet potato casserole, three kinds of pie . . .

And to think I'd actually hesitated when Jingles and Butterbean had floated the idea of having a Thanksgiving feast at the castle. Importing American customs to Santaland hadn't always worked out well, but Butterbean, who was nearing the end of his first year working at Castle Kringle, had taken charge. Every day it seemed that Santaland Postal Express delivered holiday goodies to the castle's service door: the aforementioned cranberries, pecans for pie, a crate of yams, and—most important of all—Gobbles.

Now it appeared that the castle's celebration was unraveling even as Thanksgiving was taking hold everywhere else in Santaland. Once the elves in Christmastown had gotten wind of the castle's celebration, they'd launched plans of their own. Twinkle's Fried Pie shop had collected and cooked down enough of the town's leftover Halloween pumpkins to supply the whole land with pies and pumpkin pie filling. Bella Sparkletoe, who owned Sparkletoe's Mercantile, read about the Macy's Thanksgiving Day Parade and now everyone was in a frenzy of preparation for the Sparkletoe's Thanksgiving Day Parade down Festival Boulevard in Christmastown, which would include floats, a marching band, a giant helium balloon, and of course, Santa on his sleigh pulled by nine reindeer.

Santaland's parade had one advantage over New York City's: We had the real Santa Claus. My husband, Nick, wasn't wild about inserting a big celebration right as Santaland was gearing up for the big Christmas push, but I sold him on the idea by assuring him that it would just be a one-day disruption. Then the Events Committee decided that having the parade the day *before* Thanksgiving made more sense, given that everyone would be busy cooking and visiting on Thanksgiving Thursday. So the one-day celebration had morphed into two days . . . and then another Thanksgiving event had cropped up.

Nick was the only Claus who lacked enthusiasm for the new holiday. His cousin, Amory, and his wife, Midge, were planning their own pre-Thanksgiving feast—a potluck, no less—up at Kringle Lodge at the summit of Sugarplum Mountain. "To kick off Thanksgiving week," Amory had said when he extended the invitation. I'd tried to explain that Thanksgiving was a single belt-popping meal. But in Santaland, celebrations are never done in a small way.

Amory discovered that Americans sometimes took as much as a week off. "They must eat *something* in all that time." He'd vowed to leave the turkey dinner for Thursday's feasting but promised to make his pre-Thanksgiving event special in other ways.

Now, though, the castle's turkey had flown the coop. Or he'd been stolen.

Who would steal a turkey?

Felice sized up Grimstock and pointed at him with a wooden spoon. "What about him?"

The bird's red, leathery head poked higher out of its feathery cowl neck. He let out a guttural hiss.

"We are not serving buzzard to our Thanksgiving guests," I said.

Felice's lips screwed up. "Don't come complaining to me about having roast musk ox again, then."

I wasn't giving up on Gobbles quite yet. "Where was the bird last seen?" I asked Salty.

"Right here in this cage."

"Cage? It's more like a turkey chalet." Felice shook her head. "I'm too busy to bother over a missing bird. Let me know if he shows up."

She stomped away.

"I don't see what's so wrong with providing a nice cage," Salty said. "Gobbles is an honored guest."

Honored and doomed.

And now gone.

I peered at the cage. Come to think of it, it *did* look a little like a chalet. The structure was made of wood frame and glass, with a vaulted roof that allowed for easy movement to care for Gobbles. Easy elf movement, that is—I was a foot taller than the average elf and had to duck my head inside of it. Given how cold it was at the North Pole, the turkey house was heated enough that Grimstock had his wings extended to cool himself. Fresh wood shavings were strewn all around, giving the bird dwelling a surprisingly clean smell.

"Well, I can see now why you think Gobbles didn't leave on his own," I said, inspecting the digs with an almost envious eye. "No bird in his right mind would abandon such nice accommodations."

"We should call Constable Crinkles," Salty said. "Don't they always say that the first twenty-four hours after someone goes missing are the most crucial?"

I wasn't sure that Constable Crinkles would be that great a help in this instance. Santaland's premier lawman wasn't famed for his investigative prowess. "Maybe before we alert the law, we should make double sure Gobbles isn't around here somewhere."

Jingles nodded. "I'll have Butterbean direct a thorough, castle-wide search just as soon as he gets back."

"Back from where?" I asked.

"He's picking up some helium canisters for his parade balloon," Jingles said.

I frowned. "Does Butterbean know about helium balloons?"

Jingles waved a hand. "Oh, Butterbean knows about *everything*. It's amazing the things he comes up with."

Butterbean had come up with some questionable projects in the past, but since he was the mastermind behind Santaland Thanksgiving, I was willing to cut him some slack. It was he who had found Gobbles online and ordered him—not without a hitch, of course. I didn't fault him too much for that. Grimstock had turned out to be more of a curiosity than a nuisance.

"If anyone can locate Gobbles, it's Butterbean," Jingles said.

I lacked his confidence. Castle Kringle and its grounds were vast enough for a whole flock of turkeys to get lost in. The castle rose behind us like something out of a Bavarian fairy tale. Its gray walls, towers, and turrets had the perfect backdrop of Sugarplum Mountain, which overlooked picturesque Christmastown in the valley below. One wing of the castle, the Old Keep, was unused now, but even in the "modern" section I still occasionally stumbled across a room or stairwell new to me, and I'd lived there for over two years.

Of course, for a turkey to have gotten *into* the castle would indicate that he really had been stolen—either by someone on the staff or a Claus family member. That seemed unlikely, too.

I floated another possibility. "Maybe someone just accidentally left the cage open, and Gobbles wandered off."

Ever since the word of the live turkey's arrival had spread in Santaland, people curious about the bird had trekked up Sugarplum Mountain from Christmastown and sometimes from the even more distant elf sister village of Tinkertown to get a glimpse of him. That was why it was impossible to tell from the ground near the cage who might have taken him.

The snow outside the turkey chalet was covered in bootie prints.

"It was locked," Salty said.

"Someone could have locked it after Gobbles was gone without seeing that he wasn't inside," Jingles said.

"If he wandered off," I said, "it's the grounds we should be searching, not the interior of the castle."

Salty shuddered. "I hate to think of what could happen to him alone outside."

I hunched in my puffy coat. Like Gobbles, I was from "the south"—what Santalanders called any place below the arctic circle. "He probably doesn't like the cold." I wasn't very cold tolerant, either.

Jingles clucked. "And heaven help him if Lynxie finds him before we do."

Salty looked more panicked than ever. Lynxie was my sister-in-law Lucia's pet—a cat-lynx hybrid that was one hundred percent hellcat. My calves had the scars from his claws to prove it. If the cat loved to ambush me, no doubt he would be over the moon to find a fat, helpless turkey bumbling around.

And Lynxie was an indoor-outdoor cat. Nowhere would be safe from him.

"I'll talk to Lucia," I promised Salty. "We can keep Lynxie confined somewhere until Gobbles is located."

Jingles folded his arms. "Good luck with that." He'd also been the victim of Lynxie's pounces, and he knew how stubborn Lucia could be about that animal.

"I'm going into Christmastown this afternoon," I said. "If Gobbles hasn't turned up by then, I'll stop by the constabulary and report him missing."

"Thank you, Mrs. Claus," Salty said.

"We'll find him." Maybe this was promising too much, but the poor elf looked like he needed a dose of optimism.

And, Lynxie notwithstanding, I truly didn't want to believe anyone in Santaland would harm Gobbles.

I headed back into the castle to get warm and search for Lucia. It was November, but the castle, as always, had signs of Christmas everywhere: Twinkle lights graced the ceiling, evergreen bows and candles festooned side tables and doors, and now seasonal sprigs of holly and mistletoe had begun to appear, attached by colorful ribbons to the finials of stair rails and lampshades, and over doorways.

Outside Nick's office, raised voices caught my attention. It wasn't often that anyone yelled at Santa Claus. I stopped, leaning in to eavesdrop more closely. Lucia's voice rose above the others. "Why argue over this?" she asked. "It's ridiculous!"

When I ducked my head in to see what the problem was, a wave of animal musk hit me. Nick's office was filled with reindeer—two of them large, muscled bucks that would have made the room feel crowded all on their own. I could tell at once that they were leaders—old, proud reindeer who'd earned the right to be called by the name of their herd. One I recognized was Comet, and the other was the head of the Dasher herd. You could always distinguish a Dasher because they were notoriously vain—coats shining to a high gloss, hooves blackened with polish, work done to augment antlers.

Next to them stood Lucia, and behind her, near the door as if he didn't quite want to be involved in the discussion, was Lucia's reindeer friend, Quasar. Quasar, unlike the other two, was a misfit reindeer. He walked with a crooked gait and would never win any speed or agility prizes. His erratically fizzling red nose marked him as a descendent of the great Rudolph, but he chose to live here in the castle as Lucia's friend, not with his herd. He nodded hello to me.

At the end of the office, Nick sat at his desk, strikingly handsome and Santalike in his red coat with its snowy white wool trim. Even when he was sitting down you could tell he was a tall man, with dark hair and a beard starting to go salt-and-pepper. Not the portly, jolly Santa of the Clement Moore poem and Madison Avenue—his cousin Amory better fit that description. Of course, I preferred the real flesh-and-blood Santa.

"We are *not* show ponies to be trotted out for some idiotic pageant," Comet was saying, holding his muzzle high. "This parade was sprung on us after our autumn reindeer games were well underway."

"They're *always* underway," I couldn't help blurting out.

The large reindeer swung their heads toward me and dipped their antlers in greeting, but turned back to the subject at hand quickly. Lucia, Nick's sister, who had the appearance of a Viking queen kitted out in the clothes of a reindeer wrangler, shot me a look that conveyed how unwelcome my interjection into the conversation was. Her job within the Claus family was to liaise with the reindeer herds, and she clearly didn't appreciate any caustic remarks.

"We can't ask our herds to sit out vital contests in order to flounce about in this parade," Comet said. "Of all the elves and people in the North Pole, Santa, *you* know best what's at stake."

The whole point of the reindeer games—which truly went on all year long, and heated up to a frenzy in the last months of autumn—was to choose the strongest reindeer with the most stamina to pull Nick's sleigh on Christmas Eve. Reindeer took these competitions *very* seriously.

"I do," Nick agreed. "Believe me, no one wants reindeer to participate in the parade if they would rather not."

The other large reindeer snorted. "And pray tell, who would be pulling your sleigh in the parade if not us? Musk oxen?"

Nick shifted uncomfortably. He obviously didn't want to tread on any hooves. "Surely the games are far along now.

Those reindeer *not* in contention for the finals could be in the parade."

"The *losers*, you mean," Comet said acidly.

Comet had always reminded me of all the frustrated coaches who'd taught my PE classes in school. Personally, I found the Comet herd annoying, but reindeer, as Lucia often reminded me, had a different mindset from elves and people. They were the Spartans of Santaland, competitive and prickly, and their ways were older even than the elves'. Reindeer lived outside in the cold, braved polar bears and snow monsters, and provided both the muscle of daily transportation and, since the day Blitzen the Great first leapt through the air and flew, the magical lift beneath Christmas itself.

That, apparently, entitled them to be competitive jerks. At least, their leaders were jerks, and the herds went along with the survival of the fittest mentality. Yet I'd met many rank-and-file reindeer who were more laid-back.

Nick rubbed the full whiskers at his chin for a moment. "Some of the floats are going to be motor powered. I could ask that my appearance be on a mechanical float, not the ceremonial sleigh."

The reindeer reps nearly went apoplectic.

"And make it look as though the reindeer are shirkers?" Comet asked, aghast.

Lucia finally stepped forward. "So you don't want to lower yourself to appearing in a mere parade, but you don't want Santa to appear without you, either?"

"*I* never said that," Dasher said. "All of Santaland is going to be at this event. Reindeer *should* be involved."

"Then do as Nick suggested and involve the reindeer who aren't in contention for pulling the sleigh on Christmas Eve," Lucia said. "Hold a mini tournament to decide, if it makes you happier."

"Or better yet," I piped up, "let any reindeer interested put their names forward and draw nine reindeer from a hat."

Comet and Dasher gaped at me as if I'd just sprouted horns. "*Not* have a contest?" they asked in unison.

"What would be the point of that?" Comet added.

"It would just be a random selection," Dasher said. "What would it prove?"

Lucia crossed her arms, twisting her lips thoughtfully. "It wouldn't *prove* anything, but it would let other reindeer participate for once. Even the misfits."

They gasped. So did I—but only because Lucia and I rarely agreed on anything.

"*Misfits?*" Comet was beside himself. "Pulling the great sleigh?"

She laughed. "The sleigh's just going to fly down the mountain and land on Festival Boulevard, where it will move in a straight line for half a mile. Even fawns could handle that."

Dasher's nostrils flared as he swung back toward Nick. "You said this is going to be a ceremonial event—the opening of the Christmas season." He added in a lower voice, "A Cupid told me that there would be a photographer from the *Christmastown Herald* at the event. Surely we don't want *misfits* on the front page of the newspaper?"

He spoke so witheringly of misfits while Quasar was right there. I felt furious on Quasar's behalf, and Lucia practically had steam coming out of her ears.

Nick stood before the room could erupt into a clash between his sister and the leaders of the two largest herds. Lucia was a reindeer advocate, but she was partial to *all* reindeer, not just the fastest and fittest.

"My sister makes an excellent suggestion," Nick said. "No one, least of all myself, wants this new holiday to disrupt longstanding reindeer traditions. And as April said, a drawing would give more reindeer an opportunity to step up and take a more visible role."

Comet and Dasher were two gobsmacked reindeer. "B-b-but—"

"The newspaper!" Dasher said. "They might even feature a photograph on the front page."

Nick nodded. "I'll call Snug Brighthearth over at the *Herald* and ask him to give the reindeer games extra prominence this month."

It was hard not to roll my eyes. Reindeer games already took up most of the sports page.

"That is my decision," Nick continued. "The parade team will be decided by random drawing."

The two emissaries were conditioned to follow orders from Santa, but there was no disguising the fact that the edict rubbed their fur the wrong way.

"It will be as you say." Dasher bowed his head.

"But the great herds will not be happy," Comet added. "And if I have my way, they will not be participating."

"Then the lesser herds and the misfits can step up," Lucia said.

The other two shuddered from wither to flank, but said no more before they clopped out of the office.

When they were gone, Nick let out a breath and sat down again.

"That was tense," I said.

Lucia laughed and flopped into a chair opposite the desk, stretching out her long, booted legs. "That was nothing. You should have been around the day the Comets and the Prancers tied for the reindeer relay. There was almost a war."

"W-will misfits really be allowed to pull Santa's sleigh?" Quasar asked.

"If their names are picked in the draw," I said. "Why not?"

His nose blazed briefly and then fizzled out like a falling star. "I have several f-friends who might put their names in the hat."

I gave him a pat. "You should put yours in, too."

His head bowed modestly. "I-I don't know . . ."

Nick smiled at me. "I was surprised to see you during the middle of a reindeer parlay, April. Was there something you needed?"

"I heard Lucia's voice." I moved closer to the desk, then turned to her. "I was hoping that Lynxie could be put in a secured place for a while. Gobbles is missing, and Salty and Jingles are worried that Lynxie might decide to treat himself to an early Thanksgiving feast."

She frowned. "You want me to lock up Lynxie?"

"Just until we find Gobbles."

"How did Gobbles get out?" Nick asked.

"We're not sure. Salty swears his cage door was locked, so it might be that someone stole him."

"If someone stole him, they're likely to be hiding him somewhere secure," Lucia said. "Assuming they haven't already given him the ax."

The idea filled me with dread. "Please don't tell Salty that. He'd have a nervous breakdown."

She laughed. "Does he think Gobbles is being invited to Thanksgiving dinner to tell jokes?"

"Of course not, but—"

"I don't know why there's so much fuss over one chunky fowl," she continued. "He probably tastes just like any other bird. I'd much rather have a big plate of musk ox."

"You might get your wish," I said. "According to Felice."

Nick's face filled with disappointment. "Really?"

I nodded, and we exchanged a moment of mutual sympathy. Nick had never had a full turkey dinner, and I'd been talking it up for weeks. "The sides will still be good, though. The sides are really the best part."

"The point is," Lucia said, "if Gobbles has been kidnapped, he's not likely to be somewhere Lynxie can get to."

Nick laughed. "I wouldn't have thought Lynxie could get into my bathroom, either, until he took a chunk out of my leg while I was shaving one morning."

"He won't like being locked up," Lucia warned.

"It won't be for long." As soon as the words were out of my mouth, though, I realized I was making yet another promise I couldn't be sure of keeping.

Chapter 2

The Sparkletoe's Thanksgiving Day Parade's route was going to take us straight down Festival Boulevard, but today the Santaland Concert Band was having a marching drill in the empty sleigh parking area next to Christmastown Municipal Hall.

Given that we'd all just learned to march in the past two weeks, we were doing pretty well. Another month and we'd probably look pretty good. Unfortunately, the parade was just days away, and our conductor, Luther Partridge, was in despair.

"JoJo, do you *know* your left foot from your right?"

The trombone player drew up his shoulders in offense. "It was just a temporary slipup."

"Getting it *right* is the slipup with the trombones," Smudge, my fellow percussionist joked, making a light *ba-dum-chink* rap on his snare drum. He smiled over our friend Juniper, who played euphonium and stood in front of us. She shook her head at him, but smiled back.

JoJo pivoted toward us, and his resentful gaze landed squarely on me. JoJo was a Hollyberry, a famously cantankerous elf family, and he'd recently been elected to Tinkertown's village council. Full of this new self-importance, he was now more than ever watchful for slights and insults, like an exposed nerve in search of a sharp pin.

"I heard that!" he told me indignantly.

"*I* didn't say anything," I said.

I was in no position to sneer at anyone. It was all I could do to walk in a straight line with a huge bass drum strapped to me by a shoulder harness. I felt like an upright turtle with the shell on the wrong side. It didn't help that I was cold-natured. Most of the elves were wearing light wool coats, but I was in three layers of wool and a puffy goose-down parka.

Luther blew the whistle that he kept hanging around his neck. Everyone jumped at the piercing sound.

"Now, now," Luther scolded us. "This is just a happy Thanksgiving parade. We're all friends here, right?"

"Yes," I said, even as JoJo Hollyberry tossed another glare back at me. I in turn shot an exasperated look at Smudge, who was trying not to laugh.

"This time around, we're going to add in our twirlers," Luther continued.

My sister-in-law Tiffany Claus stepped forward. In addition to being an elite amateur ice skater in her youth, she'd also been a high school twirler. In the space of just a few weeks she'd assembled a majorette line for the march: herself, Nick's tall, gangly limbed cousin, Elspeth Claus, and an elf named Cookie. The trio was mismatched in both height and skill, although maybe when they were in uniform the disparities wouldn't be so glaringly obvious—they were going to be wearing band uniforms with pleated skirts instead of the wool pants the rest of us wore.

Elspeth Claus seemed to have the hardest time getting the knack of things. At the last rehearsal, one of her thumb flips went wild and clunked Luther upside the head. Since then, Luther had been adding the twirlers incrementally while Tiffany drilled them on the sideline.

A bit of left-right confusion notwithstanding, the band was getting the knack of marching—as long as we weren't playing music. It was when we had to play actual songs and march at the same time that things deteriorated. Luckily, all I had to do was keep a simple, steady downbeat on the bass drum.

Simple in theory, at least.

"All right," Luther said, "'Over the River and Through the Woods.'"

A few groans met his announcement.

This is my fault. When the subject of having our band march in the parade had first come up, Luther had picked my brain for traditional Thanksgiving songs. Elves were so fond of holiday music, they just couldn't believe that there weren't Thanksgiving carols. "Over the River and Through the Woods" was the only one I could think of off the top of my head, and Luther had taken the ball and run with it, creating a marching band arrangement on his own. It was a sweet tune, but it seemed a little stilted, especially as a slow march.

It was a relief for everyone when the band could play the Christmas tunes we'd also chosen for the march. We knew our Christmas songs backwards and forwards.

As I stood at the back of the column, the bass drum strapped in front of me, my biggest fear wasn't sounding bad or losing the beat, it was falling. Walking on Christmastown streets was a precarious activity for me at the best of times. The ground's surface was permanently packed snow and ice. I worried that I'd lose my footing and fall on my butt with my bass drum crushing me like a bug.

Luther blew his whistle and then raised his hand. "Ready?"

We all stood at attention. The moment before we started moving was our best look—it was usually all downhill from there. Once we started marching, our tight formation slackened, "Over the River" morphed into a confused ramble, and

Luther's conducting became ever more frenzied, as if he hoped to hold us together through sheer arm power.

Despite our shortcomings, the sound of our playing was like catnip to passing Santalanders. A crowd gathered at the fringes of the parking lot to watch. Elves love music, and a marching band was a real novelty. Some had found the words to the song and sang along as we played.

After over two years in Santaland, I recognized most of the faces in the crowd. The majority were smiling, although I couldn't help noticing a couple of snowmen leaning toward each other as if exchanging snarky commentary.

"Crisp! Crisp!" Luther barked over the combined noise of the band and the singing spectators.

Periodically an elf who got out of step would have to do a little skip-hop to get back onto the right footing. This brought hoots from the spectators.

I glanced across the crowd, annoyed, and then was distracted by something completely unexpected: my friend Claire. Like me, she was a human, but she was short enough to be an elf; her yellow and green Oregon Ducks knit hat caught my eye more than anything else. She wasn't standing around watching the marching drill, but walking away from us, deep in conversation with an elf I didn't know very well personally but who was instantly recognizable: Blaze White-wreath. Handsome, always sharply dressed in the flamboyant fashion of the elf elite, Blaze was the scion of a successful Christmastown family who dealt in properties. Juniper sometimes called him the Don Juan of Santaland.

Deep in conversation, Claire and Blaze leaned in close to each other. Very close. They were practically touching heads.

I frowned. Claire, who hailed from the same seaside town in Oregon that I did, was visiting me for the second time. Last Christmas she'd gotten involved with an enigmatic North Pole private detective named Jake Frost. She was hopeful that things would work out between them, despite being from very different worlds. Jake had visited her in Oregon, and from what I could tell, things had not gone entirely smoothly. Jake didn't fare well in the relative warmth of Oregon—Claire reported that he sweated like a fiend the whole time in the sixty-degree heat. Afterwards, he'd seemed glad to return to his home in the Farthest Frozen Reaches, the wilderness north of Santaland's Christmas Tree Forest border. I knew Jake loved Claire, but he didn't seem as optimistic about their relationship's chance of survival as she was.

He certainly hadn't expected her to be back in the North Pole so soon. Neither had I.

Seeing how absorbed she was in her conversation with Blaze—one of Santaland's most eligible elf bachelors—I began to wonder if Jake had good reason to doubt that their relationship would last. In our single days, Claire had been the queen of holiday flings. Her sudden interest in the Don Juan of Santaland could auger doom for her romance with Jake.

"April!"

Luther's whistle blast brought everyone to a ragged halt.

I turned, only to discover that my bandmates were halfway across the sleigh park from where I stood.

"You were supposed to turn!" the conductor bellowed at me.

Heat rushed to my cheeks as I slid-scooted back over to the band. "Sorry," I said.

"Everyone, please concentrate!" Luther entreated. "Okay, let's try this one more time—for Mrs. Claus."

JoJo Hollyberry turned back to smirk at me.

I flushed in marcher shame. I'd been so distracted by Claire that I'd forgotten what I was doing. I never could resist a mystery.

I wasn't the only one who'd been distracted by the couple,

either. Up at the front of the line, Bobbin, our piccolo player, was doubled over, cupping his nose in his hands.

"What's the matter with you?" Luther asked him.

"I got whacked by Elspeth's baton. That thing's like a lead pipe!"

Elspeth Claus was scrambling to pick up her sparkly stick, but her gaze was pointed in the same direction mine had been—at Claire and Blaze disappearing down the street. She did not look pleased.

"You need to watch your back," I warned Claire when we met up at the We Three Beans coffeehouse after my marching band practice had finished.

She smiled at the alarm in my voice. Caution wasn't her watchword. "Why?"

A tug at my sleeve interrupted my answer. I turned and looked down. JoJo Hollyberry was glaring up at me. The trombone case propped next to him was almost as tall as he was.

"You're cutting line," he said.

"Sorry," I said, "I didn't see you when I walked up."

The words only ruffled him more. Elves could be prickly about humans not noticing them. "You weren't looking," he said.

Juniper, who had joined Claire and me, was even less diplomatic. "For the love of Christmas, JoJo, just let it go for once in your life."

"And by all means," I added quickly, trying to make peace, "just go ahead of us."

"I don't need your permission," he huffed. "I was here first."

Muttering about Clauses and Christmastowners thinking they could get away with anything, he picked up his trombone case and ordered an eggnog Frappuccino at the counter.

Eggnog drinks at coffee shops still seemed like heresy to

me, but after two years in Santaland I was reaching a point of
acceptance. I also tried not to take JoJo's attitude personally.
Hollyberrys and Clauses had a history. A Claus had been responsible for the death of JoJo's cousin, Giblet, and though
justice had been served in that case, the Hollyberrys were naturally still unsettled by one of their own meeting a violent
end. According to most Santalanders, Hollyberrys were champion grudge holders. I didn't want a misunderstanding in the
coffee queue to throw fuel on the feud between the two fam-
ilies.

After we finally placed and collected our orders, Claire,
Juniper, and I snagged the prized table next to the fireplace. I
craved thawing out by the fire almost as much as I craved caffeine. The low timbered ceilings and comfy—if slightly too
small for me—chairs gave the whole coffee shop a cozy air.
Holiday tunes played through the overhead speakers, and
elves at tables sang along to Judy Garland's version of "Have
Yourself a Merry Little Christmas."

"So what's this about watching my back?" Claire asked.
Though a newcomer, she looked much more comfortable
than I felt in the elf-sized furniture. I was half a foot taller than
her and always had to fight the urge to hunch in elf spaces.

"You were walking with Blaze Whitewreath a little while
ago," I reminded her.

She laughed. "Is that all? From the tone in your voice, I
assumed I'd inadvertently committed some unforgivable Santaland faux pas."

Juniper nearly choked on her eggnog latte. "You were
talking with Blaze?" From the excitement in her voice, you'd
have thought Claire had bumped into a rock star. "What did
he say to you?"

"He was, uh, interested in how long I intend to stay in
Santaland." She cut her gaze away toward the fire, and I could
see a flush rising in her cheeks.

What was she flustered about? I'd been on multiple vacations with Claire, so it didn't surprise me that she could attract male attention. She packed a lot of sex appeal into her five-foot frame. What did surprise me was that she seemed to be welcoming Blaze's hitting on her, given how she felt about Jake. She'd even gone to visit Jake's home in the Farthest Frozen Reaches last year, and if a woman who liked town life as much as Claire did could stand a week in a frozen wasteland full of snow monsters and exiled criminal elves, it had to be true love.

Or so I'd assumed.

"Is everything all right between you and Jake?" I asked.

"Oh sure—except that I'm here and he's off in his snow cave."

"But isn't that just because of his business?" Juniper asked. "Otherwise, I'm sure he'd want to come to town."

Jake was the North Pole's best private detective. Actually, except for the young elf and a snowman who worked for him, he was the only private detective hereabouts.

"It's his business, all right," Claire said. "He's got a case. Some old elf miner was found dead and his hoard was stolen. I didn't even know they had miners out there."

"Golly doodle, yes," Juniper said. "The Farthest Frozen Reaches is where all the lumps of coal come from. The worst criminals from Santaland are sent to work in the mines." She frowned. "But if he was working in the coal mine, the miner wouldn't have his own hoard."

"It wasn't coal," Claire said. "It was some kind of gem."

A jewel robbery! I was intrigued. No wonder Jake hadn't been around much for the past week. "What kind of gems?"

"Nothing I'd ever heard of." Claire said. "Tugtu-something?"

Juniper's eyes went wide. "Tugtupite?"

"That's it," Claire said.

"You've never heard of tugtupite?" Juniper asked, surprised. "They're beautiful stones, mostly of red and pink. Tugtupite is an Inuit word for reindeer blood."

"Okay, but I don't see what the fuss is about." Claire scowled into her coffee cup. "It's all a bunch of thieves and ruffians up there anyway. The whole point of the place is to drop criminals in the middle of nowhere and let them deal with each other, isn't it? Like Australia."

"Even when Australia was a penal colony, it had laws," I pointed out.

"Then it had one up on the crazy place to the north of here."

Oh dear.

"I keep telling Jake that if he wants to grow his business, he should relocate to Christmastown," Claire said, her frustration coming through loud and clear. "There's more to keep him busy here."

Juniper laughed. "There's not even enough crime to keep Constable Crinkles in business. It's mostly baking and housekeeping over at the constabulary."

"Actually, I need to go over to see Crinkles when I leave here," I said. "I might have a job for him."

Juniper and Claire both sat up straight. "What?"

"Someone's snatched Gobbles." I filled them in on the details of the missing bird.

"That's terrible," Juniper said. "Poor thing. If he's lost, or kidnapped, he must be terrified."

"Poor us," Claire said. "What are we going to eat on Thursday?"

I remembered the roast musk ox Felice had threatened. Even in the hands of the best chef in Santaland, musk ox was always a little tough. "I wonder if it's too late to order a backup turkey."

Juniper brightened. "Hollywell's Cornucopia has frozen turkeys on order." The Cornucopia was the largest grocery in Christmastown. "Aunt Twizzle picked hers up this morning. You should get on their list."

"That would be a good strategy," I said, "even if Gobbles is found and we end up with one turkey too many."

"There's no such thing as too much turkey," Claire said.

"That's how I feel about pie," I said.

"I can't wait for Thursday." Juniper's ecstatic expression turned more thoughtful. "Do you really think that Constable Crinkles will be able to find a kidnapped bird?" she asked me.

"Well . . . it couldn't hurt to have him try."

"I have an idea!" She straightened, and her eyes brightened mischievously. "We should send out a call to Jake. Tell him that we're *desperate* for his missing-bird-locating services."

Claire shook her head. "He would never interrupt his tug-whatever case to come here on a turkey hunt."

"Not even if you asked him to?" Juniper said. "It would give you all a little more together time."

Claire crossed her arms. "We'll have enough of that."

I was perplexed. Like Juniper, I assumed Claire would jump at any pretext to lure Jake back to town to be with her. Much as I loved hanging out with Claire, I didn't kid myself that she was staying in Santaland for the Thanksgiving holiday on my account.

"But if you're only here for a short time—"

"If he wants to see me, he knows where I am." There was an amused glint in her eyes, but the stubborn tilt of her chin spoke volumes even before she added, "I'm not going to beg for attention, and I'm not going to stoop to luring him back on a flimsy pretext like a missing turkey."

Would she stoop to luring him back with rumors that she's involved with Santaland's Don Juan?

"It's not a flimsy pretext," I said. "Gobbles really is missing."

"That makes two missing turkeys, then," Claire quipped. "Gobbles and Jake."

Juniper and I exchanged a baffled, raised-brow glance. Claire was so adamant, we made an unspoken agreement to drop the idea of summoning Jake. *Far be it from me to intervene in someone's romantic problems*, I thought. *Most of the time.*

"I should make *Missing* signs for Gobbles," I said.

Juniper looked at her watch. "I can design a little poster at the library this afternoon if I have time. Do you have a picture of him?"

Did I have a picture . . . ? Over the past three weeks, Gobbles had become the most photographed fowl in Santaland. My phone was overloaded with action photos of Gobbles in the snow, Gobbles in close-up, Gobbles with various Claus family members, Gobbles with the elf children who trekked up Sugarplum Mountain to get a peek at him, Gobbles with Grimstock . . .

We scrolled through the photos to find the best turkey headshot.

"I like that one," Juniper said, pointing to a close-up of the turkey's head.

I studied it. "The one before showed off his wattle better."

She swiped back and considered the other picture.

Claire twisted her lips. "You two are hilarious. He's the *only* turkey in Santaland. It's not like people are going to angst over facial recognition if they come across him."

She was right. Still, if a thing was worth doing . . .

"Send that wattle one to me," Juniper told me. "I'll make up a poster before my shift begins and email it to you."

As I was thanking her, a shadow fell over our table. I looked up and felt my stomach clench with dread. Nick's cousin Elspeth loomed over us. For some reason, Elspeth and

I had never gotten along. She was around Nick's age—just a few years older than I was—and single, living in a château near Castle Kringle that was the home of an elderly family member named Mildred Claus. All the ingredients were there for a friendship between us, but our personalities had never meshed. Quite the opposite. Elspeth always seemed to think that I was trying to undermine her.

Today, however, her ire was directed at Claire.

"Hey, Elspeth," I said in an overly bright voice. I wanted to nip whatever was bugging her in the bud. "Would you like to join us?"

She flicked a glare at me before homing back in on Claire. "I saw you with Blaze."

Claire met her gaze coolly. "I'm sure a lot of people saw us. We were walking downtown together on a busy public sidewalk."

I wanted to wave my arms like warning flags. Meeting Elspeth's rudeness with cool hostility was bound to escalate whatever conflict Elspeth was trying to gin up.

Then again, being nice to her never seemed to help much, either. With Elspeth, nothing really worked.

Her gaze narrowed on Claire. "What did he say about me?"

Claire laughed. "Funnily enough, you weren't the center of our conversation. In fact, your name never came up."

"That's surprising, since we're . . . involved."

Unflappable, Claire sipped her coffee and held eye contact. "If you're involved, then you shouldn't worry about his walking down a public sidewalk with me."

"I'd been wondering why he wasn't returning my calls lately," Elspeth said. "It got worse when you arrived in town."

Claire just looked amused. "So your ex was ghosting you, and now he's ghosting you more?"

Elspeth's face turned candy-cane red.

Juniper jumped in. "What you're insinuating is ridiculous, Elspeth. Everybody knows that Claire and Jake Frost are an item."

"Unofficially," Claire corrected her.

I glanced around. The elves around us had stopped singing and were intently watching these two women face off. JoJo Hollyberry especially seemed to be enjoying the spectacle.

"Are you sure I can't get you anything, Elspeth?" I asked. "Coffee, tea . . . ?" *Valium?*

She rounded on me, and I suddenly felt like the rodeo clown who'd distracted the raging bull from the cowboy. Mission accomplished—but now *I* was in for it. "You knew I would be at that marching band rehearsal today," she said. "You probably brought your little friend down with the knowledge that I would be busy twirling."

My patience snapped. "For pity's sake, Elspeth. I've never even spoken to Blaze Whitewreath except to say hello. I certainly didn't arrange an assignation between them to break up your romance. I didn't know there was a romance."

"Doesn't sound like there was to me," Claire remarked under her breath, just loud enough for all the surrounding tables to hear.

"When you see Blaze again," Elspeth said, "tell him he'll be sorry."

I choked back a laugh. "Aren't you being a tad melodramatic?"

Her chin rose and she gave me a withering up-and-down. "You think you're such hot stuff. Mrs. Claus! For your information, after this week *I'll* be ablaze with success, and you won't be looking down your nose at me."

"I don't look down my nose at you now," I assured her.

She let out a snort of derisive laughter. "You're always poisoning my life."

With those parting words, she turned on her heel and headed for the door.

Claire raised her brows. "I don't think she likes us."

"And tomorrow we're going to have to sit with her at Cousin Amory's holiday potluck," I said with a sigh.

"That'll be fun." Claire smiled. "Blaze has been invited, too."

Juniper shook her head. "Sounds like one party I'll be glad to miss."

Although Juniper was coming to the Thanksgiving dinner at Castle Kringle, Amory had not invited her to the lodge event. Amory didn't know Juniper very well; besides, he tended to populate his parties with Clauses and local bigwigs—like Blaze Whitewreath, the scion of a local family that had made a fortune buying and selling Christmastown properties. Knowing Amory, even JoJo Hollyberry, possessor of that new Tinkertown Council seat, would be a guest.

We finished our drinks, put our coats on, and went back out in the cold. Juniper headed to the library, and Claire and I turned our steps toward the constabulary.

The atmosphere in Christmastown made me smile. All along the street, windows were decorated with imagery straight out of my childhood—grinning Pilgrims and cartoon turkeys among construction-paper autumn leaves and pumpkins. It made me nostalgic, even though the images were wildly strange to see in Santaland. Pilgrims weren't any part of the history here, pumpkins only grew in greenhouses, the North Pole didn't have fall colors of deciduous trees in autumn, and our only live turkey was currently AWOL.

A group of elf carollers on the corner were singing "Over the River and Through the Woods," and Claire and I stopped to listen and join in. She laughed when she realized that she didn't know the words beyond the first line.

"Don't feel bad," I told her. "I only know them because the elves have been singing it nonstop all week."

I assumed Claire would accompany me all the way to the constabulary, but she stopped on a corner several blocks before we got there.

"I have an errand to run," she said. "I'll meet you back at the castle."

"Do you know how to get home?"

She laughed. "It's Christmastown, April, not some huge metropolis."

I felt bad for not having a vehicle to make the return home easier. Nick had given me a fancy hybrid sleigh, but at the moment the electric motor was having troubles. It was in the shop having its engine worked on.

"If you miss the sleigh bus, you can take the funicular most of the way up the mountain." I pointed up at Sugarplum Mountain, which rose above Christmastown. From this distance, the lights of various Claus family châteaux formed a twinkling trail of breadcrumbs leading up to the Castle Kringle itself, a fairy-tale structure of gray stone that was lit up like a beacon in the early fall twilight. "Once you get off the funicular, it's a short hike the rest of the way."

"Don't worry about me," she said. "I love wandering around—it's so beautiful here."

It sounded as if she didn't intend on waiting for a funicular or the sleigh bus. What was she up to?

Claire waved good-bye and then headed off down a side street. My curiosity about this mysterious errand intensified, and I was tempted to follow her.

She's your friend, my conscience scolded me. Asking nosy questions over coffee was one thing. Tailing her as if she were a criminal was taking curiosity too far. Besides, I already had one mystery on my hands: the mystery of Gobbles.

With a snappy about-face that would have made Luther Partridge proud, I turned my steps toward the constabulary.

Chapter 3

Visiting the Christmastown constabulary always provided a delectable side benefit: baked goods. Deputy Constable Ollie, the nephew of Constable Crinkles, loved to bake, and the kitchen of the cottage that housed the constabulary never failed to offer up some delicious gingerbread, tarts, spice cake, or cinnamon rolls. The building itself was a comfy cottage with traditional furnishings and holiday decorations festooning the mantel. The place seemed more a model home for miscreants than a police station.

On my way there, I looked forward to a cozy sit-down with tea and pastries, but as I approached, Constable Crinkles and Ollie were outside inspecting a large platform built on sleigh runners. Ollie hopped on top of it, testing the strength of the wooden boards beneath his curly-toed booties.

"Mrs. Claus!" Constable Crinkles beamed a smile at me. The round elf was dressed as always in his dark blue uniform, black booties, and hat that made him resemble a London bobby from days of old. "Our float platform for the parade was just delivered."

"I didn't know that the constabulary was entering a float in the parade." And I was on the Christmastown Events Committee. I obviously needed to pay closer attention to memos.

Ollie, a thin shadow of his uncle, gaped at me. "We couldn't sit out a big event like the city's first-ever Thanksgiving parade."

I briefly considered suggesting that law enforcement might have a role to play in crowd control, sleigh parking, and other vital matters of public safety, but as Mrs. Claus, I tried not to be too bossy. Elves governed themselves except when it came to weighty, difficult issues, which they would bring to Nick.

"Walnut's Sleigh Repair and Rental just brought our platform over," Crinkles told me.

Walnut, a self-made elf with his hand in several businesses, was one of Santaland's leading entrepreneurs. That he would have already winkled out a way to profit off the Thanksgiving parade didn't surprise me.

"How are you going to decorate it?" I asked.

"We thought we'd drape it in blue wool," Crinkles said.

"The color of our uniforms," Ollie added, in case I hadn't made the connection.

"And of course we'll add some greenery."

"Spruce it up." When neither Crinkles nor I laughed, Ollie added, "That was a pun."

Blue wool, spruce, and constables. So far, this didn't sound like something crowds would flock to.

"And of course," Crinkles added, as an afterthought, "we'll have the inflatable donuts."

I drew back. "Inflatable donuts?"

"You haven't heard? For the parade, the constabulary's partnering with Puffy's All-Day Donuts. We're taking care of the float rental, Puffy's supplying the donuts."

Constables and donuts. Some pairings knew no national boundaries.

"Ollie will be pulling the float with one of the constabulary snowmobiles," Crinkles explained, "and I'll be on the float tossing donuts at the crowd. Well-wrapped, of course."

I nodded. Free donuts was a game changer. "I wouldn't worry too much about decorations. This is going to be a *very* popular float."

Crinkles bobbed on his heels. "Once I saw that we'd be following the Tinkertown Juggle Club, I knew we'd have to bump it up a notch. They've got unicycles!"

About the only thing that could top elves on unicycles would be flying donuts.

"Where did you find inflatable donuts for the float?"

"Puffy ordered them," Ollie said. "We opted for the smiling crueller and a sexy jelly donut. Wanna come inside and see them?"

Constable Crinkles jerked to attention, as if he were remembering his manners. "Yes, come in and have some refreshments. Ollie baked orange pound cake this morning."

How could I say no to that? Elves thrived on a sugar- and carb-heavy diet and seemed puzzled at the idea of humans watching their waistlines. I mostly watched mine expand all winter and then dieted during my summer vacation in Oregon, where I still maintained the Coast Inn in Cloudberry Bay. The warm summer respite was where Nick and I unwound. It worked out pretty well, except that I was addicted to the milkshakes my friend Claire sold at her ice cream parlor there. Those milkshakes and Claire herself were some of what I missed most when summer drew to an end. That's why I was so happy to have her here now.

Only she was acting so erratically during this visit, she was practically an absentee guest. And this business with Blaze . . . was she really more attracted to him than Jake?

I put Claire out of my mind and went inside to look at the inflatables, which were blown up and standing in a corner of the constabulary dining room. They were impressive: heavy-duty plastic donuts with googly eyes and big smiles. The jelly donut had a Mae West vibe.

"You don't think she's too risqué, do you?" Crinkles squinted critically at the donut's cocked-hip stance. "This is a family event."

"I think you're okay," I assured him.

Once Ollie placed a wedge of pound cake in front of me, I explained the Gobbles situation to the constables.

Crinkles scratched one of his multiple chins. "Gone, huh?"

"Maybe he went exploring and will come back on his own," Ollie suggested.

"I don't think we're dealing with a case of turkey wanderlust," I said. "Salty swears the cage was locked."

Crinkles nodded. "Anyhow, no bird would come back of his own free will if he knows that his neck's going to be on the chopping block."

"I doubt Gobbles knows his days are numbered."

"Don't be so sure." Crinkles shook his head. "I once had a pet crow who was smarter than Ollie here."

Ollie nodded. "He beat me at tic-tac-toe nine times out of ten."

I swallowed a bite of orange cake and let out a sound of pure pleasure. Ollie might not be as smart as a bird, but he knew his way around a convection oven. "Salty and Jingles think someone stole Gobbles."

"Hm." While he considered the matter, Crinkles made inroads on his own wedge of Bundt cake. "What about Lucia? Could she have done it? She's an animal nut."

"Her fondness for animals doesn't seem to extend to turkeys. She's more concerned that Lynxie might get blamed. She's promised to keep an eye on him."

"Good idea." His gaze narrowed. "You think she'd fess up if she found a pile of bloody feathers near Lynxie?"

"I'm pretty sure she would tell me if Gobbles had already been . . . consumed."

"Well." Crinkles looked stumped. "This is a puzzler." He glanced over at Ollie. "We haven't received any reports of strange birds wandering around, have we?"

"No," Ollie said. "We haven't had much at all in the way of lost and found. Just Pumblechook's missing hat."

Pumblechook was one of the snowmen who lived in Christmastown.

"He reported his top hat missing last week," Crinkles explained, "so I loaned him one of my extra uniform hats till we can locate his."

"That was nice of you."

He shrugged modestly. "Well, we don't like to see anyone going bareheaded with the cold weather coming on."

"I didn't know snowmen were susceptible to cold heads."

Crinkles sent me a quizzical look, obviously surprised by my ignorance. "Why do you think they wear hats?"

I almost laughed. "Their heads are made of snow, though."

"Right," he said, explaining to me as if I were a child. "Snow is cold. So they wear hats to keep their heads warm."

Maybe snowman physiology was just one of those things non-Santalanders couldn't grasp. "I guess I never thought it through logically."

"My hat makes Pumblechook look like an honorary snowman constable," he said, chuckling. "We're going to put him on the float, too. He's real excited about it."

"A little too excited, if you ask me," Ollie grumbled. "He tried to arrest old Mrs. Goldball as she crossed Sparkletoe Lane the other day."

"She shouldn't have been jaywalking," Crinkles said.

"Do you have any suggestions for finding Gobbles?" I asked, before the constables were irretrievably sidetracked. "Is there a way to put out an APB for a turkey?"

Crinkles's forehead crunched up. "An AP-what?"

"An alert."

He scratched his chin. "What you ought to do is make some posters."

"Juniper's doing that this afternoon."

He brightened. "That's it, then. If you give some to me, I can post them around town. That'll alert everyone."

I nodded. "I can send you the file when Juniper gives it to me."

Crinkles twisted toward Ollie, who was cutting more orange cake for us. "Do we know how to send a file to the printing doojabber?"

"Printer's broken," Ollie said, and then his eyes widened. "Speaking of machinery . . ."

He went back to the kitchen and then came back dragging a huge metal pot with a matching lid. With a puff of exhaustion, he left it on the floor in front of me. The pot came up to my hips. It was big enough for an elf to take a bath in.

"Do you think that thing's big enough?" he asked.

"Big enough for what?"

"To deep fry a turkey."

I bit my lip. "I've never fried a turkey."

He blinked in astonishment. "What have you been doing with them?"

"Baking them? In the oven."

"But I read that frying them's best," he said.

"I'm sure a fried turkey will be great." Except if there was some problem with the equipment. That pot didn't look purpose built for frying turkeys.

I tilted my head, curious. "Where did you find that pot?"

"My cousin Crispy lent it to us. He's a weaver and uses it for yarn dyeing."

"And where did you get your turkey?"

"Hollywell's Cornucopia. I don't know if Mr. Hollywell

has any left, though," Ollie added. "I think there's a waiting list."

I really needed to get on that list.

I stood and thanked him for the cake. "I'll print some of the flyers and bring them back here."

At the library, Juniper was waiting for me with the *Missing* flyers already prepared. They looked fantastic—Gobbles's picture was prominent, and the contact information was legible.

"Thank you!" I said, taking a stack of them from her. "You're a lifesaver."

"I hung one up here on the public bulletin board and another in the employee break room."

"Ollie and Crinkles offered to distribute some, too. The more we get out, the better."

I left Juniper and spent the next hour taping up posters on lampposts and various public notice boards around the city.

By the time I'd delivered flyers to the constabulary, visited Hollywell's Cornucopia to put my name on the frozen turkey waiting list, and then rode the sleigh bus home, I'd missed dinner. At the castle, my mother-in-law was ensconced in her favorite wing-back chair in the salon when I dragged in and flopped on the sofa, exhausted. The day felt as if it had been forty hours long, and most of it had been spent outside. I was in serious need of thawing out.

On the rug before the hearth, Nick's nephew, Christopher, lay on his stomach, reading a schoolbook and absently munching on a cookie. He was almost a teenager now, and seemed to have developed the metabolism of an elf. "Hey, Aunt April," he said, tossing his hair out of his eyes to smile up at me.

Pamela, who was the very image of a perfect dowager Mrs. Claus, with a green wool suit over her suitably plump figure and her silver hair arranged in a neat bun, greeted me with, "There you are." She was tatting lace into a beautiful

circle. Her knitting and tatting were spectacular, as was her
baking. Pamela succeeded spectacularly at whatever she put
her hands to.

"What are you making?" I asked.

"Pumpkin doilies for the Thanksgiving centerpieces."

The moment the idea of a Thanksgiving celebration had
been raised, she'd drawn up an elaborate design plan for how
she wanted the table to look.

"I expected to find you elbow deep in pie crust," I told
her. We were all supposed to bring dishes to Amory and
Midge's party; Pamela had planned to make pies. She was also
making all the desserts for Thursday's meal, although Tiffany
had volunteered to make a pie, too.

I had not been invited to provide anything more complex
than a simple side dish for the party at the lodge. For some
reason, Pamela considered me prone to food disasters.

"I've already finished the pies for tomorrow," she said.
"Now I've moved on to getting things prepped for dinner
here Thursday. I unpacked some of the linens I brought with
me when I got married. The tablecloth is already on the table
if you want to approve it."

Pamela putting a tablecloth on the table four days early
didn't surprise me. Tiffany told me that one year the Christmas dinner table was set two weeks in advance. But I couldn't
believe she was asking for my approval.

"You want *me* to approve the tablecloth?"

She eyed me over her bifocals. "You are Mrs. Claus—*I'm*
only the dowager Mrs. Claus. Just be careful not to mess anything up. I have a *Do Not Enter* sign on the dining room door
now, but you can go in to look."

I laughed. "There's a *Do Not Enter* sign on the dining
room? How will we eat?"

"In the breakfast room. It's just until Thursday. As I said, people are welcome to look. We just want to keep the table setting pristine till Thursday. That's how my mother always did things. The tablecloth itself is hand-embroidered heirloom linen from my great-grandmother, but of course if you'd prefer something else . . ."

As if I would ever contradict her when it came to a precious family heirloom. "I'm sure the tablecloth will be fine."

"Fine?" Her brows raised. "I would think you'd want this to be better than fine. Back when I was growing up, our house was always perfect."

"I'm sure the tablecloth will be perfect," I said, correcting my mistake. "The centerpieces, too."

"You can always veto them if they're not to your liking."

I'd never have the nerve to veto any of Pamela's decorative choices. I rarely contradicted her about anything—not just because I was awed by her, but because she usually knew more than I did. Her domestic expertise was way beyond mine.

I searched for a way to change the subject. "Have you seen Claire this evening?"

"When neither of you showed up for dinner, I assumed you were eating together in town," Pamela said.

I sat up straighter. "Claire isn't here? She should have been back hours ago."

"So should you."

"I went to the constabulary to talk to them about Gobbles."

At the mention of the turkey's name, Pamela put her lacework down in her lap with an impatient sigh. "That bird is taking up so much of everyone's attention around here, you'd think he was a missing movie star."

"Well, he *is* supposed to be the star of the feast."

"It's ridiculous," Pamela said. "Felice should have ordered

a frozen turkey. My family always bought frozen turkeys, and we lived in prime turkey country. You can't really tell the difference."

My mother-in-law had been born in Alabama. Like Tiffany and me, she had only moved to Santaland after meeting her husband. He had been Santa until his death, and then Nick's older brother, Chris, had taken the title until he had also died. Then Nick had assumed the mantle until Chris and Tiffany's son, Christopher, reached adulthood. Technically, Nick was just Santa Regent, but he took the role very seriously.

Pamela, too, had thrown herself into the role of first Mrs. Claus and then the dowager Mrs. Claus. I could tell she didn't always deem me entirely worthy to be her successor. I was sometimes a little doubtful myself. I certainly seemed to be falling short in the place-setting department.

"I went by the Cornucopia grocery this evening," I said. "All their frozen turkeys were spoken for, but Mr. Hollywell has put in another order and hopes they'll show up before Thursday. We're on the waiting list."

"It's good that you got something useful done while you were gallivanting around town," Pamela said, going back to her handwork.

"I wasn't gallivanting," I said. "I just had to put a few *Missing* flyers out to help find Gobbles." I took one out of my bag.

Christopher stood between us, inspecting the poster. He'd been so quiet up to now, I'd almost forgotten he was in the room. "That's a good poster, Aunt April. Where did you put those up?"

"Downtown. Juniper put some at the library, and Crinkles said he'd distribute some, too."

He bit his lip. "I can put a bunch around, too, if you give them to me."

"That's very kind of you to offer, Christopher," Pamela said.

It certainly was—and I wasn't about to turn down an offer of help. "How many do you need?"

He shrugged. "How many do you have?"

I reached into my bag and gave him the ones I had left. I could always print more. "It's really great of you to offer."

"Could I put posters out instead of going to the dinner at Kringle Lodge tomorrow?" he asked.

Now I understood the motive behind this sudden helpful spirit. Christopher wanted to wriggle out of a dull family dinner. Only it wouldn't just be Clauses at Kringle Lodge. The mayor and his wife would be there, and Constable Crinkles, and if Blaze Whitewreath had been invited, no doubt all sorts of other Santaland grandees would be in attendance. Thinking about it, I felt some sympathy for Christopher. It was definitely not going to be a kid event. I was about to offer to lobby Nick to let him skip when Pamela spoke up.

"Certainly not." Her tone was emphatic. "Amory and Midge are expecting you, and it's important that you get to know the other guests who'll be there."

"Why? It'll be so boring," Christopher said. "I never have anything to say."

"Just say hello to everyone," Pamela advised him. "And once you've done that, the best way not to be bored is to learn about people—ask a question about family or work."

It was wise counsel to the future Santa—a true Mrs. Claus answer.

My instinct to let him ditch the lunch would have gone over better, though. Christopher's mouth flattened into a resigned line. "This Thanksgiving thing is really a drag." He glanced at us apologetically. "I mean, it's just meals—no candy, no fun games or scary stuff like Halloween. What's the point?"

"There's the parade," I reminded him.

He gaped at me incredulously. Little children might like parades with jugglers, marching bands, and a constable tossing donuts from a float, but when I was an adolescent I probably wouldn't have been impressed, either.

Oh, who was I kidding? Donuts would have been right up my alley at any age.

"Thanksgiving is about gratitude," Pamela lectured him. "Gratitude about where you live, the bounty of nature, the friends we share it with. Maybe all the trappings of American Thanksgiving with its turkeys and Pilgrims don't make sense here, but the tradition itself is a good one. Many countries have such a day, and in time Santaland will embrace it in its own way."

That made me smile. She was right. Elves enjoyed putting their own spin on things.

Christopher's hair fell into his eyes as he studied the *Missing* poster. "What'll happen if Gobbles is never found?"

I shrugged. "If my being on the waiting list at Hollywell's falls through, Felice said she might make musk ox roast instead."

"Again?" Pamela's hands paused. "That's not typical of Thanksgiving. I'll have to have a word with her. We've invited twenty guests."

I felt bad always letting the unpleasant tasks fall to Pamela. She was the dowager Mrs. Claus, and I'd been married to Santa for two years now. I should be able to run the castle. "I guess that's my responsibility," I said. "I'll talk to Felice."

The moment the words came out of my mouth, I knew they were a mistake. Pamela reacted as if I'd just speared her through the heart. "If you feel that way about it. I didn't mean to horn in on your duties."

"You didn't. I only meant—"

"I just try to help, to be useful."

"I know, but you do too much." That didn't sound right, either. I bit my lip. "I mean, I should probably do more."

She nodded curtly. "And I should step aside and let you handle things."

Let you screw up things, was the subtext I heard.

"Of course, I hope you won't take it the wrong way if I just make a few helpful suggestions," Pamela added.

"Of course not," I replied. And I meant it . . . at the time.

Christopher came closer to us. "Soy to the World has something called Tofurkey loaf."

I eyed him curiously. Soy to the World was our local vegetarian restaurant. It didn't seem like the kind of place where a twelve-year-old boy would hang out. "How would you know that?"

"My friend Winky's mother works there. He told me about it. He says Tofurkey's not as disgusting as it sounds."

Pamela's lips formed a moue of displeasure. "Let's hope we don't have to resort to hippie solutions yet. Even musk ox is preferable to *that*."

I gave Christopher an encouraging nod. "It might be a good backstop, though. I'll check into it."

He loped off, seeming pleased to have helped. Pamela watched him go and then swung back to me. "Speaking of Amory's, have you prepared something for tomorrow? You remember that I signed you up to bring a side dish."

I hadn't forgotten, but so far no inspiration had come to me.

Now the time for inspiration was over. Desperation time had arrived.

Chapter 4

I swung by Nick's office on the way to the kitchen. Usually he didn't burn the midnight oil—not this early, anyway. In another two weeks it would be December and he would be working nonstop through Christmas.

Outside his office, I heard him speaking with Flake, one of the manager elves of the Candy Cane Factory. They were standing over several square candy wrappers. When they saw me, Flake smiled.

"Mrs. Claus! Just what we need—a third opinion."

I hesitated, but Nick's expression beckoned me to come help them, so I hurried over to see what they were up to. I'd expected to see prototypes for Christmas candy wrappers, but these were Thanksgiving designs: cartoon turkeys, Pilgrims, and cornucopias.

Nonsensical though they were here in Santaland, Pilgrims seemed to be irresistible.

"We only have time to retool and produce two of these," Flake said. "Which do you prefer?"

"What are they for?" I asked. "I mean, clearly they're Thanksgiving-themed candies, but . . ." The Candy Cane Factory was where *Christmas* delicacies were produced.

"Santa needs something to throw from his sleigh during

the parade," Flake told me. "We want to make holiday-appropriate candy for the event."

"I thought the whole point of my being in the parade is to kick off the Christmas season." Nick arched a brow at me. "Isn't that right?"

It felt weird to be the presumptive authority on Thanksgiving. "Yes—but someone obviously put a lot of work into these wrappers."

Flake puffed up proudly. "Our creative team pulled out all the stops."

"The turkeys and the Pilgrims are the cutest," I said.

Flake turned back to Nick with a hopeful look. "It would be no trouble to make several batches tomorrow. We could use the square gift chocolates and use these wrappers. *Voilà*—Thanksgiving candy."

Nick sighed. "All right, but I'd rather we make too few and mix in some Christmas candies rather than overproduce Thanksgiving candies. We don't want waste."

"Yes, sir."

"Make sure and send a box up to the lodge ASAP for Amory to sign off on," Nick said.

The elf all but clicked his heels together before hurrying out.

I leaned against Nick's desk and grabbed a gumdrop from the candy bowl he was using as a paperweight.

"Amory's in charge of the Candy Cane Factory," I said. "Why wasn't he here to consult about this?"

"He's busy prepping the lodge for the party tomorrow. That's why I'm having some sent to the lodge. I don't want him to accuse us of leaving him out of the loop." He released a long, slow breath. "I don't want to sound like a Thanksgiving Scrooge, but this new holiday is using up a lot of bandwidth at a not particularly convenient time."

"Next year maybe we should bump Thanksgiving up to September."

His brows rose. "Can we do that?"

"Why not? American Thanksgiving moved around in the eighteenth century until Lincoln declared it the third week in November. The Canadians celebrate theirs in October. Why shouldn't Santalanders be grateful in September?"

Heaven knows I was inclined to feel more gratitude when the weather was slightly warmer.

Nick considered this, then shook his head. "We need to survive this week before we can contemplate next year."

His long-suffering tone made me laugh. "Survive? You sound as enthusiastic as Christopher. He says it's a boring holiday all about food." I tapped the foil wrappers Flake had left as samples. "Thanksgiving candy should perk him up."

"How are *you* holding up?" Nick asked me.

"Fine, except that I've discovered that I can't march and beat a drum at the same time. And I suspect Claire is carrying on a clandestine affair with Blaze Whitewreath."

He drew back, surprised. "What happened to Jake?"

"He's busy with some robbery case in the Farthest Frozen Reaches."

Nick's brow pillowed into a frown. "I'm sorry to hear that."

"There are always unsavory things going on in the Reaches, right?" I suddenly remembered something unsavory happening closer to home. "Maybe I shouldn't be so smug, though. Gobbles is still missing. Do you think he really was bird-napped?"

Nick drummed his desk blotter with his pencil. "Who could have made off with him?"

"Some large flightless bird freak?" I guessed. "Although how they think they're going to hide a twenty-four-pound turkey in perpetuity is anyone's guess."

"Maybe they plan on eating the evidence."

That possibility unsettled me. Poor Gobbles.

Although it probably didn't matter to Gobbles if he was eaten at a castle feast or devoured in secret by his current captors. Either way, he was on the menu.

Speaking of menu . . .

"I need to go to the kitchen and whip up something to take to Amory and Midge's tomorrow. Can I bring you anything? Cocoa? Decaf?"

"No, I'm going to power through a few more things and then turn in."

I leaned down and kissed him. "Don't overdo. December is just around the corner." *December Is Coming* might as well be the country's motto. During the twelfth month, no one in Santaland slept from the first day to the twenty-fifth.

On the way to the kitchen, I ran into Claire heading toward her guest room, a happy, almost euphoric smile on her face. She still had her hat on and was carrying her overcoat.

"Where have you been?" I asked. "I expected you back hours ago."

"Sorry, Mom."

I had to laugh. I did sound like a disappointed parent. "Did you run into trouble?"

"No, I was just dawdling." A secretive smile touched her lips, and for a moment she seemed like a person planning a surprise party. And I was one of the people she meant to keep in the dark about it.

I studied her more closely. She was wearing a strange sweater. Actually, it was a knit wool elf tunic in multicolored checks. "Where did you get that?"

She looked down at herself. "Blaze loaned it to me. The top I was wearing got . . . messed up."

Scenes in romance novels of a hero and heroine so lost in lust that they flew at each other in a frenzy popped into my mind. Clothing was often a casualty in romance novels. Was that what had happened to Claire's shirt?

Having just been accused of being a nag, I hesitated to press for lurid details.

Claire put a hand on my arm. "Don't worry, April. I'm just at the beginning of something, so I don't want to jinx it by talking too much. You know how it is."

After she floated away to her bedroom, I continued to the kitchen, retrieving sandwich fixings from the larder for a snack. The castle kitchen was a gleaming cavern of spotless white tile and wood cabinetry that reached so high on the walls that the elves required stepladders to reach the highest shelves. The worktables were crafted of butcher block. I cut up some bread and cheese and ate absently, still thinking about what Claire had said about not wanting to jinx the beginning of something.

When I'd first met Nick, he'd come to the Coast Inn in Cloudberry Bay as a guest. I realized later that it had been a getaway for him in more ways than one. The Clauses had just suffered a loss after his brother Chris was killed. Quiet, capable Nick, grieving the loss of his brother, was suddenly thrust into the role of Santa Regent—although at the inn he was traveling incognito. He'd taken a short retreat during the summer break to wrap his mind around how his life had changed.

Recently widowed at the time, from a husband I'd discovered had lied to me during our marriage, I'd thrown myself into running the inn and never dreamed of finding a new relationship. Yet when Nick came along, there was something in his eyes, a combination of strength and vulnerability that drew me right in. I wasn't sure I could trust anyone again, though, and something in his manner made me fear a dark secret. During those first weeks, my feelings were so wildly fragile that I felt as if I were teetering across a tightrope with something very precious in my hands. No one was perfect—

every adult had secrets. I held my breath, waiting to see if whatever Nick was hiding would shatter my trust forever.

But then Nick declared that he couldn't lead me on without revealing all his secrets to me. He hadn't been hiding a checkered past, or a messy romantic history. His big secret was that he was Santa Claus—a being I'd never believed was real, much less an eligible bachelor. On my own, I'd decided to take a chance and elope with Nick. But I'd kept Nick's identity a secret from my friends for a long time, fearing that under the cold, objective scrutiny, our relationship would pop like a soap bubble.

Was Claire still at the tightrope-walking stage with Jake? Or had Blaze Whitewreath really swayed her affections? The two men couldn't have been more different. Jake was a dark, enigmatic figure. He claimed Jack Frost as a distant relation, so it was hard to know whether he was man, elf, elfman, or something else entirely. Blaze, on the other hand, was a friendly, charismatic elf, a Christmastown Realtor whose handsome face could be seen in the discreet advertisements our municipality allowed on sleigh buses and local bulletin boards. He was a likely candidate to run for mayor of Christmastown someday, should Mayor Firlog ever decide to retire.

In personality, Blaze and Claire seemed a better match. Yet she'd been so smitten with Jake, I was convinced she'd come here to make the case that they should be together permanently. Nothing would have made me happier. Not that my happiness was the real issue. *It's Claire's business.* She'd navigated the perilous dating rapids all these years just fine without me sticking my oar in.

Right now, my focus needed to be on preparing something for Amory's party. I looked enviously at the two perfect pies Pamela had baked for the occasion: two-crust apple pies with elaborately fluted, golden crusts and an apple-shaped dough cutout in the center. They were magazine-cover worthy, like everything Pamela set her hands to. I was a competent baker, but not a dessert artiste like my mother-in-law. Running my inn had given me a competency in the kitchen, but for some reason I wasn't ever able to get things quite right here. My specialty back in Oregon was breakfast and brunch, but Castle Kringle had a full cooking staff to provide a lavish breakfast every morning. Anyway, I couldn't take eggs to Kringle Lodge tomorrow.

Or could I?

I peeked into the pantry cupboard by the cold room. We didn't need electric refrigerators in the North Pole. Most houses just had an insulated room with a window that could be cracked open to achieve the appropriate level of coldness.

Inside the pantry I found several cartons of eggs. I grabbed two of them and set about my work. A large copper pot hung on the wall, and I got it down, filled it with water, and heaved it onto the stove. When the water began to boil, I dropped the eggs in as carefully as I could, set the snowman-shaped egg timer on the counter and then waited.

In the stillness of the kitchen, the eggs seemed to be making a strange noise—a kind of whining rattling sound. I edged closer to the pot, listening.

That wasn't the eggs making that noise. I looked up at the vents and realized the eerie sound emanated from somewhere else in the castle.

I poked my head out the door into the servant's corridor . . . and came face-to-face with Jingles wearing his bathrobe, plush, curly-toed house slippers, and a long candy-stripe sleeping cap with a red puffball at the tip.

"What's that sound?" we asked in unison.

"What are you doing in here?" He ducked his head into the kitchen, frowning suspiciously.

"Boiling eggs for tomorrow."

"You're taking hard-boiled eggs to a party?" he asked.

"Deviled eggs."

His frown deepened. "Just plain deviled eggs?"

"They're delicious," I said.

And foolproof to make.

"They don't have much oomph though, do they?"

I thought about this. I'd tasted some really good deviled eggs once and had asked for the secret ingredient. "I think I can give them oomph."

He shrugged, obviously unconvinced. "If you say so. It seems a pretty odd choice for Thanksgiving week."

Suddenly *he* was an expert on the subject.

"Never mind the eggs." I pointed at the vent. "I could have sworn I heard something coming through there."

He stared up. "This part of the castle was originally part of the Old Keep. Could be that the vents weren't sealed off very well."

The Old Keep, centuries old, was the original section of the castle. It had fallen into disrepair long ago after a bit of ceiling had collapsed. The family had abandoned it for the newer, front section of the castle. The ceiling had been fixed in the Old Keep, but it was still super creepy—a dark, cold place where arctic ice rats made nests.

"Gobbles could be there," I said. "We need to check it out."

Jingles's eyes widened. *"We?"*

"Well, *I'm* going," I said.

I couldn't find a flashlight in the kitchen, but Jingles unearthed an old hurricane lantern. I was heading for the door when he stopped me.

"What about your eggs?"

They still had a minute to go, but I turned off the heat. They would continue to cook in their hot water bath. "Thanks for reminding me—I would have probably forgotten and let them boil down to black shells."

"I'm hoping that for once you'll manage to attend a Claus function without causing a food incident," Jingles said.

"I don't cause food incidents."

He darted a caustic glance my way.

Okay, maybe I had caused a few incidents. But this was not the time to dwell on past culinary failures.

"Let's go see what's in the Old Keep," I said.

We turned down several dark passages to get to the old section, stone corridors that grew increasingly dark and cold. I should have put on my puffer coat for this. And maybe brought a knife for protection. Now my only protection was Jingles, and he was letting me take the lead.

"Did Lynxie get locked up?" I whispered.

He gulped. "I believe so."

I wasn't sure if I preferred knowing that Lynxie wouldn't jump out at us, or if it would have been better to have Lynxie around to scare away any hungry, saber-toothed rodents.

The whining, knocking sound grew louder.

"That doesn't sound like a turkey," I said.

"Maybe it's a ghost."

"No self-respecting ghost would be that loud."

When we creaked open the thick-timbered door that led to the Old Keep's great hall, a strange sight met our eyes. Dead center in the vast room stood an old treadle sewing machine, surrounded by candelabras and a few battery-powered spotlights. Flowing from the sewing machine were yards and yards of shiny brown fabric. A round, blond-haired elf hunched over the machine. He had to perch at the very edge of his chair so his feet could work the pedals. At the sound of the door opening, he looked in our direction.

"Butterbean!" Jingles strode forward, shedding all his trepidation. "What are you doing here?"

"Sewing a helium balloon for the parade." Butterbean's round face squinted up at us, and no wonder. He was in a puddle of bright lights like an actor giving a monologue center stage. "The Order of Elven Seamstresses said they don't have time to make it before Thanksgiving. They're doing all the costumes for the Santaland Square Dancers."

Jingles crossed his arms and tossed the pom-pom of his nightcap over his shoulder. "We can see that you're sewing, but why are you doing it *here?*"

"I didn't want to bother anyone." Butterbean blinked at us. "I *didn't* disturb you, did I?"

Jingles and I exchanged a look.

"You only scared us half to death," Jingles said acidly. "We thought you might be a mutant ice rat."

"Then you must be relieved it's just me." Butterbean bent back over his sewing. His short, pudgy legs had a hard time reaching the sewing machine pedals.

This was the most subdued I'd ever seen Butterbean. Of course, it was late and very cold here in the Old Keep. A strange place to choose for a sewing room, even if he was trying to be quiet.

Also, something he'd said struck me as peculiar. "I've never heard of elves square-dancing."

"No one has," Butterbean said. "It's the elf clogging group. They thought square-dancing would be more in line with the Thanksgiving theme. They wanted to find something quintessentially American, in honor of Mrs. Claus."

I wondered what Past Me would have made of the idea that in the future a group of elves would be square-dancing through Christmastown in my honor. No doubt she would have thought someone had slipped hallucinogens into her Diet Coke. But Current Me realized that it was actually quite a compliment.

I studied the material cascading from the sewing machine table. It gave off a strange, rubbery smell. "Do you really know how to make a helium balloon?"

"Butterbean knows how to do all sorts of things," Jingles said. "He's a genius that way."

Butterbean's cheeks went pink, but he bridled to smother his pride. "I don't know about *genius*. It's just designing a pattern, picking the correct fabric, and stitching it all together."

"Where did you learn to do this?" Was there some kind of giant helium balloon instruction course somewhere in Santaland that I wasn't aware of?

"I looked on YuleTube," he said. "You can find out how to do anything there. Plus they gave me a link to where I could purchase the correct polyurethane-coated fabric and canisters of helium. It'll be just like the big Thanksgiving parade in New York City."

Right. All that would be missing would be about eight million people—and Manhattan.

A little of my skepticism must have shown. "It's going to be fantastic—just you wait and see," Butterbean assured me. "I've asked some of the reindeer to help me steer the balloon down the street."

Getting reindeer more involved was a great idea, especially since some of the elite reindeer had gotten their antlers in a twist over picking the reindeer for Santa's sleigh at random.

"I like your Thanksgiving spirit." Which reminded me. "By the way, you haven't heard a turkey flapping or gobbling around here, have you?"

"Gobbles?" He shook his head gravely. "No, I haven't."

That was too bad. "I hope he's okay."

"Don't fret, Mrs. Claus. I'm sure he'll turn up. You can't hide a twenty-four-pound bird forever."

That's what we all kept telling ourselves.

Anyway, Gobbles or no Gobbles, I had enough to worry about between now and Thursday. And I still had to finish my deviled eggs, which I now worried would lack oomph, or Thanksgivingness. Luckily, Butterbean had just given me an idea where to look to jazz them up.

Chapter 5

Nick, Pamela, Christopher, Tiffany, Claire, and I all piled into Nick's sleigh for the ride up to Kringle Lodge. Even in his everyday sleigh—not *the* sleigh used for special occasions and Christmas Eve—there was plenty of room for all of us.

I clutched my platter of deviled eggs in my lap as the world glided by. The sleigh had excellent shock absorbers; if it hadn't been for the six reindeer backsides in front of us, and the attendant jingling harnesses, you would have thought we were floating up the mountain. As we drove, a snowshoe hare darted across the path. I kept an eye on the cedar and fir trees bordering the sleigh path, which could be camouflaging Gobbles. Lucky thing I'd ordered a frozen turkey, because there had been no sign of that bird. Not so much as a stray feather.

Pamela, I noticed, was looking askance at the platter in my lap.

"Is something wrong?" I asked.

She cleared her throat. "Deviled eggs seems an odd choice for a Thanksgiving celebration."

"These are special." I'd told her that I'd made deviled eggs, but the foil I'd put over the plate covered what really made these eggs special.

Last night, stinging from Jingles's criticism, I'd enhanced

them at the last minute with a brilliant suggestion from Yule-Tube. As Butterbean had said, there were instructions on how to do everything on YuleTube, including making deviled eggs for a Thanksgiving celebration. With ingredients available in the kitchen, I was able to do a fair approximation of the recipe I'd found to fashion deviled eggs that looked like little turkeys.

Now, like a proud artist giving a preview of a painting, I pulled the foil covering back to reveal one of the eggs on the platter. Pamela's eyes widened in surprise. "Oh my goodness."

I frowned. "What's the matter?"

"Nothing—I just wasn't expecting an egg to stare back at me."

The turkeys were very simple: on top of a regular deviled egg, I inserted a little triangle of carrot to form a beak, and tail feathers were formed out of strips of carrot and beets. The eyes had posed a bigger problem, until I'd rooted around in the cookie-decorating drawer and found candy eyes. They were made of sugar, but hopefully that sweetness wouldn't stand out.

"I think they're cute," Tiffany said.

"Me, too," Claire chimed in loyally.

"Thanks. They came out just like the ones I saw online." My deviled egg recipe also had added oomph. No one could say I hadn't given my all to this side dish.

Kringle Lodge was situated at the edge of the timberline in the shadow of Sugarplum Mountain's summit. The lodge was a rustic design on a grand scale—a wide building of cedar and stone, with a covered porch spanning the width of the building.

The lodge's steward, Balsam, was waiting in the circular drive near the front door. He was dazzlingly handsome, with green eyes, a strong jaw, and a dimple in his chin—like Timothy Dalton in his prime, except shorter and with elfin ears.

He managed to cut a dashing figure even in the costume Midge and Amory had rigged him out in today: a Pilgrim outfit with black knee breeches, white hose, and black boots that were curly-toed in the elf style but with large buckles that matched the buckle on his black hat.

When the sleigh stopped, he stepped forward and helped Pamela step down. Two of his attendants—dressed in home-spun Puritan clothing—took the pies, which were encased in metal pie carriers tole-painted with exquisite decorations of partridges in pear trees, French hens, and swans swimming. Then the steward looked at the aluminium foil-covered tray I held. He shifted a bit awkwardly—obviously lacking enough minions to hand my dish off to. "I can take those for you, Mrs. Claus."

Clearly he didn't want to. "That's okay," I said, feeling very protective of my egg turkeys. "I'll put them on the buffet myself."

"As you wish." Even though he hadn't seemed eager to help, his voice now conveyed an ever-so-slight disdain at me for not accepting his offer.

Jingles had warned me that Balsam was a bit of a snob—which was rich, coming from the most socially persnickety servant at Castle Kringle. Jingles was so status conscious that any elf in a job of equal standing to his no doubt seemed a threat. From the moment he'd heard of Balsam's being hired last spring, Jingles had been sniffy about him.

"Balsam Tremblay? What kind of an elf name is that?" he'd asked.

"French?"

His eyes narrowed. "And what is a French elf doing in Santaland?"

"Madame Neige is a French elf," I'd pointed out.

Madame Neige was the directress of the Order of Elven Seamstresses.

Jingles snorted at my naïveté. "She's about as French as Quasar is. She was just plain old Coco Snowball when she and my father were in school together."

This news astonished me. Madame Neige was such a striking individual. "It's hard to imagine her coming from an ordinary elf family."

"Elves are like everyone else," Jingles said. "Some grow up dreaming of remaking themselves. Mark my words, Balsam Tremblay is a phony."

From the slight flutter of her lashes and her big smile as he helped her out of the sleigh, Claire seemed to have developed a susceptibility to handsome elves, phony or not.

"Welcome, miss," Balsam said.

Her smile didn't fade. "Claire."

He moved to give the impression of bowing without actually bending anywhere except a slight downturn of the head. "Miss Claire."

It was probably wise for Balsam to be cautious and formal. Amory was always letting servants go for the smallest of infractions. He'd fired his last steward for having too many wrinkles in his tunic. And then he complained that it was hard to find help who didn't mind living at the top of the mountain.

Midge and Amory had outdone themselves with the decorations. The rustic lodge hall was adorned with yellow, orange, and brown streamers. Although turkey wasn't going to be on the menu for this pre-Thanksgiving dinner, turkeys were everywhere in the décor: in the lights strung over the wide doorways, in the crepe paper turkeys atop tables and alternating with pumpkins on the mantelpiece. There were even turkey balloons hanging in a few corners. Where Amory had found those, I have no idea.

More surprising than the over-the-top decorations were Amory and Midge themselves, who greeted guests looking as if they'd just stepped off the *Mayflower*—if the *Mayflower* had been a Pilgrim luxury cruise. Amory wore black velvet pantaloons ending in silk garter ties, white stockings, and of course black shoes shined to a high polish. His black velvet doublet was shot through with gold thread and strained against his ample girth. Instead of a square collar, he had a frilled ruff, and his hat was more cavalier than modest Pilgrim. Next to him, Midge was in a Pilgrim's dress of fine linen, down to the embroidered white collar, apron, and lacy cap. The serving elves, I noticed, were also dressed in period costume, although in rough-spun browns. Even in their make-believe moments, Midge and Amory preserved social distinctions.

The main hall, with its vaulted, skylighted ceiling, was crowded with familiar faces: the mayor and the mayor's missus, Constable Crinkles, and Claus relations. So many Clauses. Kringle Heights, the neighborhood of châteaux and manor houses on Sugarplum Mountain between Castle Kringle and Christmastown, was full of Clauses and people who'd married Clauses. All Claus relations, in order to earn the family stipend, had to do some work in Santaland.

Clement and Carlotta Claus, twins who worked at the Wrapping Works, waved to me from across the room. I waved back. They were a gossipy pair, but fun to talk to. I was making my way over to them when I bumped into Mildred Claus, Nick's elderly cousin. She was standing next to Olive, her faithful elf companion. Olive served as Mildred's combination housekeeper, gardener, secretary, and cook. She was at least one and probably two decades older than Mildred, and though she moved slowly and looked feeble, the truth was that she was as tough as an old boot. Olive never said much, but I always sensed that her pale eyes saw everything.

"Did you just get here, too?" I asked in greeting. Otherwise, why would Mildred—not the most robust guest in the room—be left standing? Mrs. Firlog was sitting, and the mayor had just given up his seat to Pamela. I scanned the periphery of the room for other free chairs. "I'm sure we can find you a place to sit down."

"Oh, don't bother about me." Mildred was always self-effacing. "I'm just as happy to be on my feet. Olive read that staying upright is good for the digestion."

I glanced down at Olive, who nodded curtly. Not that Olive was the last word on health matters.

"In fact," Mildred continued, "she's building me a tilt board for Christmas."

"That's very thoughtful," I said.

"Olive's a wonder in the woodshop."

"She does that kind of work by herself?" I couldn't help taking in Olive's stick-thin limbs and hands that displayed a visible tremor. The thought of her operating table saws gave me pause. "Maybe Elspeth can help her."

A wave of doubt rippled across Mildred's expression. "We don't like to bother Elspeth. She's doing so much already."

"Really? What?" As far as I could tell, Elspeth had mostly dedicated her life to sponging off of Cousin Mildred. Olive, aged and creaky as she was, was the only servant over at Mildred's, and she performed most of the work there.

"Elspeth's been very busy practicing her twirling for the parade," Mildred explained. "She goes to her room all the time to work at it. It's a lucky thing we have an old house and high ceilings."

I nodded, remembering her whacking poor Bobbin in the schnozzle with her baton. All that practicing wasn't yielding stellar results. I had a suspicion it was mostly just a pretext for holing up in her bedroom.

"We think it's wonderful that she's getting so much exercise," Mildred said. "She hasn't been very robust this year."

She'd certainly seemed robust yesterday at the coffee shop. Which reminded me . . .

I glanced around. I'd lost Claire in the crowd soon after we'd entered the lodge, but now I spotted her standing next to one of the wide windows, deep in conversation with Blaze Whitewreath. And—oh God—JoJo Hollyberry was standing nearby, chatting with Mrs. Firlog, the wife of the mayor of Christmastown. Luckily, Elspeth was nowhere to be seen. I didn't want a repeat of yesterday's coffee shop encounter. I was a little stunned, however, at how quickly Claire had gravitated toward Blaze, who was looking handsome as usual in a royal-purple coat tunic and black velvet cap. Very understated for a prosperous elf.

Next to him, Claire was wearing a cranberry-colored wool dress, and her blond hair was pulled back in a French twist. The two would make a striking couple . . . if they weren't a couple already. It was strange not to know what was going on with Claire, especially now that she was here with me in Santaland. She wasn't usually a secretive person.

One thing I was sure of, though. If Claire's looking so good next to Blaze was striking to me, no doubt Elspeth would notice, too. And she would be fuming.

I scanned the room, then turned to Mildred. "Didn't Elspeth come with you?"

Mildred looked around, too. "No, she left ahead of us. She said she wanted to make sure that her prepared dish got a good place on the sideboard."

What a lunatic.

"I suppose she thought if she arrived too late," Mildred continued, "there might not be any room left for her platter and she'd be standing around with—"

Her gaze fixed on the foil-covered dish I was holding. "Oh dear—you're still holding on to yours. You'd better take it to the buffet. Or better yet, let Olive do it."

"That's all right," I said quickly. I didn't want to put Olive to any trouble.

I excused myself and turned to head to the dining room, but before I could walk away, Mildred touched my arm to stop me. "I meant to ask—have you found Gobbles?"

"Not yet."

"Oh dear. Will you send me one of those *Missing* posters I've heard about? I'll tack one up at the Christmastown Depression Center."

Mildred was the Christmastown Depression Center's sole volunteer. It was one of the least visited places in Santaland, so the poster there wouldn't be seen by many. Still, it was kind of her to offer. The more eyeballs on the lookout for Gobbles, the better.

"Thank you so much," I said. "I'll email you a copy of the poster after all this is over." I gestured vaguely around the room.

Gobbles seemed to be at the forefront of a lot of minds. Before I'd crossed halfway to the dining room, I was buttonholed by Joyce Chao-Claus, another of Nick's cousins. It was hard to keep track of the Claus family tree, although I knew Joyce was a more distant relation than Amory was. Joyce had married a non-Santalander like me, a man from Hong Kong. I looked around for him, mostly because wherever John Chao-Claus went, delicious dumplings followed. The couple ran Santaland's only Chinese restaurant, the Wonderland Wok in Tinkertown.

Joyce practically had to snap her fingers in my face to bring my attention back to her.

"Isn't John here?" I asked.

"He didn't want to close the restaurant for the day. It's Dim Sum Sunday." My disappointment must have shown on my face, and Joyce pinpointed its source right away. "He sent a platter of dumplings, though," she assured me.

"Oh good!" I shook my head, trying to make out as if I hadn't been thinking about those dumplings all along. "I mean, John will be missed."

Her hand clamped tightly around my arm, and she pinned a serious look on me. "April, I need to talk to you about that turkey," she said in a serious voice.

"Have you seen Gobbles?" I asked.

"No, but Hal heard he was missing." Hal was John and Joyce's son, who was eight. "He's very upset. His class visited the castle just last week to meet Gobbles. Now he's heartbroken that the bird is lost."

Aw, that was sweet. "Tell Hal we're doing our best to find him."

Joyce wasn't one to rest on assurances when action could be taken. "He'd like to help. Can you think of anything he and his little friends can do?"

Before I could answer, Christopher appeared. I hadn't noticed him, but he must have been eavesdropping on us because he jumped right into the conversation. "I can organize a search party with Hal," he suggested. "We could look around Peppermint Pond and put up some of April's posters around town."

"That's a great idea," I said, admiring this initiative and show of leadership.

Joyce was also impressed. "Would you, Christopher? That would be wonderful of you."

"Sure," he said. "I'll pick him up tomorrow—my friend Winky'll help, too." He cast an unsure glance at me. "That is, if Gobbles doesn't show up before then."

I left the two of them making arrangements to meet up. I'd have to tell everyone about Christopher's volunteering to help with the kids. He was going to make an incredible Santa someday.

I threaded my way through the guests toward the dining

room to deposit my egg turkeys on the buffet. Clement and Carlotta, who were standing near the door, stopped me. "Any sign of your turkey, April?"

I stopped. "Not yet."

"Oh, I'm sorry," Carlotta said.

"Wattle you do now?" Clement said, and he and Carlotta laughed.

I shook my head. Expecting them to take anything seriously was always a mistake. "I need to put these away." I nodded to the platter.

"Of course," Carlotta said. "Better shake a tail feather."

The two dissolved into whoops.

A few other guests were starting to filter across the hall to the dining area. Like the main hall, the dining room had high, slanted ceilings and a wall of windows overlooking the snow-covered grounds. A fire roared in the great fireplace at the end of the hall, and the lights had been dimmed, giving the room a cozy glow for such a large space. The long dining table was covered in Midge's finest linen, with a long centerpiece featuring evergreen boughs, candelabras, ceramic turkey figurines, and a large cornucopia with fake fruit spilling out of it. At each place a name card stood next to the water glass. Midge was very insistent on assigned seating. I checked out where I would be, and discovered to my relief that I was seated between Claire and Nick.

I stepped over to a long sideboard loaded down with dishes the guests had brought. As I searched for a place for my offering, something caught my eye. I gasped. A platter of deviled eggs with carrot tail feathers and cartoonish eyes stared up at me. I stepped back, unnerved.

Pamela was right. It *was* odd to have eggs staring back at me. Especially when the eggs were the ones I thought I held in my hands.

But I'd shown the eggs to Pamela on the sleigh ride up the

mountain. I peeked beneath the foil covering my platter. Same dish pattern, same deviled eggs.

What the heck was going on?

Indignation swelled inside me. Castle Kringle dinnerware pieces managed to circulate around Santaland, but what were the chances that someone else would have brought little turkey deviled eggs to a pre-Thanksgiving potluck?

I looked up and saw Lucia next to me, her gaze alternating between the plate of eggs I was holding and the one on the table. "You made *two* platters? How many eggs do you expect us to consume?"

I nodded my head toward the plate on the table. "Those aren't mine. Someone else brought those."

Some deviled egg imposter.

Lucia laughed. "Wow—same plate, same eggs. It's like they're trolling you."

I frowned. Ridiculous as it seemed, that's how it felt. But how could that possibly be true? "I didn't tell anyone what I was bringing. *I* didn't even know what I was going to make until late last night."

Lucia shrugged. Her limit on how much she could care about food kerfuffles had already been hit. "I never bother with cooking for these things. I just bring wine. Wine's the most necessary element to surviving any family gathering anyway."

I looked around for something else she hadn't brought. "Where's Quasar?" Hosts often balked at inviting him to events like this—large ruminants could be challenging dinner guests for any hostess—but Lucia usually boycotted events where Quasar wasn't welcome. "Didn't Midge and Amory invite him?"

"In their usual grudging fashion—but Quasar decided to skip it anyway. He's busy getting reindeer to sign up for the Thanksgiving parade sleigh-pulling drawing."

"That's good of him," I said. "Although a little self-defeating, isn't it? The more reindeer who put their names in the hat, the less chance Quasar has of being one of the eight who are chosen."

"He doesn't care," Lucia said. "He just thinks it's a great opportunity for reindeer to participate."

Quasar was such a good soul. "That makes me hope his name gets picked all the more."

"Me, too." Lucia's lips twisted. "I've been trying to figure out ways to rig the drawing in his favor."

My jaw dropped. "That's terrible!"

She laughed. "I'm joking. If you could see your face. You'd think I'd just committed murder."

My reply was cut off by a gasp from behind us.

Elspeth was gaping at the deviled eggs. "Is this some kind of gag? Did you steal my idea?"

I groaned. It *would* have to be Elspeth involved in the duplicate egg dish scenario. She already had a tendency to believe that people—usually me—were undermining her. Now this.

"Great minds think alike," I joked, trying to defuse the situation.

No such luck. The color in her face went from irritated pink to boiled lobster. "Seriously—look at those egg turkeys. They're just alike, right down to the googly eyes. I was planning my eggs for *weeks*. How did you find out?" She scowled. "Did Olive tell you about my eggs? I swear, that elf will stop at nothing!"

I sputtered out a laugh. Did she honestly think I sent spies to Mildred's house to pull some side dish shenanigans on her? "I swear, all I did was find a video on YuleTube. And technically, those aren't googly eyes, since they don't move. They're fixed candy eyes."

Her scowl just deepened. "What is this, retribution for

yesterday? You just had to show me up because I had an argument with your little American friend?"

"Please." I purposefully kept my voice low and calm, the way you might when talking to a feral animal. "I wasn't even thinking of you, Elspeth. I just made something fast and easy."

"*Easy?*"

Oh God. When Elspeth got into one of these states, it was almost impossible to find the correct words to get her to snap out of it. Every attempt to placate her just seemed to make her worse. It was a shame that she didn't have an Off button that I could push so I could walk away until she'd cooled down.

"I put a lot of care into my egg turkeys and their presentation," she said indignantly.

On the platter you obviously nicked from Castle Kringle. "I didn't mean to belittle your efforts."

An uncomfortable chuckle rasped out of her. "No, you just insinuated that for *you* it was no big deal." Her face collapsed into a frown. "Have you been spying on me?"

Now it was my turn to laugh. "No. How could I?"

"I was searching for recipes yesterday on my phone, in the coffee shop."

"I never went near your phone. I didn't even know you were there until you swooped down on us."

Maybe *swooped* was the wrong word to use. She crossed her arms. "You even sprinkled your eggs with paprika, like mine."

For Pete's sake. "The whole world does that." I looked to Lucia to back me up. "Right?"

She lifted her hands. "Leave me out of it. All deviled eggs look nauseating to me."

Thanks, Lucia.

A crowd was gathering around us, including Claire and Blaze. I sent up a silent prayer that Elspeth wouldn't turn around and see them. That just might cause her to snap.

"Anyway," I said, eager to put this whole stupid argument to rest. "I doubt our eggs are exactly the same. I have a secret ingredient in mine."

Elspeth's forehead wrinkled in suspicion. "What secret ingredient?"

I shrugged. "Just a little something I came up with."

She hesitated a split second, then darted her hand out to my plate. She scooped up an egg, popped it into her mouth, and started chewing.

A second later, her face scrunched up. She flapped her hands, making a noise of disgust as she searched frantically for something. Finally, she grabbed a napkin off the buffet and spat the egg back into it.

"Ew!" Claire exclaimed.

"Are you trying to poison us all?" Elspeth said, her face still puckered in revulsion. "What did you put into those?"

Fire crept into my cheeks. "Garlic."

"In deviled eggs?" Pamela blurted, horrified.

I hadn't even noticed my mother-in-law approach.

At this point, Elspeth was hopping up and down, as if she could shake the bad taste away. Then she poured a glass of wine into the wineglass at her table and glugged down half a glass.

I looked around for Nick, hoping for one supportive voice in the crowd. Unfortunately, he had been cornered by Constable Crinkles on the other side of the room. The two of them were deep in conversation.

Finally, Midge hurried forward, Pilgrim cap fluttering. "Speaking of food, why don't we all start finding our places and serving ourselves?" She looked distastefully at my egg turkeys, which I was still holding in front of me like a cater waiter. With the tips of her fingers, she took the plate from me. "Let's just set these aside for now, shall we?" She looked around. "Balsam?"

The steward wasn't in the room, but a serving elf who was filling water glasses at the long table set her pitcher down. "I'll take them, madam."

"Thank you, Star," Midge said. Bending to the elf's ear, she lowered her voice and added, "Just take them to the kitchen."

The guests started making their way to the buffet.

A hand touched my shoulder and I turned to find Nick standing close to me, looking puzzled. "What was that about?"

I made sure Elspeth wasn't watching before rolling my eyes. "Elspeth has the crazy idea that I copied her egg turkeys."

My explanation didn't seem to clear up his confusion any. "That brouhaha was over a plate of eggs?"

"You know how Elspeth is. Drama queen. She's probably just put out because Claire's been cozying up to Blaze White-wreath."

At this news, Nick turned sharply, following my gaze. "What do they see in him?"

"According to Juniper, to the female elves of Christmas-town he's the star at the top of the tree."

Nick's brow furrowed.

"Or Claire might just be trying to make Jake Frost jealous."

"Jake's not here, so how can she make him jealous by talking to Blaze at a party?"

"News travels fast in Santaland. I'm sure word will even reach beyond Mount Myrrh soon." When he didn't respond, I asked, "Are you worried about her leading Blaze on?"

Nick guffawed at that. "I'm more concerned for Claire. Blaze doesn't have a great track record for long-term relationships."

Now it was my turn to laugh. "He's met his match, then. If it's a battle of heartbreakers, we'll see who slays whom."

By the time Nick and I finished our little tête-à-tête and got into the buffet line, most of the other guests had already bellied up to the trough.

Not that there was any danger of running out of food on that long buffet table. Even though some dishes had been cleared out, there was still enough left to feed half of Santaland. I greeted Lettuce, Kringle Lodge's main chef, when I finally reached the carving table in the buffet line. She was one of the few lodge elves not decked out in a period getup. She wore her usual white chef's uniform topped off by a high white hat. Lettuce was Butterbean's sister. Butterbean had been employed at the lodge, too, until an unfortunate accident last year had caused Amory to fire him.

"What would you like, Mrs. Claus?" she asked.

There was no turkey—that was to be reserved for Thursday—but Amory hadn't skimped on the meat offerings. Guests had a choice of honey ham, roast goose, or a musk ox roast so large it looked like an entire haunch. Lettuce had to lift onto the curly toes of her booties to see around the roast to talk to me.

"I'll try the goose," I said, and Nick repeated the same order for himself. We made our way down the rest of the sideboard, heaping our plates with all the offerings from the lodge kitchen and the guests at the gathering. Dishes leaned heavily on cranberries and pecans as theme ingredients. My only complaint was that the mountain of mashed potatoes Lettuce and her kitchen elves had prepared was nearly gone. Knowing that Nick loved mashed potatoes, I decided to go without for the sake of him and the few other guests in line behind us. *No greater love*, I thought.

When I was done, I turned to take my seat at the dinner table. My place was between Claire and Nick, but I was dismayed to see that Elspeth was directly opposite me. She would be staring across the table at me and, worse still, Claire, who was seated next to Blaze Whitewreath. I suspected a place-card switcheroo had taken place to achieve that coincidence. Claire could be sneaky.

Remembering what Mildred had said about Elspeth not being as robust as usual, I couldn't help noticing that she did look awful. Her complexion was off—sallow, almost green, like a cheese going to mold.

"Elspeth, are you feeling okay?" I asked.

Her lips tightened. "I was fine until I ate that grotesque egg of yours."

Again with the egg. My sympathy for her began to melt away, especially when I noticed that she had taken what looked like a triple helping of mashed potatoes.

She gulped down some wine. "I've been trying to wash that disgusting taste out of my mouth. I'm not sure I ever will, though."

I'm Mrs. Claus. I can't cause another scene at a dinner party. No matter how much I wanted to upend a gravy boat over the woman's head, I would rise above it.

I looked around the table. Everyone was waiting patiently for the last buffet laggards to be seated before digging in. Midge was talking to Pamela; Crinkles and JoJo Hollyberry were chatting about the parade; Claire and Blaze were deep in conversation in low voices; Mildred was smiling, eager to be pleased by everyone and everything, while Olive sat watchfully in a chair behind her. Apparently the old servant hadn't come to eat, just to look after Mildred. Which seemed silly. What could go wrong at a dinner?

Besides, Olive wasn't even paying attention to Mildred. Her narrowed eyes were focused on Elspeth.

I glanced across the table again. Elspeth had gone from green to a sort of mottled purple. Alarmed, I leaned forward. "Elspeth?"

She took another long drink of wine, but her shaking

hand lost control as she tried to put the glass back on the table and she knocked it over. It broke, and a deep red stain spread over Midge's cloth.

Mayor Firlog, Elspeth's neighbor, hopped up to avoid being splashed—too late. The red wine had already stained his maroon-and-yellow checked tunic, too.

"What's going on?" he asked.

"She's sick," I said, growing afraid for her.

Elspeth nodded, clutching her stomach for a moment before lifting her trembling hand. Her index finger pointed at me.

"April." Her voice was barely a rasp. "Help—"

Her bloodshot eyes widened.

Was she frightened of me? Was she accusing me of—of what?

Before I could find out, Elspeth collapsed facedown into her extra large helping of mashed potatoes. Then, after a heave and a shudder, her body went still. Deadly still.

Chapter 6

For half a heartbeat, silence descended on the room. I couldn't believe what I was seeing; no one could. One minute Elspeth had been her whingeing, annoying self, and the next she was just . . . facedown in her mashed potatoes.

Gone.

A shrill cry from Mildred rent the silence. Nick was the first to react, jumping out of his chair and rushing around to the other side of the table. I followed, and we pulled Elspeth upright. If she wasn't dead, having her face smothered in food wasn't going to help her.

The moment I touched her, however, it became very clear to me that the situation was beyond dire. Her body was an unresponsive sack of flesh, and a fixed unseeingness had settled into her eyes. Those glassy orbs unnerved me. Just a minute ago they had been sharp with indignation. She had even used her dying moment to shoot me one last evil eye and point a red-polished finger at me.

Why? What did she mean by saying my name, followed by "Help"?

"Give me a hand laying her on the carpet," Nick said to me.

It was good one of us was focused on the emergency . . .

although I didn't hold out much hope for saving Elspeth. At first, I was surprised that Nick didn't perform the Heimlich maneuver, but instead started CPR. He was right, though. Whatever had happened to Elspeth hadn't seemed like choking. Not long ago I'd performed the Heimlich maneuver on Constable Crinkles when he'd choked. He hadn't been able to speak, and had barely been able to move. In her last moments, Elspeth had lifted her arm to point at me. The way she'd spoken my name would haunt me.

When I looked up, Crinkles was standing over us. Other guests formed a semicircle around him. JoJo Hollyberry was frowning at Elspeth, and then he aimed that frown at me. His stare was no less accusing than Elspeth's had been before she'd collapsed into her meal.

Mildred broke through the line, her face contorted in fear. "Elspeth?" Her desperate eyes sought Nick's. "Is she going to be okay?"

His voice lowered. "I can't find a pulse. I'm sorry."

Hands over her face, Mildred tipped back her head and howled in grief. The sound sent a shiver through me. Elspeth had lived at Château Mildred for years, but it took this terrible moment to make me realize how close Mildred felt toward her.

"I'm so sorry, Mildred," I said, crossing toward her.

She collapsed into the nearest chair. Elspeth's, as it happened. Her place card remained next to her shattered wineglass.

Clement reached for the water glass to give it to Mildred, I supposed with the misplaced notion that it would do her some good. As if shock and grief were matters of poor hydration. In moments like these, most gestures were simply done out of love, not usefulness.

Thinking quickly, I piped up, "No—don't."

Clement shot a surprised look at me. "Why not?"

"That was Elspeth's water glass."

"I don't care," Mildred said.

Nick put a hand on Clement's arm. "Best not."

Nick and I turned to Constable Crinkles, hoping he would understand the problem. The lawman looked as baffled as Clement. "I don't see the harm. I could use a drink myself."

"This might be a crime scene," I said.

Mildred gasped. "You think someone *killed* Elspeth?"

"April just meant that it could be a possibility," Nick said.

Mildred's eyes were unfocused, bewildered. "I just assumed she choked."

Nick shook his head. "I don't think so. She was talking right before she died."

He shot an anxious glance at me, no doubt remembering Elspeth saying my name.

"Murder!" Crinkles exclaimed, as if this were a new concept to him. "Who would do such a thing?"

The same question had begun percolating in my brain. I studied the faces hovering around us. Midge and Amory, panicked Pilgrims, were slack-jawed with shock. Pamela, Tiffany, and Christopher also looked stunned; Tiffany circled her arms around her son as if she could create a force field between him and death. Across the table, Claire's eyes were huge, and Blaze had a comforting arm around her. Lucia had hiked one hip against the dining table, and wore a thoughtful frown as she sipped some wine. Clement and Carlotta had retreated to the back of the room as if to observe from a safe distance. Their usual japing smiles weren't in evidence now. Now they looked as solemn and apprehensive as everyone else. The mere mention of the word *murder* had shifted the atmosphere in the room.

The serving elves and Lettuce, who'd all been hanging back in a doorway, parted when Balsam strode into the room and addressed himself to Midge and Amory. Their over-the-top Pilgrim outfits seemed out of sync with the mood of the room now. Amory had at least removed his silly hat, revealing his bald, pink skull.

"I've phoned Doctor Honeytree," Balsam announced with solemn formality. Then, with more consideration than the rest of us had shown, he placed a large cloth into Midge's hands. "I thought this might be needed . . . to cover Miss Claus."

"Thank you, Balsam," Midge said.

She, Amory, and Nick draped the cloth over Elspeth's lifeless form. It was a tablecloth, I could see now, of creamy white linen with brighter white snowflakes embroidered around the edges. A makeshift shroud, yes, but a fitting one for a Claus.

Quietly, Olive wove through the huddled guests and went to Mildred's side. She whispered something in her employer's ear.

Mildred nodded and then turned to Amory and Midge. "Olive thinks we should go home. It's been such a shock." Her gaze moved back to Elspeth. "I just hate to leave her here like this."

Nick crossed to her and put a comforting arm around her. "She'll be taken care of—Doc will see to that."

The thought seemed to comfort her. "Doc brought her into the world."

Doc Honeytree had brought almost everyone born in Santaland into the world.

Mildred took a tissue that Olive offered her and dabbed her eyes with it. "It's going to be so strange returning to the house without her."

"I'll take you home," Nick said. He flicked a glance at me and I nodded. There was nothing for Mildred to do here now. Waiting for Doc to get here and then take Elspeth away would be agony for her. Château Mildred wasn't the most comfortable place on Sugarplum Mountain, but it was her home and she'd be more comfortable there.

Nick escorted her out. On his other arm was Olive. My heart ached at the kindness he showed the two old ladies.

Tiffany approached Midge and Amory now. "Christopher and I will follow Nick to Mildred's," she said. "Maybe we can be of use there."

Mostly, I could see, she wanted to get Christopher away. Pamela went with them.

After the group bound for Mildred's had gone, Clement and Carlotta stepped forward to address Midge and Amory next. "We'll take our leave, too."

I frowned and turned to Crinkles. "You don't want *everyone* leaving, surely. Shouldn't you be talking to everyone?"

His blue eyes widened and blinked. "About what?"

"About Elspeth's death."

His lips formed a tight *o* in his round face, as if he were about to whistle but ran out of air. "I guess I probably should take some statements." He patted his breast pocket, then turned to Amory. "Do you have a pencil and a little notepad?"

"I can get you that," Amory said, looking eager to escape if only for a moment. My guess was that he wanted to escape to the well-stocked liquor cabinet in his office.

Carlotta and Clement didn't look pleased with me. "Thanks, Miss Marple," Carlotta muttered.

Crinkles tutted. "Now, don't blame Mrs. Claus. I have to ask questions."

"Why bother?" a strident voice piped up.

JoJo strode forward. He'd dressed in green-and-red checks today, with green-and-white striped stockings. "Elspeth Claus was poisoned. We all saw it, and who did it. April Claus poisoned Elspeth."

"I did not," I said.

How could he accuse me of murder? Sure, there was no love lost between Hollyberrys and Clauses, but JoJo and I were bandmates.

"Please." He tossed his head slightly back so that the jingle bell on his elf cap tinkled. "She ate that egg of yours. What did you put in it?"

Heat flooded my face. "That's ridiculous. Elspeth didn't even swallow it."

"That's right," Carlotta said, jumping to my defense. "She had to spit it out because it . . . tasted so foul . . ."

Hardly a ringing endorsement of my cooking's trustworthiness. Carlotta shot me an apologetic look.

"She must have swallowed trace amounts of whatever April Claus laced it with," JoJo said. "Let's hope that Doc Honeytree can pinpoint exactly what poison you used."

"I did not poison Elspeth."

"Of course you didn't." Claire turned and addressed all the people assembled around us. "None of you have known April for as long as I have. She wouldn't kill anyone. Or anything. The very idea is preposterous. She even catches and releases spiders she finds at her inn."

I swallowed back a groan. Claire couldn't have chosen a worse example to use as a character testimonial. Being kind to spiders didn't carry much moral weight in Santaland. Spiders were few here, and elves were vulnerable to any kind of venom. No one was more sensitive to this than JoJo Hollyberry, whose cousin, Giblet, had been killed by a spider bite.

"Isn't. That. Nice." JoJo's words themselves dripped with venom.

Claire, looking more doubtful now at the awkward silence in the room, persisted. "I know April isn't responsible for this."

"Naturally you're going to stick up for your friend." JoJo turned and addressed himself to the gathered guests like one of the prosecutors on *Law and Order*. "I saw those two at the We Three Beans yesterday. Elspeth confronted them about something, and there was a fight. Ask anyone who was there. The whole coffee shop witnessed it. Elspeth even mentioned something about poison."

"That was just a little argument over—" I bit my lip before I could drag Claire's name into this, which I absolutely didn't want to do. "Elspeth and I just didn't get along all that well . . ."

My words dribbled away into silence. Nothing seemed to come out right.

JoJo arched his brows as if to say, *See?*

The others stared at me, and I could tell at least a few of the elf guests seemed to be swayed by JoJo's arguments.

"We had misunderstandings," I admitted. "She always thought I was undermining her or something crazy like that." *Way to speak ill of the dead, April.* The more I babbled on, the guiltier I probably seemed. "I never would have harmed her, though."

"Did anyone else hear this argument?" Crinkles asked everyone.

"I was there," Claire said. "*I* was the one Elspeth was angry at. She'd seen me walking down the street with Blaze and seemed to think it was an insult to her."

"Were you and Elspeth an item?" the constable asked Blaze.

"At one time," he admitted. Then he shook his head regretfully. "Poor Elspeth. Are we actually sure someone did kill her? Perhaps she died of natural causes. People have heart attacks, even at dinner."

Crinkles considered this. "That's true. I guess we'll have to wait for Doc Honeytree to give us his professional opinion."

Blaze nodded gravely. "I'd like to offer to pay for any funeral expenses for Elspeth. Even though we were no longer involved, I still care about her." He swallowed, and immeasurable sadness filled his expression. "*Cared.* I can't believe I have to speak about her in the past tense now."

The gravelly sorrow in his voice seemed genuine, and it obviously convinced quite a few others. The room fell silent except for the ticking of an old, ornately carved cuckoo clock, and a few guests—women, mostly—were dabbing at tears as they looked at Blaze.

During the wait for Doc Honeytree, everyone began to filter away from Elspeth to the other side of the room. Guests gathered in clusters to speak in hushed tones.

Midge and Amory came over to where I stood with Claire.

"Well, this isn't *quite* the party we'd envisioned," Midge said in a low voice.

Amory looked a little put out. "A lot of food gone to waste—and that honey ham was imported. I guess it would be bad form to serve it now."

"Yes," I agreed. Although, frankly, my stomach *was* a little grumbly. I glanced regretfully at my loaded plate on the table.

Midge sighed. "It's just like Elspeth to do something like this."

"Die?" Claire asked.

Realizing how her words sounded, Midge backtracked. "Don't get me wrong. It's a tragedy, of course. But it seems very odd that she died *here*, during dinner."

"Unless she really was poisoned," Amory said. Looking at me, his eyes widened. "Not that I think *you* did it."

"Heavens no," Midge chimed. "Anyway, we all know Elspeth could be difficult."

So they didn't think I did it, but they'd understand if I did?

I frowned, remembering something. "Mildred said that Elspeth hadn't been feeling well recently."

"Well—there you are." Midge seemed oddly pleased with this tidbit of gossip. "Natural causes—just like Blaze said."

"In which case we're missing out on dinner for no reason at all." Amory eyed the ham again.

Midge clucked at him. "Put it out of your mind. We could hardly start eating while she's lying there on the floor."

He sighed. "No, I suppose you're right."

"Poor Elspeth." Claire shook her head. "It doesn't sound as if she'd win any popularity contests around here."

"Mildred was very upset," I said.

Midge's brow broke out in a network of lines. "Now *that* was surprising, wasn't it? I never thought she cared all that much for Elspeth. But I suppose once you live together for a long time, you just get used to each other."

Amory leaned in toward her. "Like you and me?"

She fluttered and gave her husband a loving swat on the ruff. "I think if I died in the middle of dinner, you probably would just carry on eating."

He grinned at her. "That would depend on what was on the menu."

Their bantering was interrupted by Doc Honeytree's arrival. As usual, the old doctor was dressed all in black from stovepipe hat to the tips of his booties. It made for a dramatic entrance.

"Finally." Amory straightened. "I'd better go have a word."

I wanted to talk to him, too. Walking in behind the doctor was his nephew, Algid, who had recently started working with him. Algid was thin and almost cadaverously pale. He tended to stay in the laboratory; a sighting of him making a house call was uncommon.

Doc crossed directly to where Elspeth lay, dropped into a knee-cracking squat next to her, and pulled back the table-cloth. "Hm."

It was always amazing to me that the old doctor could see anything through the glasses he wore. The lenses were as thick as the bottom of a Coke bottle. He pulled his gaze away from Elspeth to look up at his nephew. Very subtly, Algid nodded. They'd noticed something about her appearance.

Crinkles bobbed nervously. "See, we were thinking that Elspeth must've died of natural causes."

"Not likely." Doc Honeytree creaked back up to standing with his nephew's aid.

"Why?" I asked.

"Discoloration on her lips, bloodshot eyes." Doc shook his head. "That combined with what you told me over the phone about how she flopped over into her mashed potatoes, it's a clear case of poison."

Gasps went round the room, and my stomach churned in dread.

"We'll need to take samples of everything you know Elspeth ate or drank here," Doc told Amory. "And keep samples of the rest for a day or so until we can look at the contents of her stomach."

JoJo Hollyberry stepped forward. "There's no need to do an autopsy to find out what Elspeth ate. We all saw it—she had one of those killer eggs that Mrs. Claus brought."

"But she didn't swallow it," I said.

Doc frowned. "Didn't swallow it? Then how in the blue blazes did she eat it?"

"She spat it out," I said.

"Because it tasted awful," JoJo said pointedly. "Elspeth mentioned that several times."

Doc Honeytree looked over at his nephew, then nodded toward the buffet. "Algid, make sure you bag one of those eggs, and little bits of everything else besides."

Algid nodded and snapped on a pair of latex gloves. He

even had evidence-collection bags at the ready. It was very by-the-book for Santaland.

JoJo was like a dog who'd just sunk his jaws into a particularly tasty, grizzly bone. He wasn't about to let it go. "It's a stroke of luck that none of the rest of us ingested one, or half the guests might be dead right now."

"There was no poison," I insisted. "Elspeth just didn't like the garlic."

Doc Honeytree's face fell. "You put garlic in your deviled eggs?"

"It's supposed to give them oomph. I found the recipe on YuleTube."

Midge gaped at me. "You needed instructions to make deviled eggs?"

Surprised, confused, and pitying faces stared back at me.

"I wanted to make them look special," I said in my defense.

But the eyes of the identical egg turkeys Elspeth had prepared mocked my pretenses of originality.

JoJo puffed up and rounded on Constable Crinkles. "Aren't you going to make an arrest?"

"Who?" The constable looked baffled. "April? For putting garlic in her deviled eggs?"

JoJo shook with frustration. "For killing Elspeth. The egg turkey was the only thing the woman ate. And then she died a short time later. We all saw it, plain as a pine cone. She even pointed at Mrs. Claus—her dying gesture." He turned toward me, his eyes pinpricks of accusation. "With her dying breath, the poor woman begged us for help. Mrs. Claus is a murderer."

Chapter 7

"I did not murder Elspeth," I insisted for the thousandth time.

When Crinkles and I arrived back at the constabulary, Ollie met us at the door and helped us off with our coats, hats, and mufflers while Crinkles filled him in on all the details. Word of Elspeth's death at the lodge had reached Christmastown—gossip flew as fleetly as reindeer in Santaland—but the deputy was surprised to see me brought in for further questioning. Technically I was not under arrest, Crinkles had been careful to explain to everyone as he handed me into the sidecar of the constabulary snowmobile. But it had looked enough like an arrest to silence JoJo Hollyberry—at least for the moment.

"The only thing I'm guilty of is putting too much garlic in my deviled eggs."

Ollie's face collapsed in shock as he hung Crinkles's scarf, decorated with a reindeer and Christmas tree pattern, on the coat rack. "You put garlic in your deviled eggs?"

He clearly considered that a crime against cuisine. He wasn't alone, apparently.

"Guilty," I said. "But that's all I'm guilty of."

We continued through to the dining room area. The inflated donuts were still on display, and now a complex craft project was underway. The table was covered in old copies of the *Christmastown Herald*. A tub of some kind of gluey substance sat on the table along with piles of newspapers that had been cut into strips. In one corner of the room there was a shipping box big enough to hold an average-sized kitchen stove, although right now it was full of inflated rubber play balls—the cheap, multicolored kind sold in basket bins in grocery stores. Several of these balls had been coated in newspaper strips and were perched on the table to dry.

"What's all this?" I asked.

"It's Ollie's papier-mâché project," Crinkles explained. "For the parade float." He looked sheepishly at the mess. "I didn't know I'd be bringing back a suspect—er, guest. Don't worry—we'll have tea in the living room."

At the mention of tea, my stomach rumbled. I was starving. But I was still fascinated by the crafty chaos on the table. "What do papier-mâché rubber balls have to do with the constabulary float?"

Ollie reached over and gingerly held one up. "When they're dry, I'll decorate them to look like they're donut holes covered in powdered sugar or chocolate or sprinkles. They'll form the decorative edge of the float platform."

"A donut hole border," I said. "I would never have thought of that."

Ollie sighed in frustration. "I'm beginning to wish I hadn't thought of it, either. I've got a lot of holes to make before Wednesday, and it's more involved than I expected—each step has to dry."

"While I'm here, I can help you," I offered.

The deputy's eyes lit up. "Will you? That'd be great." He looked over at his uncle. "Hey, Unc, are there any other suspects in Elspeth's murder that you could bring in?"

Crinkles put his hands on his round hips. "I can't arrest people just to help with your craft project. I told you we should just do a snowy border with some of that white batting they sell at Sparkletoe's Mercantile."

Ollie sniffed. "*Everybody* does snow borders. I want our float to look unique."

Crinkles sent me a long-suffering look. "You don't have anybody else in mind as suspects, do you?"

I gave him the benefit of the doubt and assumed he truly wanted to find out what had happened to Elspeth, not just bring in more people to papier-mâché rubber balls.

"There were plenty of people at Kringle Lodge today who weren't overly fond of Elspeth," I said.

"I'm no expert in the ways of Clauses, but for elves, being not overly fond of someone doesn't usually lead to murder."

Crinkles scratched his double chin. "That business of her pointing at you before she collapsed . . . Why would she have done that?"

"I wish I knew. She also said the word 'Help.' JoJo Holly-berry seemed to think she was warning everyone against me."

Elspeth probably died thinking I'd murdered her. That thought depressed me.

"JoJo's always been a cranky elf, even for a Hollyberry . . ." The constable's lips turned down. "But then there's the whole issue of the egg. Everybody saw her eat it."

"And spit it out," I reminded him.

"There are poisons in the world that work with just tiny amounts, I hear," Ollie chimed in helpfully.

I sank down in my chair. If I didn't know better, even I would think I'd killed Elspeth. All the evidence made me look guilty.

The constable tapped his fingers. "Did you notice the way the serving elves were watching what was going on?"

"You can hardly blame them. It's not every day someone dies during a dinner party."

For a moment, his face tensed as if the act of thinking was physically painful for him. "Or it might have been something more sinister. After all, Elspeth had a heaping plate of food— well, we all did." He lowered his voice regretfully. "It all looked delicious, too. I'm fond of honey ham."

I narrowed my gaze on him. "But no one saw her eating anything besides the egg."

"So? Who's to say she didn't sneak a little nibble of something on the way to the table? I do that sometimes myself. She might have popped an hors d'oeuvre into her mouth. Even a cracker or a piece of bread."

"Poison bread?" I asked doubtfully.

"Well . . . something." He shook his head. "There was lots of food on that buffet, all brought by different people. And for a while, no one else was in that room. No one was watching the food."

Ollie looked up from where he was methodically plastering pasty newspaper over a sparkly pink rubber ball. "Sounds to me like it all depends on the egg," Ollie said, "and whether or not it was poisoned."

"Yup," Crinkles agreed. "We'll just have to see what Doc Honeytree's nephew finds."

Ollie looked at me with hopeful eyes. "And while you're waiting . . ."

I nodded. "Toss me one of those balls."

I managed to cover an entire rubber ball in soppy newspaper strips before my first visitor arrived. Of course it was Juniper.

"I hurried over as soon as I could get away from the library," she announced breathlessly. "What's going on?" Before I could explain about Elspeth and the egg, however, she was completely distracted by Operation Donut Hole. "What's all this?"

Ollie told her about the parade float, finishing with, "Would you like to make a hole?" he asked her. "If you do, you can come back tomorrow when it's dry and decorate it yourself."

Juniper could never resist a craft project.

After we were both ensconced at the table, up to our elbows in the mess, it occurred to me that I'd forgotten to send Juniper a text to tell her I'd been brought in for questioning. "How did you know I was here?" I asked her. "Did Claire call you?"

She blinked. "Gosh, no. Nick did."

Nick, of course, had been the first person I'd sent an SOS out to. He'd promised to come by as soon as he'd gotten Mildred settled at home and made sure she was okay. He must have been doing a thorough job of consoling; I hadn't heard from him since.

Claire hadn't appeared yet, either, but she'd at least texted to ask if I was okay. I affirmed that I was, and that my staying here was just for appearances until they discovered that my deviled egg had not been fatal.

Have business to tend to, and then I will find a way to drop by. Let me know if you need anything!

What business was she talking about? She was on vacation.

Blaze was the business, I guessed.

Don't worry, I texted back. **Hope to be home soon.**

And by *soon*, I meant sometime before Thanksgiving. I didn't want to spend Claire's entire visit in the hoosegow, even if it was a very homey hoosegow.

Smudge came by the constabulary to walk Juniper home. I wasn't overly surprised to see him. He and Juniper were exes, but they'd become friendlier lately. Maybe friendlier than I'd realized.

"What's going on with the balls and the newspaper?" he asked.

When it was explained to him, he shook his head. "That's pretty crack-brained."

"But extremely addictive," Juniper said.

"Really?" He sat down and picked up a ball. Soon, he was as immersed in the activity as the rest of us.

There was something irresistible about slapping soggy newspaper onto a surface. It reminded me of a solar system project I'd done when I was in elementary school. I'd lost an entire weekend of my life to that project and hadn't even minded.

While we worked, Ollie pulled a batch of muffins out of the oven and served them on dainty holiday plates. Meanwhile, Crinkles put on some Christmas music—a mix of Bing Crosby and other golden oldies. A knock on the door heralded the entrance of Lucia and Quasar.

Nick's sister took one look at us sitting around the table and tossed her blond braid over her shoulder. "I see you're doing hard time."

"The Christmastown equivalent of making license plates." I tried to make light of being here, but the truth was that I'd been hoping that Nick would be the next one through the door. Yes, he knew the only possible peril at the constabulary would be the risk of eating too many rich desserts. But I was still being held on suspicion of murder. Didn't that rate a spousal visit?

Lucia inspected the newspaper-covered balls sitting on the table. "What the heck are those supposed to be?"

"Donut holes," Juniper said cheerily, as if it were obvious.

Lucia's lips twisted skeptically, but she took a seat and was soon swept up into the activity. Quasar even got in on the act, dragging strips of paper through the liquid in the tub.

After Clement and Carlotta showed up, the constabulary living room was starting to feel like the Marx Brothers' overstuffed stateroom in *A Night at the Opera*. If one more person opened the door, we all might just explode out onto Festival Boulevard. "Not a bad way to spend your time in the slammer," Clement remarked archly.

Some slammer, I thought.

The group continued to work, singing along to the next song, "God Rest Ye Merry Gentlemen." The room grew so noisy that we didn't hear anyone come in until Nick in his red suit filled up the doorway into the dining room. Behind him, like a pale, thin shadow, stood Doc Honeytree's nephew, Algid. He was wearing a warm black elf cap but still wore his white lab coat.

My pulse picked up. I knew I was innocent, of course, but what if something had gone wrong with the egg Algid had tested? Someone might have tampered with it.

The table quieted as everyone looked up expectantly, which left just the sound of Bing Crosby. Crinkles leapt up to turn off the music. "What did you find out?"

"Excuse me for coming instead of my uncle," Algid said. "He had to be called away to Tinkertown. There was a three-sleigh collision."

"No fatalities, I hope," Crinkles said.

"Oh no. An elf dislocated his arm, and apparently two of the reindeer involved in the accident got into an argument, so Uncle Doc's having to do a bit of patching up of antler puncture wounds."

Road rage, Santaland style.

Lucia frowned. "Did Doc say which reindeer?"

Algid shook his head.

"What about the egg?" I asked, unable to keep the impatience out of my voice—and the worry.

"The egg was just a deviled egg," Nick said. "April didn't poison anybody."

I sagged against the back of my chair. Knowing I was innocent was one thing. Being cleared was still a huge relief.

Constable Crinkles looked relieved, too. He obviously didn't relish locking up Santa's wife for murder. "Guess you're free to go, Mrs. Claus."

Juniper beamed at me, until a moment later her smile faded. "If April's egg didn't kill Elspeth, what did?"

"I'm going to have to do more testing." Algid looked anxiously at Nick. "I just wanted to make sure the constable understood that Mrs. Claus's egg was not the cause of death."

"Thank you." I realized now that this was where Nick had been—putting pressure on Algid to move my egg to the top of the testing queue.

"We're going to have to look at . . . well, other things."

He meant the autopsy, to see what else Elspeth had eaten.

"We should have more findings tomorrow," Algid said.

Constable Crinkles smiled at me. "I guess you're free to go, then."

I wasted no time gathering my things. To my surprise, no one else followed suit. Santalanders: give them holiday music, hot beverages, and a craft project and they were immovable.

"I'm going now," I announced over the strains of Ella Fitzgerald singing "Winter Wonderland."

Juniper smiled at me, then nodded at Smudge, who didn't seem inclined to budge until the last rubber ball in the box was papered. "Don't forget marching rehearsal tomorrow," he called out, completely focused on smoothing down a strip of newspaper.

It felt as if we'd just had a rehearsal, but that had been yesterday. Luther had insisted we drill every other day in order to get us ready in time for the parade. The parade was Wednesday, so tomorrow would be our last rehearsal.

Outside, Nick handed me up into the sleigh. Then he

brought out a wool blanket and tucked it carefully around me. The reindeer team—the same one that had driven us up to the lodge this morning—seemed happy when he gave them the command, "Home." It had been a long day for them, too.

I could tell by the way they began to buck and hop that we were going to take the fast route. Instead of driving through Christmastown and then winding up the mountain path through Kringle Heights to the castle, the reindeer took off at a bounding sprint. Then, with a stomach-churning lurch, we were airborne.

I tensed, and Nick slipped an arm around me. "Seemed like a good night to take the shortcut."

My teeth chattered. Sleigh flight still wigged me out, but to Nick this was the shortest and simplest of hops. Nothing at all like the grueling round-the-world trip that he would be taking in another month's time.

And yet, even in my slightly terrified state, I could appreciate the beauty of the night around me. The northern lights were casting a green aura around the night sky, and as always, I was dazzled by how large and bright the stars were at the North Pole. On a clear night like this one they seemed almost bright enough to reach out and hold.

Their brilliance and the warmth of Nick's nearness soothed me. After a day like today, it was good to be reminded of the wonderful things in life. I tried not to take it for granted.

I burrowed down and smiled. "When December rolls around, people always say we should make the spirit of Christmas last the whole year. Me, I think the spirit of Thanksgiving could last all year round, too."

"Not a bad idea," Nick said. "I'm thankful every day that I have you in my life, April."

I nestled closer to him. "And to think I spent part of the afternoon worried that you'd forgotten me."

"I was worried about you. I went to Doc's and made Algid check on the egg before anything else."

"Thank you."

He looked down into my face, his dark eyes twinkling. "It was pure selfishness on my part. I didn't want to spend a night apart."

We kissed, and for a moment I forgot to be nervous as our sleigh skimmed along through the air, with snow-tipped tree-tops below and glorious stars above.

Chapter 8

What a relief to be sleeping in my own bed. All afternoon I'd wondered if, come bedtime, I'd still be confined in the constabulary's jail cell, which of course was perfectly comfortable. Sinking into my own foam-topped mattress and snuggling with Nick beneath our down quilt, though, was much nicer.

And yet sleep eluded me. Long after Nick dropped off, I lay on my back, staring up at the ceiling. The suspicion that I'd missed something today at the party at the lodge kept creeping over me, making my brain itch.

I combed through everything Elspeth had said. The argument over the egg turkeys seemed so trivial, none of her words struck me as significant. Then I sifted through my conversations with Mildred. The one thing that stood out for me was when she said that Elspeth hadn't been well lately. In spite of Doc's observations, perhaps Elspeth really had keeled over from a longstanding illness or some other natural cause.

Doc had said the discoloration on her lips indicated poison, though. And Doc would know if Elspeth had been sick.

Besides, the sudden, quiet violence of Elspeth's attack hadn't appeared natural at all.

It wasn't that I thought no one at the lodge today was capable of murder. I just didn't want to believe that someone I knew had followed through with such a heinous impulse. Elspeth wasn't my favorite person, but I never wanted her to die. I'd just wanted her to be less irritating.

While Nick snored gently beside me, I went over the timeline. If some guest at the lodge killed her with food, the murder had to be premeditated. Midge's putting place cards at the table meant that anyone who strolled through the dining room could have found out where Elspeth was going to be. The killer could have left a small coating of poison on her spoon, or in her water glass.

Or her wineglass. Elspeth had been chugging wine to wash down the awful taste of my egg.

Which was such a drama-queen move. Honestly. Even with the garlic, it was still just an egg.

I love garlic, I thought sleepily.

Before I could nod off, a strange sound reached my ears, one that wasn't Nick's gentle snores. A repeated wail that was almost like a hiccup. I sat up, tilting my head and straining to hear it more clearly. Had that been a gobble of distress? Was Gobbles inside the castle?

I'd ordered my frozen turkey, so—if it arrived in time—finding Gobbles wasn't quite so critical to the success of our first Thanksgiving dinner. But Gobbles was a helpless creature, and I didn't like to think of him wandering around snowy Santaland all on his own. Or worse, in the clutches of some evil birdnapper.

The ghostly gobbling reached my ears again. I had to go investigate, no matter how much I dreaded crawling out from under the quilt.

I flicked the blankets off quickly; holding my breath as if I were taking a polar bear plunge, I shoved my feet into my shearling slippers and pulled on my boiled-wool robe. When Madame Neige from the Order of Elven Seamstresses had brought the robe to me as a wedding gift, I was skeptical that

I would ever wear it. Now, two years later, I shrugged it on as if it were a second skin. A toasty, much-needed second skin.

I tiptoed across the bedroom and took special care opening the thick, arched door that led to the hallway. Its hinges creaked, and I didn't want to wake Nick. In fact, I waited until I was outside to light the candle I'd swiped from my bedside table. Most of the hallways of Castle Kringle had fairy lights strung along the ceiling, which remained dimly lit all night. But there was no knowing what dark corner of the castle that eerie gobbling was luring me toward.

I'd expected the noise would take me to the Old Keep, but this time I pinpointed the sound as coming from the kitchen. As I crept closer, I realized that it wasn't a turkey making the sound. What I was hearing was a woman's sobs.

When I cracked the door, two elves stood in the dark kitchen. One, a female, was clearly distraught. She had on an overcoat and a thick outdoor cap on her head. Two suitcases sat on the floor next to her.

The light from my candle caused the two to pivot toward me.

The two elves were Butterbean and his sister, Lettuce, whom I'd last seen that afternoon at Kringle Lodge.

"What's going on?" I asked. "What's wrong?"

The two exchanged edgy glances, and Lettuce wiped her bloodshot eyes. "I was let go," she confessed.

I stepped through the swinging door and let it close behind me. "Amory and Midge fired you?"

Butterbean nodded frantically. "Without any notice!" he said, incensed. "It's unfair."

Unfair as well as foolish. Good cooks were hard to find, and I knew from dining at the lodge that Lettuce was a wizard in the kitchen. "Did they give you a reason?"

Lettuce blew her nose. "Mr. Amory Claus said he didn't have to give me a reason, but when I insisted, he told me that

I couldn't be trusted now after the disastrous dinner. He seems to think that *I* was responsible for Elspeth Claus's death because I was in charge of the food."

"That makes no sense," I said. "Doc Honeytree and Algid aren't even certain of which food caused Elspeth's death."

Butterbean folded his arms. "Amory didn't care—he's scapegoating my sister!"

Amory was an idiot. "I'll have a talk with Midge and Amory tomorrow." Emphasis on Midge. She was usually more reasonable than Amory. "I'm sure you can get your job back."

"Absolutely not. How can she go back there?" Butterbean asked. "Her cooking integrity has been impugned."

She frowned at him. The thought of *not* going back to the lodge clearly distressed her almost as much as having been fired. "But I like the lodge."

"Don't be foolish," Butterbean said. "There's a whole world available in Santaland—you can't let personal feelings limit you."

Personal feelings toward . . . what? Kringle Lodge? Her fellow elf colleagues? Amory?

"What else can I do?" she lamented. "Where else can I work?"

As one, the two round-cheeked faces swerved in my direction.

On the spot, I made a snap decision. "You're welcome to stay here until this can be sorted out. I spoke to Doc Honeytree's nephew this evening. He's bound to discover the cause of death very soon."

Anxiety filled her eyes. "But what if he really does find that some dish I prepared caused the death?"

Butterbean bobbed on his heels, suddenly a pint-sized Perry Mason. "Even if they did discover one of the dishes from the lodge caused the woman's death, that wouldn't necessarily mean that Lettuce put the poison in it, would it,

Mrs. Claus? Anyone going through the kitchen or dining room could have tampered with the food." His brow darkened. "Even Amory Claus himself."

It was clear that Butterbean, once Amory's protégé, still clung to a little bitterness at the way Amory had dropped him like a hot potato. Amory's managerial style didn't exactly inspire loyalty.

Having Lettuce here made me realize she might be able to satisfy my curiosity about what had gone on at the lodge after Crinkles had taken me away to the constabulary. "Did Amory talk to any of the other servants about what happened today?"

Lettuce lifted her chin indignantly. "I don't know. I mind my own business. All I know is that Mr. Amory wouldn't even listen to what I had to say."

I tilted my head. "What did you have to say?"

She hesitated. "I don't like to point fingers."

"If there's a murderer loose at the lodge, maybe you should. Anybody might have been killed. Imagine if a serving elf had simply grabbed a nibble of one of the dishes."

"Well . . ." She looked down uneasily, then said, "It's just a hunch, more than solid proof."

"It's about Star," Butterbean blurted out. "She's a wackadoodle."

Star? After a moment, I remembered the serving elf who'd been filling glasses from a water pitcher. Could that pitcher have contained something besides water?

If it had, half the table would have keeled over.

"What did Star do?" I asked.

Lettuce's round face tensed in concentration as she remembered all that had happened today. "When we were all in the kitchen, someone mentioned that there was some kind of friction between Elspeth Claus and another woman over that elf, Blaze Whitewreath."

I hoped no color showed in my face at this reference to Claire. "What about it?"

"Well, it was sort of an open secret among all the staff at Kringle Lodge that Star has a huge thing for that Whitewreath character."

"A crush on him?" I asked, for clarification.

"I guess that's what you'd call it," Lettuce went on, "although it seems silly to me. She's a servant, and his family were some of the richest elves in Santaland. She might as well pin her hopes on marrying the man in the moon."

"I've never understood that guy's appeal," Butterbean grumbled.

"He's handsome," Lettuce and I said in unison.

Butterbean shook his head. "And as for being from such a rich family, everybody knows Blaze was adopted as a baby. No one knows how humble his origins really were. He acts better than all of us, but he might have been born a wild elf, for all we know."

I almost laughed. Wild elves, those denizens of the Farthest Frozen Reaches, were usually scruffy in appearance, about as far from Blaze Whitewreath as possible. If Blaze Whitewreath had wild elf blood, he would be a spectacular triumph of nurture over nature.

"Some of the other maids at the lodge tease Star about her crush," Lettuce said. "I never paid much attention, but I could tell something was odd today. Star came down to the kitchen completely rattled. When someone asked why, she said 'He's here.'"

"So she saw that one of the guests at the lodge was an elf she had a crush on?" I asked. "That doesn't strike me as much of a motive for murder."

"Maybe Star was angry that he seemed to be involved with not one but two other guests," Butterbean said.

"And decided to kill one of them?" I asked. "Why not both?"

"Could be that Star just didn't get the opportunity to take out the other lady," Lettuce suggested.

I shuddered. That *other lady* was one of my best friends in the world. It would be terrible if by visiting me, Claire ended up in danger.

"I think I'll go up to the lodge tomorrow"—I looked at the kitchen clock—"today, I mean, and talk to Star."

Lettuce gazed up at me hopefully. "And you'll speak to Mrs. Midge on my behalf?"

I promised I would, adding, "And until the lodge takes you back, you can work in our kitchen."

"As cook?" Lettuce asked.

"Of course." With the big Thanksgiving feast coming up, Felice surely wouldn't mind having an extra pair of hands to help.

Speaking of Thanksgiving . . . "You all didn't hear gobbling down here, did you?"

Butterbean's eyes went saucer wide. "No."

I guess it really had all been Lettuce's sobbing. My tired brain had just imagined ghostly gobbling in the night. "Well, never mind."

After making sure Butterbean had room in his quarters to accommodate his sister, I left them. But not before Lettuce thanked me profusely, both for taking her in and for promising to speak to Midge on her behalf.

"I'll never forget your kindness," she said.

I went to bed feeling almost saintlike.

Chapter 9

My sainthood didn't last beyond my morning shower.

Jingles thumped down my coffee tray as I still sat at my dressing table in my robe. "What madness possessed you?"

I reached for the coffee, in desperate need of a caffeine jolt. After my late night, my alarm clock rattling me awake had felt like a cruel joke. I was disappointed to see there wasn't a pastry included on the tray. Felice usually sent up a little something for me to nibble on—a breakfast appetizer.

"Possessed me to do what?" I asked.

"To hire Lettuce to be cook."

"It's only temporary." I poured cream into my cup. "Once I talk sense to Amory and Midge, they'll take Lettuce back. Until then, I imagined Felice would welcome the extra help."

Jingles huffed out a laugh. "Felice does not *welcome* other cooks into her kitchen. She's a wooden-spoon-wielding despot."

That explained the treatless tray this morning. "I'm sure she'll calm down."

He gaped at me. "It's an armed camp down there. The morning scrambled eggs all ended up on the walls, and two batches of scones were ruined. The family had to have toast for breakfast."

"Oh." I gulped down more coffee. Middle-of-the-night decision-making was rarely the sharpest.

"When I was talking to Butterbean and Lettuce, it seemed like a reasonable idea."

"Butterbean." The castle steward's lips turned down in a dramatic frown. "He should never have put you in that awkward position."

"It wasn't his fault. I interrupted them talking. I thought I heard gobbling in the night, but it turned out to be Lettuce crying." I tilted my head, regarding him. "Your bedroom's not far from the kitchen. I'm surprised they didn't wake you up, too."

"After the night we thought we heard Gobbles and it turned out to be Butterbean, I decided to sleep with earplugs."

"I should try that myself."

He crossed his arms and drummed his gloved fingers against his elbows. "Butterbean should have sent his request to hire his sister through *me*. That elf is taking too many liberties around here."

I lifted a hand before he could get any more wound up about correct castle procedure. "I'm going up to the lodge today to have words with Amory and Midge. I'm sure I can convince them to give Lettuce her job back. This will all blow over."

Jingles's lips pursed. "I hope so. This is a very bad week to have a kitchen war."

"Message received. I won't interfere in kitchen staffing decisions in future."

"Message . . ." He looked befuddled for a moment, then he gasped and reached into the pocket of his tunic. "I almost forgot—I found this letter taped to the door this morning."

I inspected the plain white envelope he handed to me. *Mrs. Claus* was printed across the front in round, grammar school-perfect letters.

"Which door?" I asked.

"The castle entrance. I saw it when I retrieved the newspaper off the porch."

I unfolded the letter. *Stop the search—or else!*

The letters were also hand printed, but they'd been written in red ink to imitate dripping blood. At the bottom, instead of a signature there was a red outline of what looked like a bird's claw print.

Jingles' face went pale as he read over my shoulder. "The birdnappers have sent you a threat."

As if the past day hadn't been traumatic enough.

"What are you going to do?" he asked. "Call off the search?"

I refolded the note. "That would be giving in to turkey terrorism." If anything, my curiosity was aroused more now. This message struck me as peculiar. As did the fact that it was left on the castle's front door. That indicated someone close to the castle . . . unless someone had made a special middle-of-the-night trek up the mountain to deliver this one-line warning.

"So you're going to take it Constable Crinkles?"

I tapped the envelope against my palm. The constable had a murder on his hands. I didn't want to distract him with our turkey situation now.

"Keep this under you cap." I didn't want word of the threat to get out, especially to Nick. He might worry that I was really in danger.

Jingles nodded eagerly. "My lips are sealed."

"And bring Salty to see me in the breakfast room."

His eyes goggled. "You think he did it? Are we going to fire him?"

"No one's getting fired," I said.

But I did want to check Salty's frame of mind. A note like this didn't seem his style, but he was the castle employee who was closest to Gobbles. If he was hiding the turkey to save him from the ax, he might have concocted a letter like this.

While Jingles went to find Salty, I dressed carefully in wool pants and a sweater set. My schedule today was going to take me up to Kringle Lodge and back down to marching band practice this afternoon, and I wasn't sure I'd have time to come back to the castle to change clothes. Sometime today I also needed to visit Mildred, and check up on how she was doing.

In the breakfast room, I discovered Jingles hadn't downplayed the kitchen friction. All the chafing dishes were empty. You'd think the castle had no cooks at all instead of one too many.

The groundskeeper came in while I was nibbling on toast.

Salty twisted his cap in his hands as he stood before me. He always looked a little awkward inside the castle. His elf coveralls looked comically rustic in the immaculate holiday décor of Castle Kringle. He rubbed one brown bootie against the opposite calf as if to pull up his sagging striped stocking.

At first I wondered if he was nervous about being confronted with the letter, which I placed on the table in front of me. But he didn't seem to notice it.

"Any word on Gobbles?" I asked.

His face sank into gloom, which was all the answer I needed. "No—I was hoping *you* might have heard something, ma'am."

"No." I tucked the letter away. I fairly was sure he hadn't written it now, and its contents would only upset him.

"Oh." He looked dispirited, then made an effort to put on a more positive face. "There is some good news. Walnut's

Sleigh Repair and Rental delivered your sleigh this morning. It's fixed now and is ready for you to use."

"Wonderful." I tried to perk him up. "And I'm still hopeful about Gobbles. Christopher had some ideas for getting some of the younger kids involved in hunting for him."

Salty's eyes widened in horror. "Hunting?"

"*Looking*," I said quickly.

He nodded, clearly relieved to hear it. Although what he thought was going to happen to Gobbles once he was found, I couldn't say.

"That's good news about my sleigh," I repeated. "Thank you."

He nodded and bowed out of the room as if I were the Queen instead of Mrs. Claus.

After breakfast, I stopped by Claire's guest room. I expected to find her still asleep, but she was up and at 'em, putting the last touches on her makeup.

"I'm going up to the lodge this morning," I told her.

In her reflection in the mirror, a blond brow arched at me. "Taking another look at the scene of the crime?"

"Amory fired his cook yesterday. I'm going to ask Midge to rehire her." I ducked my head. "And I might do some other poking around while I'm up there."

"I'd just let the doctor take care of it," she said. "They're bound to find out what food was poisoned sooner or later, and after that it'll be a snap to figure out who the culprit was."

Would it really be that simple? As Ollie had suggested last night, someone could have planted the poison. And by *someone* I was now beginning to substitute *anyone*.

"I have to go to town later," I said. "I'll swing by after I'm done at the lodge and pick you up."

"Don't bother. I'll probably have already left by the time you're finished up there."

"Where are you going?"

"Christmastown," she said, as if it should be obvious. "I'll hook a ride with Lucia, or as a last resort I can always ask Blaze to pick me up."

Blaze again. "You sure are spending a lot of time with him." I sank down on the bed. "Tell me honestly, is something going on between you two?"

The way it came out, the question sounded both nosy and prudish. And Claire's set smile made me realize she wasn't going to answer it anyway.

"Let's just say that Blaze is key to my plans for the future."

"Are you trying to make Jake jealous?"

"As if." She laughed. "I'm not sure Jake is the kind of guy who gets jealous. He's part ice cube."

She was joking, but Jake really was odd.

She brushed her hair back. "My dealings with Blaze are all about what *I* want."

I lifted my hands in frustration.

Claire finally twisted so that she was facing me, not just talking through a mirror. "I'm sorry. I don't really want to be evasive—it's just the timing. By the end of today I'll be able to tell you everything."

"That's good, because my curiosity is driving me nuts."

"I think you'll be pleased." She laughed. "I'll give you a hint: It's sweet."

I let the matter drop. I supposed I should be happy that I had such a self-sufficient guest, given all the distractions going on. I needed to get the day jump-started.

Having my sleigh back improved my mood. I loved whizzing up the mountain's snow path. The electric motor didn't have as much power as a gas snowmobile would have, but it was still as fast as a reindeer, and silent. As Mrs. Claus, I was rarely on my own, and the freedom having my own sleigh gave me was intoxicating. I felt like a teenager with my first car.

Balsam, back in the red-and-white lodge livery he usually wore, appeared at Kringle Lodge's door after my knock. His eyes registered surprise. Clearly he wasn't expecting to see me today—or maybe he wasn't expecting any visitors. A lot of noise was coming from the house behind him.

"Mrs. Claus, it's good to see you . . . free."

"The egg proved my innocence."

"Indeed?" His brows drew together in confusion. "If you've come all this way to see Mrs. Midge Claus, I'm afraid you'll be disappointed. She went to town earlier this morning."

"Too bad." I should have called first. "I guess Amory's gone, too."

"Oh no—he's in his study." He stepped back. "If you'll follow me . . ."

I couldn't blame Amory for holing up in his study this morning. Every elf on staff seemed to be busy in the lodge's dining room and the great hall, cleaning, dusting, and scrubbing. Multiple vacuums were running—the noise was so intense that I covered my ears. The table was cleared, the furniture was all put back in its usual place, making it clear that the owners of the house wished for nothing more than to erase all memory of the day before. A few flaccid turkey balloons hung from doorframes as a lingering reminder, though.

In his office, Amory was nursing a glass of something in a whiskey glass. Staying seated, he welcomed me with all the enthusiasm he would have shown if the grim reaper had walked into his home. Wordlessly, he nodded to the empty chair opposite his desk.

"You're not at work," I said.

He drew up as if I'd insulted him, then nodded to a box of candy on his desk—the Thanksgiving candies I'd seen Nick and Flake discussing. "I approved these. Have one."

He'd probably approved those yesterday.

"No, thanks," I said.

"Probably just as well. Flake sent the candies over with a note about how they're supposed to be Top Secret." He took a slug of whiskey. "Anyway, am I supposed to think about candy inventory when someone's died beneath my own roof? You might have noticed that there's quite a lot of work to do around here."

Yes, and I'd noticed everyone besides Amory doing it. "Did Crinkles give you permission to clean up the death room?"

He let out a snort. " 'Death room'? What is this, *CSI Santaland?*" He shook his head. "This Thanksgiving week you sold the country on hasn't worked out great so far."

"It's not really supposed to be a week," I said. "Just a day, really."

"Trying to talk elves into toning down any celebration is always futile."

As if it hadn't been his idea and his alone to kick off Thanksgiving week with an elaborate Sunday dinner potluck. I scooted forward in the leather club chair. "I had a conversation with Lettuce last night . . ."

That was as far as I got. Amory clucked impatiently. "Good riddance to her. I hope you showed her the door, too."

"No, of course not."

"The more fool you, then. We can't keep people in our houses who are trying to kill us."

"No one knows how Elspeth died yet. Yesterday everyone thought *I* did it. Firing Lettuce was incredibly premature."

"I call it taking the initiative. Even if you had poisoned that egg, would anyone remember that?"

I sputtered. "If Santa's wife had become a mad poisoner? That would stick in people's minds, yes."

"Okay, yes, maybe it would." He pointed at me, not ready to cede the argument. "But at the same time, everyone will always remember that the deadly dinner happened here, in this lodge. Years from now, they'll be pointing out that this is where some poor woman face-planted into her mashed potatoes."

"I still don't see how it follows that you had to fire the cook."

He steepled his hands like a professor explaining a basic concept to a dense student. "Look at it this way, when the ship goes down, the captain is supposed to go with it. Now, the captain didn't personally smelt the iron that was penetrated by the torpedo that hit it, did he?"

God, he was crazy. "No . . ."

"Yet the captain's supposed to go down with the ship anyway. That's not fair, either. Most likely the captain of that ship just joined the navy because it was a family tradition, or he liked the uniform. And maybe that's why Lettuce became a cook. It's just too bad she had to preside over a fatal feast. But *someone* has to be held accountable." He leaned back, pleased with himself and his nutso analogy.

"I'm not sure that justifies firing an innocent elf."

He frowned impatiently. "Now when people receive an invitation to have dinner here, they'll think, 'Isn't that where that woman was poisoned?' but in the next moment they'll remember that the cook got the sack and so it's safe to accept an invitation to dinner here."

"That is a completely crack-brained reason for firing a cook," I said. The man *looked* like Santa Claus, but he had the personality of Daffy Duck. "Did you even bother to question the rest of your staff about where they were and what they were doing yesterday?"

He leaned back in his chair, frowning. "Why would I have bothered with that? You were in custody."

"But you knew I didn't do it." I paused, giving him plenty of time to agree with me. Silence stretched awkwardly.

"Well, we all saw her eating that egg of yours," he said.

I rolled my eyes. "I wish I'd shown up empty-handed yesterday. Those eggs have caused me nothing but trouble."

"*You?* What about me? Now I don't even have a cook."

My head felt as if it might explode. "Because you fired her!"

"Yes, thank you, April. I know that. I've just explained why." He leaned back in his chair and grumbled, "Midge was mad about it, too. She's in town at the EEA trying to find a new cook."

At least Midge had some sense. The EEA was the Elfworks Employment Agency. Maybe if I saw her in town I'd have more luck talking to her.

"Had you noticed that Elspeth was sick?" I asked. "Before yesterday, I mean."

"I never noticed Elspeth much at all. She tried to borrow money from me once, though." He laughed. "Talk about barking up the wrong tree."

I leaned forward. Finally, something concrete. Money pressure often provided a motive for murder. "When was this?"

His brows knit in thought. "I don't know. Two months ago? Come to think of it, she *did* look a little sickly that day. I remember thinking it would do her good to get out of the North Pole for a bit, but I didn't actually suggest it."

"Why not?"

"She'd just told me she was broke. I couldn't very well advise her to take an expensive vacation when I knew she didn't have any money, and I had no intention of loaning her any."

"Did she say why she needed the money?"

"I think she wanted to move out of Mildred's. Who could blame her? Dreary place."

"But free."

He grunted and took another drink. "Free sometimes comes with its own hefty price tag."

He was in a position to know. Amory lived in Kringle

Lodge for free. In exchange, he had to maintain the old structure and had to commute all the way down the mountain and over to Tinkertown to work at his job as chief executive of the Candy Cane Factory.

"For a while I worried Elspeth would ask to move *here*," he continued. "She seemed to be hanging around with some kind of expectation along those lines. But Midge must have told her that wouldn't work out. Midge and Elspeth were never close."

Poor Elspeth. The only person who liked her was Mildred, the person she couldn't stand living with.

"Didn't Blaze Whitewreath say that he and Elspeth were still friends?" Amory asked.

"Blaze seems to have a lot of women friends." I remembered what Lettuce told me. "Including one here under your roof. Star—one of your serving elves."

"First I've heard of that."

"Lettuce told me that it was well-known that Star had a thing for Blaze. In fact, she seemed to think that Star might have been inclined to harm Elspeth because she was Blaze's girlfriend."

"Ex-girlfriend."

"Still, it might be worth asking Star about, just to make sure she didn't have a motive to murder Elspeth."

"These elves." Amory sighed, stood, and crossed to the bellpull by the fireplace. "Still, I suppose you're right. I believe Star is feeling under the weather today. She didn't serve at breakfast." He tugged the pull. "Not that it was much of a breakfast, without our cook. You wouldn't have someone you could recommend, would you?"

"Yes," I said. "Lettuce. You shouldn't have let her go to begin with."

He shook his head, but before he could reply, Balsam

came in. "Ah, Balsam—there you are. Mrs. Claus here wants
to talk to Star. If you would be so kind as to take us up to her
room?"

"Yes, sir. Please follow me." As Balsam led the way up the
stairs, he turned to me and said in a low voice filled with concern, "I hope Star isn't in any trouble."

"Mrs. Claus just wants to ask her a question about yesterday."

Balsam's lips turned down tightly, and we finished the
climb up the servants' narrower staircase in silence. Amory
was winded when we reached the top, and we both had to
duck slightly. The ceilings followed the point of the roof, so
that the whole floor was just an inverted V overhead. It was
good that elves lived up here, because their cubbyhole cells
didn't allow for much head room.

Balsam knocked at one of the doors. After a moment, Star
the elf cracked the door and peeked out anxiously. Her nose
was red, and her eyes grew bigger at the sight of us all.

"Mrs. Claus has come to speak with you," Balsam said.
"About yesterday."

She shook her head. She had a sweet face, now that I
looked at it, with green eyes—slightly rheumy today—and
blond hair that fell in a bob around her chin.

"I-I-I don't doh anything about what happened yesterday," she stuttered, her voice congested.

"I'm mostly interested in what you can tell us about Blaze
Whitewreath," I said.

The name caused her to take a sharp intake of breath.

"May I come in and talk to you for a bit?"

She shook her head, clearly frightened. "Doh, please—"

It was the wrong answer to give in Amory's presence. "*No?*"
he asked irritably. "Why not? What are you hiding in there?"

"I'm sick and—"

Amory pushed Star aside and bulldozed through. Balsam and I followed more hesitantly. The room was so tiny there was barely room for all four of us, and Amory and I had to stoop. Amory let out an exclamation, but I was so concerned about not whacking my skull against the ceiling that it took me a moment to process what I was seeing: The walls were covered with images of Blaze Whitewreath. Most were from advertisements and flyers for his real estate business that Star must have picked up off of bulletin boards, but she'd also clearly photocopied the same photograph of him with a raised chin looking sensually into the camera. Copied it several dozen times, in fact, and made a collage out of them so that it covered the sloping ceiling above her bed. The effect was Blaze Whitewreath in fly vision.

On top of the bed—her sick-day reading—was a hardcover of *Property and Profit* by none other than Blaze Whitewreath.

"I haven't done anything wrong," she said, looking ill in more ways than one as she stood before us in her quilted housecoat.

"Someone said you seemed agitated yesterday when you first noticed that Blaze was a guest at the party," I said.

Her cheeks colored. "Well, of course. He was right there. I was afraid I'd spill something on him."

"And did you feel any animosity toward the women he talked to?" Amory asked. "Elspeth Claus, for instance?"

Her eyes took on a derisive gleam. "He never did talk to *her*. She even arrived early to hang around—probably waiting for him. But he dumped her months ago."

"And you know this how?"

She ducked her head. "I might have hung around his office a few times, and like, bumped into him in other places. Just public places, like Merry Muffins or whatever."

"You stalked him?"

"I never *said* anything to him."

Amory shook his head.

Star sneezed, then repeated, "I didn't do anything wrong."

"I'm going to have to talk with Midge about this."

The young elf was on the verge of tears. I felt sorry for her. She was as obsessed with Blaze as some kids were obsessed with pop stars. Also, as fanatical as she was, I had no doubt that she was watching Blaze's every move while he was at the lodge.

"You never saw Blaze talking to Elspeth yesterday?" I asked.

She shook her head. "She was never good enough for him. If her last name wasn't Claus, he never would have looked twice at her."

"Hey—that's my cousin you're talking about," Amory said, obviously forgetting that he'd been fairly dismissive of Elspeth himself.

"Did Blaze ever go near Elspeth's place at the table?" I asked.

"I don't think so. His place card was on the other side." Star bit her lip. "Elspeth Claus went back outside to talk to someone right after she got here, but I'm not sure who it was she went out to meet."

"You didn't look, out of curiosity?"

She shrugged. "I didn't care about *her*."

Mildred had told me that Elspeth had wanted to arrive early. An assignation made more sense than worrying about the placement of her dish on the buffet. Was her meeting with Blaze? We didn't know when he had arrived at the lodge. Maybe he had also come early to talk with Elspeth. But what in the world would they have spoken about?

I recalled something weird Elspeth had told me at the coffee shop. *After this week, I'll be ablaze with success, and you won't be looking down your nose at me.* Was *ablaze* mere coincidence? Blaze was one of the biggest real estate wheeler-dealers in Christmastown.

Finally, Star was put out of her misery and allowed to go back to bed.

Back downstairs, Amory flopped into his desk chair and leaned back. "The things that go on under your own roof that you never know about!"

Balsam cleared his throat. Amory and I hadn't noticed him following us downstairs.

"I'm sorry, Balsam, do you need something?" Amory asked.

"I just wanted you to know that I have advised Star to take the pictures down."

"Probably best," Amory agreed. "Or at least cut back a little."

Balsam remained rooted where he stood.

"Anything else?" Amory prompted.

"Just that . . ." The butler seemed hesitant to speak. "In regard to something Mrs. Claus was asking Star about. I, too, saw Elspeth Claus go out the back way not long after she arrived."

I swiveled to face him. "Did you see her with anyone?"

"Yes, ma'am," he said. "That is, I saw a figure—a man, I believe. But I didn't pay close attention. All that stood out for me was a glimpse of color as I passed by the window. I saw purple."

Amory chuckled. "Well, that's jolly. All we have to do is sort through the dozens of guests who were here yesterday and figure out which ones were wearing purple, and then we'll have a list of the people who *might* have been talking to

Elspeth about something that *might* have been important or might have meant nothing at all."

"Yes, sir," Balsam agreed.

But before he backed out of the room, the butler caught my eye. And I could tell that he and I were remembering the same thing: Blaze Whitewreath had been wearing a purple coat.

Chapter 10

What had Blaze been talking to Elspeth about at the lodge before everyone else had arrived? Had it simply been a chance encounter—they just happened to bump into each other outside the lodge's *back* door? I doubted that. When I'd spoken to Mildred before the dinner, she had intimated that Elspeth had very purposefully wanted to go to the lodge on her own, and left Château Mildred before anyone else.

Perhaps she'd intended to arrive early to hit Amory up for money again. But surely even someone as self-absorbed as Elspeth would know that it would be easier to extract plasma from a garden gnome than to get Amory to reverse his decision to not lend her money.

She might have met Blaze to ask to borrow money from him, though.

For all I knew, Elspeth and Blaze had ridden up to the lodge together.

Of course, there was nothing wrong with any of this, per se. Certainly nothing criminal. But this alleged clandestine talk indicated that Blaze still had some kind of relationship with Elspeth that he hadn't mentioned yesterday.

I just didn't trust him. It made me uneasy that Claire seemed to be so wrapped up in him, too. Obviously she wasn't as obsessed with him as Star was. And it wasn't his fault that a young serving elf had developed the crush to end all crushes on him. Yet he seemed too slick for his own good. *The Don Juan of Santaland.* What were his designs on Claire?

I nipped by Mildred's on my way to marching band rehearsal. Château Mildred was one of the older houses in Kringle Heights. What made Mildred's house unique was that from certain angles it resembled a horror-movie house—dark stone, with multiple gables and carved gargoyle cornices. You'd almost expect to see bats flying out of it at twilight. At this time of day there was still plenty of sunlight, yet glancing up I couldn't help noticing the silhouette of Grimstock perched on an eave. What was he doing here?

More puzzling still, why was Constable Crinkles's snowmobile parked in front? As I pulled up alongside the snowmobile's sidecar, I decided that Crinkles was probably just checking on Mildred. The constable might be a bit of a bumbler as a lawman, but his heart was as big as Sugarplum Mountain.

Maybe I would show him the threat letter I'd received. It couldn't hurt to get his opinion on the matter.

I reached under the seat of my sleigh and retrieved the tinned Castle Kringle fruitcake I'd remembered to grab from the kitchen pantry before I left that morning. The castle Clauses had sent flowers to Château Mildred, but fruitcake was the customary condolence gift when visiting the bereaved in Santaland.

I only knocked once at the door before it was swung open by Olive. The sight of her shocked me. Instead of a cap, the wizened old elf had a thick white bandage around her head.

"Olive! What happened?"

The diminutive servant opened her mouth to speak but was cut off by Crinkles, who appeared in the hallway behind her. "There's been a home invasion!"

"*Here?*" I'd never heard of such a thing happening in Santaland. "Did you catch who did it?"

"No." Crinkles cast a furtive look outside. Satisfied that no criminal was lurking out in the driveway, he beckoned me inside. Olive shut the door behind us.

"They attacked you?" I asked her as she led the way to the big salon. It was unbelievable.

"He clubbed her from behind, the coward," Crinkles said. "Olive says she never got a good look at him. Just saw a glimpse of black clothes."

Mildred's house was sparse on decorations and Olive usually kept it as neat as a pin, but today disorder reigned. Upholstery had been slashed, sending stuffing bubbling out of furniture, and a knickknack cabinet stood gaping open, its contents spilled on the floor.

This was horrific.

In the living room, the walls were stone and plaster, discolored from centuries of smoke from the enormous fireplace. The château had almost burned down once; no amount of scrubbing seemed to lift the black from the stone. Mildred was laid out on a velvet sofa that now looked as if Edward Scissorhands had been at it. An afghan crocheted in alternating red and green granny squares covered her. "Oh, April. Thank you for coming." She looked at the tin in my hand. "And you brought a fruitcake. How thoughtful."

"Are you okay?" I asked.

"I'm fine. I wasn't even here. I'll never forgive myself for that," she lamented. "Poor Olive was all alone."

"Where were you?"

"In Christmastown. It might sound disrespectful to Elspeth's memory, but I thought that with this new holiday coming up, it was more important than ever to keep the Depression Center open. No one showed up, of course."

No one ever did.

"That doesn't sound disrespectful to me," I said. "And it's probably lucky that you weren't here. You might both have been attacked."

"Olive's managed to get most of this room tidied up, but the rest of the house is a mess. Upstairs is even worse than down here."

"Was anything stolen?" I asked.

"As far as Olive and I can tell, they didn't take anything."

"But why would they have torn up all your rooms? Maybe you just haven't realized what's missing yet."

"That could be." Mildred frowned until an idea occurred to her. She leaned forward and clasped my hands in her bony ones. "Maybe *you* would notice something missing from Elspeth's room."

Crinkles bobbed on his bootheels. "Fresh eyes—always a good idea."

I readily agreed, though their logic didn't strike me as sound. I'd never been in Elspeth's room, but I was burning with curiosity to see it now. Whatever happened here this morning, it had to be related to Elspeth's death. "Maybe something obvious will jump out at me."

I went up the stairs and across the landing, which had a stained-glass window of a wintry sleigh scene centered above it. The small suit of armor that had always stood sentry at the top of the stairs—a priceless elf antiquity—had been knocked over. Its big-eared helmet had rolled several feet away from the body. The desecration of the antique upset me. What cretin had done this?

The staircase landing overlooked the main room, so I could see Mildred still on her couch. Poor woman. To have lost Elspeth yesterday and then be the victim of this break-in today. What was going on with Santaland? Murder wasn't unprecedented—but a murder and then this break-in?

Whoever had gone through the upstairs had been as destructive as they were thorough. All the bedrooms had been turned inside out. The first one I poked around in had to be Mildred's, given the clothes on the floor and its connection to a smaller, more Spartan room that looked like Olive's. It had her scent: lavender and mothballs.

Mattresses were flipped over and slashed open, the contents of drawers spilled on the floor, clothes pulled off hangers and any pockets turned inside out. Books had been dumped out of bookshelves onto the floor, paintings had been yanked off the walls with such force that the hooks of some had been pulled out of the plaster, leaving jagged wounds in the walls.

No wonder Mildred and Olive couldn't tell what had been stolen. In this chaotic condition, taking fast inventory would be impossible. The women had an awful job ahead of them. Putting this all to rights would take weeks.

In what was clearly Elspeth's room—the walls were pink and inspirational word décor popped out from walls and shelves: *100% Inspired!* and *Hello, Gorgeous!* and *The World Needs More YOU.* Her room had received the same treatment as Mildred and Olive's had received. The difference was that Elspeth had more stuff—more clothes, tchotchkes, drawers full of clutter. Again here, the mattress and box springs had been pulled to the floor and slashed open. A large suitcase had been upended, its contents spreading across the bed frame slats.

I picked my way around the mess, seeing bits of clothing and other possessions I recognized, including some things of mine—a necklace I'd lost over a year ago, and a favorite cashmere sweater I'd thought I'd misplaced—among the debris. It looked like Elspeth had a little magpie stash of goods she'd pinched. I grabbed my sweater and when I bent to pick up my necklace, next to it was a gold Arpels brooch. It hadn't been stolen. I'd seen Elspeth wearing it on several occasions, and she'd told me it was an heirloom she'd inherited from her mother.

It was a gorgeous piece, and valuable. And the so-called burglar had just left it.

I began to question the robbery motive. The only robber exposed here was Elspeth. What was going on? If it wasn't greed for gold that had instigated this vandalism, what had? Was this all an elaborate threat? There seemed to be a lot of that going around today—although the severity of this attack made the letter I'd received this morning seem trivial.

In a daze, I returned downstairs. Mildred and Crinkles watched me with interest to gauge my impression. In the interest of not speaking ill of the dead, I decided to not mention the fact that Elspeth seemed to have a kleptomania problem.

"I'm so sorry." I seated myself and inspected the tea trolley Olive had just wheeled in. Olive always put together a dependably tasty tea. "It's such a mess up there. Did you only see one burglar, Olive?"

"She said she never saw anyone clearly," Mildred answered for her. "I suppose it's entirely possible that the man who hit her could have had an accomplice."

"Was it a human or an elf?"

"She couldn't say with any certainty."

"It's hard to believe one individual could have been so destructive. Do you remember how long you were unconscious?"

Olive scowled, and Mildred spoke for her. "She wasn't out the whole time. She woke up in a closet and could hear the person tearing things apart. It wasn't until after she heard the burglar leave that she managed to get the door open. They had pushed a solid oak étagère against the closet door, but Olive has a lot of strength."

No kidding. In size-to-strength ratio, she must have been

like an ant. An ant who, even on the worst day, always laid on a good cream tea, I thought as I wolfed down a scone with clotted cream. My morning toast hadn't stuck with me.

"So she escaped and called me," Mildred continued, "and I telephoned the constable. We keep one of the most modest households in Kringle Heights. Who would do this to us?"

"The same person who killed Elspeth," I said. "It's too much of coincidence that she was killed just last night, and the very next morning her home was viciously robbed."

"I never thought of that," Constable Crinkles said.

The rest of us had the grace not to comment on what that said about his detecting skills.

So far this morning I'd discovered two suspicious, unidentified characters: a man in a purple coat talking to Elspeth, and another mysterious man who tore up her house. Could they be one and the same?

I considered my prime suspect: Blaze Whitewreath. But why would he have done this? He was wealthy enough to have left expensive jewelry around and fled the country.

I took a sip of tea. "Was Elspeth planning a trip?"

Mildred straightened in surprise. "I don't think so. Why?"

"There was an overturned suitcase on her bed. It looked like it had been packed."

She shifted, uncertain. "Elspeth never said anything to me about a trip."

Constable Crinkles gobbled down a crustless cucumber sandwich. "Odd time to take a trip. You'd think she could wait till January."

Yes. The lead-up to Christmas was a busy, magical time of nonstop activity in Santaland. Most Clauses wouldn't have left Christmastown before Christmas for love nor money.

But what if it was for both love and money?

"I know who did it," Olive announced.

Her voice, so rarely heard, shocked Crinkles and me. It

managed to sound both high and gravelly, like a bear on helium. We leaned toward her expectantly, while Mildred made a *tsk*ing noise. "Now Olive, we don't really need to—"

"It was Elspeth." Olive's mouth was a thin, resentful line in the wrinkles and folds of her face.

I nearly choked on my tea, and directed a side-eyed glance at Crinkles. He looked as confused as I felt.

"Olive, Elspeth is *dead*," he said.

That detail didn't faze Olive. "She sent an assassin to kill me. He was a ghost's cat's-paw, that's what he was."

A ghost's assassin? In Santaland? "Why would Elspeth have done that?" I asked.

"She wouldn't have." Mildred jumped up, fluttering her hands before her. "Olive, why don't you take April's fruitcake into the kitchen and put it in the pantry before we forget."

It was the lamest of pretexts to get rid of someone.

The wizened old elf sent her employer a disappointed look, but finally turned to go. The tea trolley's wheel squeaked as she rolled it to the kitchen.

Mildred turned back to us, lowering her voice. "You'll have to forgive Olive. Yesterday upset her, and this morning . . ." She shook her head.

"I can see that," Crinkles said.

We could hear it, too. From the kitchen came sounds of cupboard doors slamming, and crockery breaking. I assumed Olive was stepping on already broken pieces, not destroying more.

"Is the kitchen torn up, too?" I asked.

"Oh yes," Crinkles said. "Big mess in there. Broken dishes everywhere, and bags of flour scattered all over the flippin' place." He glanced over apologetically at Mildred. "Pardon the expression."

"It's a lucky thing Olive gets up early to do the baking,"

Mildred said. "We're set for two days, at least. I suppose I'll have to have the Cornucopia deliver some groceries, though."

"I'll send some of the castle elves down to help you clean up the mess." I lowered my voice. "And I'll call Doc Honeytree to come take a look at Olive. That blow to her head might have given her a concussion."

"It obviously rattled her wits," Crinkles said.

I pinned a serious gaze on Mildred. "Unless you think there's some reason for her to say what she did."

"No!" She blinked. "That is to say . . . Olive and Elspeth were never the *best* of friends. Elspeth could be . . . imperious. Even unpleasant."

Yup. Mildred's assessment at least showed that *she* hadn't lost her wits.

"But her saying this about Elspeth—" She twisted the napkin in her hands into a tight spiral.

"I'm sure you're right—it's just the blow she took." Constable Crinkles slapped his hands on his thighs and rose up out of his chair. "I should get back to the constabulary and write up a report about this."

And I needed to get to Christmastown for my rehearsal. I rose and said good-bye to Mildred. "If you need anything else," I told her, "anything at all, just let me know."

"You're very kind."

I followed Crinkles out the door. I hopped on my sleigh, which the constable inspected with admiration.

"Very snappy," he said. "What can it do?"

"Twenty-five miles per hour."

He whistled.

"Of course I've never pushed it that high."

"Seats four?"

"Or five elves."

He laughed and rubbed his belly, which strained against

his thick black belt. "Probably depends on the elves in question."

I smiled and turned the key in my ignition.

And frowned.

"That's a quiet motor," Crinkles said in awe.

"It's a dead motor." I leaned back in my seat, swallowing a curse. "Walnut's Sleigh Repair said they'd figured out the problem."

"Probably your battery."

I groaned. Why did transportation troubles always strike at the worst moments? "I don't have time to deal with this. I have to get to marching band rehearsal."

I'll say this for Constable Crinkles, he never trivialized the problems of others. In fact, he looked as alarmed as I felt. "The marching band for the parade?"

As if there were multiple marching bands in Santaland. Until three weeks ago, there hadn't been even one.

"Hop in with me," he said. "We'll get you there by the downbeat."

I couldn't refuse that offer. I ran back into Mildred's so that she'd know why my sleigh would be parked in her driveway all afternoon. Then I jumped into the constabulary sidecar. Crinkles took off so fast, I had to grip the dash in front of me. I felt like Robin to his Batman, only without seat belts.

"It's not life or death," I reminded him, and he slowed up slightly. I took the opportunity to send off a text to Jingles, asking him to send help to Mildred's. Then I called Doc Honeytree and suggested he pay Olive a visit to make sure she didn't have a concussion.

"She seems a little . . . disoriented," I said.

"Dizzy?"

"Physically she looks the same as always, but she was saying some off-the-wall things."

"I'll be over there as soon as I can harness the sleigh," Doc promised.

I hung up, feeling slightly better.

"*Disoriented* was a kind word for what happened back there," the constable said. "Olive seemed nuttier than the fruitcake you brought."

I sent him a look. "She's been through a terrible ordeal."

"Of course." He shook his head. "I just can't remember when there's been such an outbreak of naughtiness." He bit his lip. "But if the home invasion was tied to Elspeth's death, like you say—without ghosts coming into it—why did they tear up Mildred and Olive's things, too?"

"I'm willing to bet they did that after they didn't find what they were looking for in Elspeth's room."

He frowned. "You mean you think they were looking for something specific?"

I remembered Elspeth's brooch. "I can't imagine any other reason for someone to be so thorough, and yet leave valuables behind."

He nodded. "Good point—I'm going to mention that in my report."

I was a little confused about whom this crime report was being written for, but I supposed all departments had procedures to follow.

My mind was completely absorbed in the who and the why of what had happened. What had Elspeth been involved in, and why had there been a packed suitcase in her room? Was she taking a trip, or—as Amory had indicated back at the lodge—was she just planning to finally move out of Mildred's?

And who knew about her plans? I had one guess: Blaze Whitewreath. Maybe that's why she had met him early at the lodge yesterday. Blaze was a Realtor. She might have wanted to consult with him about finding her own place to live.

Christmastown was an old village with strict building standards, so there weren't many apartment buildings. Juniper lived in one of the few in town, and she said that the waiting list was long. He could have been helping her with that.

But they'd stepped *outside* to talk. Why confer about real estate in such a clandestine way?

What exactly was the Don Juan of Santaland up to?

Chapter 11

Crinkles pulled up to the sleigh park just as the Santaland Concert Band was mustering to march. I thanked him and scrambled over to the equipment sleigh where the bass drum was waiting. As I struggled into my harness, Smudge darted a glance from me to the constable's snowmobile.

"Did you get arrested *again*?"

"Very funny. My sleigh broke down. The constable gave me a ride."

Juniper hurried over, her forehead crinkled in worry. "I heard that there was more trouble up at Kringle Heights today. Is Mildred Claus okay?"

I gave them a shorthand account of what had happened at Mildred's, not mentioning Olive's talk about Elspeth—or Elspeth's ghost—hiring a hit man to attack her.

"How awful!" Juniper said. "I'm so glad that nothing worse happened to Olive, though. She could have been killed."

My steps faltered. Whoever had cracked Olive over the head and tore up that house was clearly ruthless. If it was the same someone who was responsible for Elspeth's death, was it significant that they'd decided to spare Olive's life this morning?

Or maybe they'd intended to kill her or assumed they had.

The old elf was tougher than she looked. Her attacker wouldn't be the first to underestimate Olive.

Funny, though, how Mildred hadn't wanted us to hear much of what Olive had to say. Granted, what Olive was saying didn't make sense. But it reminded me of what had happened at the lodge, when Olive had whisked Mildred away quickly after Elspeth had died. Almost as if she didn't want anyone asking her and Mildred questions.

Were those two hiding something? I'd thought Mildred had seemed honestly bewildered by the home invasion, but maybe she knew more than she was letting on. She'd only reluctantly admitted that there was no love lost between Olive and Elspeth.

How had Olive described her assailant? A flash of black.

I glanced over at Smudge. As usual, he was wearing black. He gaped back at me. "What?"

I shook my head. "Nothing."

Suspecting Smudge of the violent home invasion at Mildred's made about as much sense as suspecting Doc Honeytree—also a black-wearer—would have. Smudge might have attitude, but he wasn't evil.

Speaking of evil, JoJo Hollyberry was shooting me the evil eye. We'd last seen each other when he was demanding I be put away, and now here I was on the loose. Awkward. Nearby, another elf with that Hollyberry look also stood staring at me. Who was he?

At the front of the band, my sister-in-law Tiffany was doing an impressive toss, spin, and catch with her baton to applause from passersby. She was used to the limelight from her skating career. Her fellow twirler, Cookie, was barely managing to do a basic twirl. Elspeth hadn't been any good, either, but with her gone, our majorette line was going to be very lopsided.

Growing impatient, Luther clapped for us to get into formation. I was still fidgeting with my bass drum as I stepped into place. It was hard to maintain equilibrium with twenty-five pounds hanging in front of you via a shoulder harness. Not to mention that Gulliver-like feeling that being a human in a mostly elf marching band gave me.

"Just to remind you," Luther announced, his voice almost a yell, "our playing will mark the start of the parade. We and all the other marchers will be lined up on Sparkletoe Lane—all except Santa and his reindeer, who will muster at Castle Kringle. Our cue to begin playing will be when Santa's sleigh is first spotted coming down Sugarplum Mountain. Santa will land on Festival Boulevard as the parade is underway and wait for all the marchers to pass before he joins the procession at the end. Any questions?"

"What's the music order?" Bobbin piped up.

"First we'll play 'Over the River and Through the Woods,' and then 'Winter Wonderland' . . ."

Running down the playlist took a while; each mention of a song got a cheer from the crowd gathering around. Elves loved Christmas songs because they loved singing along, and everyone in Santaland knew all the words to every Christmas carol or song, down to the most obscure, least-sung verses. Since we were alternating every Christmas song with another repetition of "Over the River," they would probably have that one memorized soon, too.

When we finally started playing and marching, I was surprised how much improved we were. Proof positive that panic and desperation could work miracles.

The band was on its second loop around the parking lot when something curious appeared in the corner of my line of sight. A diminutive, two-segment snowman was gliding down the street, muffler streaming. I knew him—his name was Pocket. Behind him, clinging to his icy shoulders, was a young elf: Quince. I hadn't seen them in over a year. The inseparable duo worked for Jake Frost.

Had Crinkles called Jake Frost in to help with investigating Elspeth's murder?

Without thinking, I peeled off from the band formation and hurried after them, waiting until I was a bit beyond the crowd before I called out their names. Electric-powered snowboards for snowmen had been all the rage last year, until too many snowmen fatalities had ended the fad. Pocket, clearly, was the kind of snowman who didn't mind living dangerously. Hearing his name, though, he slowed, and Quince turned to wait for me to catch up. I was out of breath by the time I reached them.

Quince laughed when he recognized my face over the drum. "What are you doing?"

"I'm playing bass drum in a marching band. What are *you* doing?"

His gaze cut left, and he bit his lip.

"Visiting family?" Pocket answered for him.

Uh-huh. "You're an orphan," I reminded Quince.

He shrugged. "I thought I'd drop by the orphanage."

I wasn't buying that for a second. Quince had been a problem kid, and last year he couldn't wait to run off to the Farthest Frozen Reaches to work with Jake Frost. The idea that he'd darken the doors of the Santaland Home for Orphaned Elves again was almost laughable.

"Is Jake with you?" I asked.

There were so many reasons to hope so. Even discounting the fact that he needed to be here for Claire's sake, Jake was Santaland's only professional private detective. I was dying to ask him what he thought of the details of Elspeth's death, and now the break-in at Château Mildred. He might even be able to help with our missing turkey.

"He's . . . not available right now," Quince said.

His evasiveness didn't fool me. "Where is he? Has he heard about the murder?"

The elf's eyes widened. "Somebody was murdered?"

"Elspeth Claus."

"That's nothing to do with us." He shifted impatiently. "Look, it's good to see you and everything, but I shouldn't be standing out here. I'm supposed to be at Municipal Hall."

"What for?"

He and Pocket exchanged an eye-rolling look—or I assumed Pocket was rolling his eyes, too. It was hard to know with chunks of coal.

"I won't tell," I insisted.

Quince finally relented. "We're looking for a wild elf by the name of Stumpy Shivers."

I frowned. "I don't know that name."

"Jake hopes the hall of records might produce some record of the Shivers family."

"So Jake *is* here." He wouldn't have sent Quince and Pocket all the way from the Farthest Frozen Reaches by themselves just to look up an elf's birth certificate.

"I've got to go," Quince insisted, "and you'd better watch out."

"What for?"

He nodded to something over my shoulder. "A band director who looks like he wants to add another homicide to the week's tally?"

A tingling apprehension washed over me. The music had stopped. Sure enough, when I turned, a red-faced Luther was thundering toward me. Quince and Pocket vanished, and suddenly I was standing in the road being berated for abandoning the formation and leaving my fellow musicians without a strong downbeat.

"I'm sorry," I explained, "I had to talk to someone. It was very important."

"We *all* have important things going on, April. You just can't charge off as the mood strikes you. What if everyone decided to do that?"

It was the old grammar-school teacher argument to make students behave, and it still worked on me. Heat rose in my cheeks, and I apologized again for being so thoughtless and selfish.

Shamed, I went back to finish the rehearsal.

"Your days are numbered, Mrs. Claus," JoJo Hollyberry muttered as I passed.

I turned abruptly, nearly whacking his trombone slide with my protruding drum. "Is that a threat?"

Could *he* be the one who'd left me that letter this morning? The tension between us didn't have anything to do with turkeys.

He bristled. "Miss high-and-mighty bass drummer."

"You're ridiculous," I shot back.

Although, to be honest, we *both* probably seemed ridiculous at that moment.

Luther shushed us. "May we continue now?"

The marching resumed, although JoJo flicked mocking glances back at me at every opportunity. It was unnerving, and more than once I fumbled the beat or slipped on the ice underfoot.

After rehearsal, I was unloading the drum on the equipment sleigh when a delegation approached comprised of Luther, Tiffany, JoJo Hollyberry, and that spare Hollyberry JoJo had brought with him.

"This is my cousin, Skip," JoJo said. "Why don't you try it out," he ordered his cousin, pointing to the drum I'd just wriggled out of. Skip hurriedly started shrugging on the harness.

"What's going on?" I asked Luther.

Luther looked regretful—but not overly so. "I'm sorry, April. We've decided to make a few changes. JoJo tells me that his cousin is quite a good percussionist, and after today . . ."

My face went red. "I didn't know that today's rehearsal was some kind of test."

Luther lifted then dropped his arms as if he were helpless in the matter.

"At least, we don't have to worry about Skip being thrown in jail before the parade," JoJo said.

My jaw dropped, and I turned back to Luther. "I was wrongly accused, so you're replacing me?"

"*Moving* you," he corrected. "And actually moving you to a much more visible—albeit less essential—spot in the formation. You'll be twirling on Tiffany's right."

Twirling? I blurted out a laugh. "I barely know how to twirl. I mean, I fiddled around when I was a kid . . ."

"You don't have to do much." Tiffany stepped forward. "I'm going to be doing the complex routines. All you and Cookie have to do is march beside me and do a basic hand twirl. I know you can manage *that*."

It still felt like a demotion. "I can't believe I'm getting kicked out of the band."

"Not kicked out," Luther corrected. "Repurposed."

Seeing how upset I was, Tiffany handed me a baton. "And look—you'll get to honor Elspeth by using her baton. Mildred told me to take it last night."

I held it. Naturally, Elspeth had added glitter and fluttering streamers to the rubber ends of her baton, which made it heftier than I remembered those metal sticks being. I gave it an experimental twirl.

It actually *was* kind of cool.

Resigned, I asked Tiffany, "What else should I know?"

"Just get used to carrying it around. Think of it as an extension of your arm."

I did a wrist twirl and then held it at my side. It was hard to think of something that sparkly and fringy as part of my arm.

"You'll be great," she assured me. "Just try not to do anything fancy and end up dropping it."

She didn't need to worry about that.

"I'll go by Mildred's again tonight and see if she can find Elspeth's twirling skirt for you, too," she said.

The twirlers were wearing the Santaland Concert Band's uniform, only with a wool skirt instead of pants. Not exactly flashy, but Christmastown was too cold to march in flashywear.

"There might be some trouble about that." I told her everything that had transpired at Mildred's. Tiffany looked shocked.

"Poor Mildred! I'll go over there directly."

"What happened?" Juniper asked when I'd rejoined her and Smudge.

"I've been repurposed."

She lifted her chin, genuinely upset on my behalf. "Maybe I'll twirl, too, and then the band can try to find another euphonium."

"It's okay," I said. "It's just for the parade."

I hoped.

"Would you like to join Smudge and me at We Three Beans?" Juniper asked.

If only I could. It would have been cathartic to go over the indignity of having my drum taken away from me—by a Hollyberry, no less—but I'd already wasted enough time on marching band self-pity.

"Thanks, but I can't. I have to track down someone."

Juniper's forehead pillowed in a frown. "You're not going to try to capture a murderer single-handed, are you?"

"No."

In fact, I was going to do the opposite. I was going to track down the very man who could find a murderer for me.

Chapter 12

There was one place where I was reasonably certain I could find Jake, at least eventually: the Gingerbread House, the inn where he usually stayed when he was in town. I headed there after rehearsal.

"Halt!"

At the shouted command, I stopped. A snowman wearing a blue constable hat had his coal-eyed gaze focused on me. It was Pumblechook, the one Crinkles had loaned his hat to. "Just a moment there, lady," he said.

"Is something wrong?" I asked.

"I should say so," he said. "You looked mighty suspicious skulking along the sidewalk."

"I wasn't skulking, I was hurrying."

"That's your story, is it?"

I couldn't believe I was being interrogated by a snowman. "Don't you recognize me? I'm not a criminal, I'm Mrs. Claus."

"Do you have any ID to prove that?"

"Pumblechook, you *know* I'm Mrs. Claus."

"Ma'am, if you're not going to cooperate, I'm going to have to take you in."

Take me in? I tried not to laugh. "You're a *snowman*."

"Giving me guff isn't going to help your case any."

Oh, for pity's sake. Plop a constable hat on a snowman, and suddenly he was Joe Friday. "There is no case." I sighed. "I'm looking for someone."

"Thin fellow, all dressed in black?" he asked. "Gang of folks with him?"

I blinked. Could Quince and Pocket be considered a gang? "Maybe . . ."

"He went thataway."

I looked at the snowman, whose two stick arms protruded from both sides of the middle segment of his body. "Which way?"

"The way I'm pointing."

"You have two arms pointing in opposite directions," I reminded him.

"How many left-sticked snowman have you ever met?" He released a snuffle. "I'll give you a hint. It rhymes with sun."

I tilted my head. "One?"

"Shoot. It was supposed to be none." He tried again. "How about . . ." It took him a moment. "Rhymes with hero."

Zero, then. And his right stick was pointing toward Twinkle Street. "Thank you!"

I set off in the direction he'd pointed me to. Behind me, he called out, "I'm letting you off with a warning this time."

I waved without looking back.

I hurried down Twinkle Street, slowing only once to admire a hardware store's display of Pilgrims fashioned out of brooms and mops.

Up ahead, I saw a flash of black. Only it wasn't Jake. It was Christopher, bundled in his black wool toggle coat. A young boy and a teenage elf the size of the boy were with him. They all stood around a pole looking at one of Juniper's *Missing* posters for Gobbles.

Not Jake, then.

I smiled in spite of my disappointment. I'd forgotten that Christopher had promised to put up *Missing* posters with Hal. And that other boy must be Christopher's elf friend, Winky.

When I hailed them, they looked up, surprised. Boys, I noticed, sometimes had a slightly furtive look, even when they were performing good deeds.

"Thanks for doing that," I said when I caught up to them. Christopher nodded. "Oh hi, Aunt April. This pole already had a poster. We were wondering if we should put another one on it—either below this one or on the other side of the pole."

There was space for another one, although a smaller bill was posted—a sort of public service announcement from the Cornucopia market warning about the proper temperature and time people should cook their turkeys.

It's Bigger than a Goose: Allow Plenty of Time!

Below that was a chart with cooking times listed by weight.

"Don't cover up the Cornucopia flyer," I advised. "And don't worry about running out. I can always print up more copies."

Christopher inclined his head in the direction of the pole in question. "This old poster's already a little torn, too. I think I'll go ahead and replace it."

The weather was always unpredictable in November. It was a shame we couldn't laminate the posters so they could last longer. But that would add a lot more time and money to the operation, and I was hoping we'd find Gobbles before the signs wore out, or before the birdnapper's patience wore out.

I thought again about that letter from this morning. The threat had seemed specific to me—and to Gobbles, of course.

Would the letter writer stoop to hurting children helping in the search? That possibility turned my blood cold. I didn't mind putting myself in danger, but these were just kids.

"Thank you all for helping," I said, "but once you finish putting out these posters, you should go home. You've already done enough."

Goodness was supposed to be its own reward, but after Gobbles was found, I would have to do something nice for the boys—maybe give them front row tickets to next year's big iceball playoff match.

"We could do more," young Hal said. "We just want Gobbles to be safe."

I patted him on the shoulder of his puffy coat. "You've already made a big difference." Kids like these made me feel optimistic about the future of the world.

"We still have a lot of posters." Christopher stared up at me. "Are you giving up looking for him?"

Judging from the thickness of the bunch he was holding, the kids must have run off some posters on their own. His stack looked as thick as the one Juniper gave me when this all began.

It was hard to believe that was only two days ago.

"Of course I'm not giving up. I just don't want you all to stay out after dark."

"We won't," they chimed.

I left the boys to do their postering and continued on toward the Gingerbread House. Taking in the streets along the way, it looked as if Christopher's crew had their work cut out for them. Most every pole, lamppost, or window was festooned with autumn-colored streamers, turkey or pumpkin lights, or Pilgrim-themed decorations, and occasionally all of them were mixed together in a kind of Thanksgiving décor trifecta. But few poles as yet had *Missing* signs on them. Every bare pole seemed like a missed opportunity to locate Santa-land's favorite turkey.

Before heading back to the Gingerbread House to wait for Jake, I took the opportunity to email Juniper to see if she could make more copies of the poster today. Even once the boys were done, I could put a few up.

Sure thing, Juniper texted back. **Someone took down the copies I put up here at the library.**

I had a flashback to the pictures being yanked out of the walls by their hooks at Mildred's.

Vandals?

What was going on in Santaland?

If they were, they were tidy vandals, Juniper answered. **They left the stick pins neatly lined up at the bottom of the cork board.**

I supposed that tidy vandals were preferable to the ones who'd caused all the mayhem at Mildred's.

Not far from the Gingerbread House, I nipped by Gert's Pretzels cart for some sustenance. I ordered a pretzel and also a big mug of hot spiced cider to go. Stakeouts were always easier with something to munch on and a warm beverage.

In keeping with the holiday, Gert was wearing a Pilgrim hat, although I noticed that she had a wool hat underneath it. Wise accessorizing, given the cold. On the corner nearby, another group of elf Pilgrims was singing "Over the River and Through the Woods." I never thought I'd want to hear more Christmas carols in a non-December month, but here we were.

"Nice day," Gert said.

It was freezing. Of course, it was always freezing here. I supposed she meant it was nice because the sun was out. At this time of year the sun rose late and set early, so every minute of sunshine was a good minute.

"Sure is," I agreed, suppressing my shivers.

"Liar." Laughing, she handed me my mug of cider. "Here—this'll warm you up."

Everyone in Santaland was aware that I was a wimp when it came to the cold.

I knew the liquid would be too hot to take a sip without burning my tongue, but I was grateful to wrap my hands around the cup. "You haven't seen Jake Frost around today, have you?"

Gert's lip twisted. "Usually he's an easy one to sight when he's in town, but with so many elves running around in Pilgrim getups, somebody in black doesn't stick out so much anymore."

Arching a brow, I nodded toward her hat.

She laughed. "You know the saying—when the walruses come to town, best grow tusks."

I nodded. "Someone dressed in black—maybe as a Pilgrim—broke into Mildred Claus's house today, attacked Olive, and tore up everything."

"I heard about that." Of course she'd heard—the pretzel cart was a Christmastown nerve center. "I hope Olive's okay. She's old to get whacked on the head like that."

"I sent for Doc to check on her. I'm hoping Jake Frost might be able to help find who did it."

My phone vibrated in my pocket, and I looked down, expecting a text from Juniper or Nick. It was from Pamela.

I'm sure you won't forget to pop by the Cornucopia and check on the frozen turkeys.

Translation: She knew I *would* forget—and I had.

On it! I replied, and added a thumbs-up for good measure.

"Speak of the devil."

Gert's words made me worry that I'd look up and Pamela would catch me eating pretzels instead of running turkey errands, but of course Gert had no idea whom I'd been texting with. She nodded her head at Doc Honeytree's sleigh coming down the street. The old doctor sat erect in his black stove-pipe hat and black frock coat in the driver's seat, although I assumed it was his reindeer, Hotfoot, actually steering the sleigh. Doc Honeytree's distance vision was not the best.

I thanked Gert and hurried over to waylay the doctor. Hotfoot saw me and stopped, bowing his head in greeting even before Doc had pulled up the reins.

I climbed onto the sleigh seat next to Doc. "Have you been up at Château Mildred?"

His head bobbed in a curt nod. "I have."

"How was Olive?"

"Fine, considering that goose egg lump on her skull."

"I guess she couldn't fake that," I said.

"Fake it?"

Something had been off at Mildred's place. I sensed a secret there, and it bothered me not knowing what it was.

"Why would she fake her attack? You think Olive had anything to do with that break-in?" Doc narrowed his eyes on me. "You saw the state of that house."

A flush of shame crept into my cheeks. "Yes."

"You think she did that and then clunked herself on the head to cover up—what?"

"I'm sorry—I was just thinking aloud. Of course she wouldn't have done anything like that. But she was saying that *Elspeth* had done it, or hired an assassin."

"Head trauma. It can disorientate a person."

"Into thinking ghosts have hired hit men?"

"Into all sorts of delusions." He frowned at me. "I'm shocked that a Claus could even insinuate such a thing about one of their own. Olive has served Mildred faithfully for decades, and she was the victim of a vicious attack."

I sank into the seat, ashamed now for being both untrusting and a disloyal Claus. "It's been a confusing two days."

"You of all people should know how pernicious false accusations are," he said.

He was right. "Is there any more information on what happened to Elspeth?"

"I was just at the constabulary telling the constable our findings. Elspeth ate something laced with arctic wolfwort."

Arctic wolfwort? "I've never heard of it."

"It's a flower. Quite pretty, with lacy blue petals. But when they're dried and powdered, they're highly poisonous to elves and humans."

"Would it have killed her immediately?"

"If she was poisoned with a concentrated dose, and she obviously was."

"And she wouldn't have been able to taste it?"

"She might have noticed an off or bitter taste. At least, that's what Algid tells me. I'm not likely to take a chance and sample any myself. You'd have to be crazy to do that."

"What if it was in Elspeth's wine?"

He shook his head. "Algid tested the bottle of wine that had been opened. Said it was fine."

"But someone might have put something in Elspeth's glass," I said. "Did anyone test it? She broke it."

He sighed. "A serving elf must have cleared it away."

A serving elf named Star, for instance? If she had some suspicion that Blaze had killed Elspeth, what wouldn't she do to protect him?

And of course, Midge and Amory were having the lodge cleaned from stem to stern this morning. But were they scrubbing away memories of a bad party, or scrubbing away evidence of a crime?

"Was this the first time you suspected Elspeth was being poisoned?" I asked the doctor.

He looked at me, uncomprehending.

"Mildred told me that Elspeth hadn't been feeling well for a long time. Did she ever consult you about nausea?"

I half expected him to scold me again, or to claim doctor-patient confidentiality, but instead he answered, "She had heart-burn. I gave her some pills for that, but just recently she said it had gotten better."

"Could indigestion have been caused by small doses of wolfwort?"

"It would have to be very small or very dilute not to kill a person." He scowled. "What are you getting at?"

"You said a person would have to be crazy to give herself low doses of poison. Do you think Elspeth could have been such a person?"

"Why would she have done that?"

"To garner sympathy?" Remembering what Amory had told me, I hazarded another guess. "To guilt someone into giving her money?"

He looked astounded. "First you tell me that Olive could have whacked herself in the head, and now you've got some cockamamie theory about Elspeth poisoning herself."

"I'm just trying to look at all the possibilities."

He scowled. "Well, I think your theory is a load of rein-deer flop. I knew Elspeth. She didn't like to suffer. She would never have put herself through anything like that on purpose. She certainly wouldn't have risked her own life."

"But those symptoms you mentioned—the long-term nausea. That could have been something trying to poison her."

The folds in his face deepened like an old Shar-Pei as he scowled at Hotfoot's rump. "Well . . . I suppose. But who would have poisoned her?"

"Someone who was tired of her," I said.

There were elves and people aplenty who'd been annoyed by Elspeth. Fatally annoyed? Who could that have been?

At that very moment, a Christmastown municipal sleigh bus glided by. And on the side of the bus was the ubiquitous smiling face of Blaze Whitewreath.

Chapter 13

The sun was starting to set by the time I finally spotted the bladelike figure of Jake Frost wending his way up the street toward the Gingerbread House. When I stepped out of the shadows, I thought I glimpsed fear flash in those gray eyes of his for the first time.

But in the next instant, his lips turned up in a wry smile. "If you ever get tired of being Mrs. Claus you could hire yourself as a hiccup remedy."

His stab at deflection couldn't make me forget that genuine alarm I'd detected in his eyes. If Jake Frost was jumpy, something in the universe was very wrong. I poked him with Elspeth's baton. "What's going on, Jake?"

He frowned. "What is that thing, a star-spangled self-defense stick?"

"It's a twirling baton. Don't avoid my question."

"I'm sorry. What was it you wanted to know, exactly?"

"For starters, how is it that you've barely seen your girlfriend visiting from three thousand miles away?"

"Claire knows why." His expression turned stony. "Work took me away."

"Work that's making you jump at shadows."

"It's been a long day and I wasn't expecting a crazy woman with a sparkle stick to jump out at me."

I probably did look a little crazed, so I let the remark pass. "Do you know what's been going on here these past two days?"

"I've overheard a few things." His eyes suddenly filled with worry. "Claire wasn't involved in any of those incidents, was she?"

I thought of Blaze Whitewreath and his possible involvement in Elspeth's death. Blaze, who was with Claire all the time.

"She might be more involved than she knows."

His dark brows raised in question. He clearly had even less idea than I did about what Claire was up to. The street was probably not the best place to discuss the matter.

"Come on—I'll treat you to an early dinner," I said.

The Midnight Clear diner was just down the block. It was an old-school North American establishment—the type with vinyl booths, Formica counters, endless menus, and bottomless cups of coffee—er, eggnog. Places like it might be disappearing in the United States, but the Midnight Clear was as popular as ever here. Of course, it kept its Christmas lights up all year, and the jukebox, filled with holiday favorites, was always playing.

We took a booth in the back. A waitress in red and green turned over our waiting cups and poured not coffee but cups of hot cider, and left to give us time to look at the menus. Jake plucked one out of its place next to the sugar dispenser and made a show of looking at it. But I knew he was just giving me an opportunity to fill him in on everything that happened.

"Elspeth Claus was murdered at Kringle Lodge yesterday," I said. "Doc Honeytree says she was poisoned by something called arctic wolfwort. Do you know it?"

His brows knit. "It's a flower. You see it in summer when certain areas thaw—even in parts of the Farthest Frozen Reaches."

"Apparently a flower that, if dried and powdered, is deadly if ingested."

He frowned. "So someone gave powdered wolfwort to Elspeth at the party?"

"Calling it a party's a bit of a stretch," I said. "Elspeth's face-planting into her mashed potatoes cut the festivities short. But get this—she'd complained about feeling sick for months, until just recently."

"So?"

"So I think someone might have been trying to poison her before," I said.

"Why did it take them so long to finally kill her?"

"Maybe they were just waiting for an optimal moment, when someone else could easily be blamed. Like me." I told him about the kerfuffle over the egg turkeys, and spending the evening in jail.

He frowned. "Why would you put garlic in deviled eggs?"

Oh, for heaven's sake. "It's not like I'm the only one."

"They must have tasted really bad, though," he said. "You mentioned that Elspeth said she was trying to wash the taste away. If it was the wine that was poisoned, the aftertaste of your egg must have been so bad that she didn't taste the wolfwort in her wine."

My breath caught. "The more of the wine she drank, the more of an off taste she received."

"Which just made her drink more, trying to get rid of it."

Jake's comments convinced me that we'd pinpointed the poison vehicle. "Doc said the wine had been tested and was fine—but Elspeth broke her wineglass when she was sick, and the elves cleared it away."

"Out of efficiency, or were they purposely destroying the evidence?"

It was the same question I'd asked myself about Midge and Amory's cleaning job.

I frowned. "Why would someone kill Elspeth and then tear up her house?" I gave him the details of the home invasion at Mildred's, and even confessed my misguided suspicion of Olive.

He whistled under his breath. "It *has* been an eventful few days in Santaland. Almost makes the Farthest Frozen Reaches seem tame."

Almost was doing a lot of heavy lifting in that assessment.

"At least we haven't had any rampaging snow monsters here lately."

"Monsters come in all forms," he said darkly.

Could Blaze Whitewreath be a monster in disguise?

The waitress came over to take our orders and I told her that cider was all I was having. Gert's pretzel had been pretty filling.

She turned more hopefully to Jake.

He glanced at the menu. "I'll have the Glorious Sandwich of Old."

"Mayo?" she asked.

He shook his head.

"Fries or rings?"

"Fries."

I was disappointed. The onion rings were fantastic here. I wasn't above a little ring scavenging.

I set my disappointment aside and asked, "What kind of monster are *you* looking for?"

"A wild elf named Stumpy Shivers made off with a fortune in jewels."

"Tugtupite," I said.

He looked surprised that I knew that detail. "That's right."

"And you've tracked Stumpy back to his family here?"

"No. Evidently he has no family left in Santaland—or any family, period. His father, Stumpy Shivers Senior, was exiled to the Farthest Frozen Reaches for crimes against reindeer."

The reindeer of Santaland were protected. Killing them was forbidden, and slaughtering them for consumption was considered especially monstrous. I assumed that was the "crime against reindeer" the elf had been convicted of.

"Stumpy Senior lived thirty years in exile and fathered two sons with a wild elf woman," Jake said. "But five years ago, the Shivers family perished in a blizzard. All but Stumpy Junior."

"And now he's a jewel robber. The rotten apple didn't fall far from the tree in the Shivers family."

"I tracked him to the border of Santaland, but I fear he wound his way through the Christmas Tree Forest and has come to Christmastown or Tinkertown to meet an accomplice to fence those jewels."

"Have you checked with Snuffy Greenbottle?" The old elf ran a dodgy secondhand store in Tinkertown.

"That was the first place we went. Snuffy swore he'd never heard of Stumpy Shivers."

Jake fell silent while the waitress delivered his sandwich, then he picked it up and waited until she was out of earshot before speaking. "Stumpy killed the miner he stole the jewels from. It's not surprising. The scuttlebutt in the Reaches is that he killed his own brother, Stinky."

No wonder Jake had seemed jumpy. He was on the trail of a psychopathic elf. It made me uneasy, too. I reached for a French fry.

"Help yourself," Jake said.

I chewed it thoughtfully. "You said his family was wiped out in a blizzard. How could he have killed his brother?"

"The brother's body was never found—just the bodies of the parents." He shrugged. "The fratricide talk might be a load of chestnuts. Horrible things can happen out in the Reaches during a blizzard. Elves wander off, get lost, and their bodies get covered with snow and sometimes disappear forever."

That was the reason being exiled to the Farthest Frozen Reaches was the punishment for heinous crimes in Santaland. For some it would be tantamount to a death sentence, but even for those who managed to scratch out a living in the wastes beyond Mount Myrrh, it could be a life sentence of misery.

"Then again, if the gossip is true, that really worries me," Jake continued. "An elf who would kill a lone prospector is bad enough, but if that elf has already killed his own brother? It's hard to imagine scruples preventing him from murdering anyone who got in his way."

I picked up another fry. They lacked the batter-fried magnificence of the onion rings, but they were delicious all the same. "I wonder what his brother did to make Stumpy think he needed to get rid of him."

Jake shrugged. "Who knows? All the accounts I heard indicated that Stinky was the nicer brother."

"Maybe that was the reason for their rivalry—people liked Stinky more. He might have been his parents' favorite."

"Sibling rivalry doesn't always need a reason." He took a sip of coffee. "Word among elves is that Stumpy was always rotten—the kind of kid who would hit birds with his slingshot just for the fun of it. And he turned into a ruthless adult."

For some reason, connecting Stumpy to what had happened with Elspeth's death and the trouble at Mildred's hadn't occurred to me until just then.

"Do you think Stumpy Shivers attacked Olive and ransacked Château Mildred?"

"It would be strange if the arrival of a notorious criminal had nothing to do with a rare crime wave, don't you think?"

It made more sense than Elspeth's ghost being the culprit.

"Sure, but why would some elf from the Farthest Frozen Reaches need to tear Mildred's place apart?" I wondered.

He drummed his fingers on the table. "I'm not sure. I want to go by Mildred's and show her the sketch I have of Stumpy."

"There's a sketch?" I scooted forward on my bench seat. "Can I see it?"

He reached into his jacket and pulled out a paper that had been folded into quarters. I took it and opened it up. The drawing conveyed little more physical detail than one of those *Wanted* posters from the Wild West days would have. The elf in the drawing appeared shaggy and unkempt, with long hair parted in the center falling over his big ears. His eyes were hard, dark points and too small for his face. His mouth was a grim, lipless line in his unshaven face that showed a hint of cleft chin. A truly unappealing elf.

I pushed the sketch back across the table and sat back.

"You should make a *Wanted* poster and put it around town," I said. "An elf like that would stick out like a sore thumb in Christmastown."

"He might be wearing a disguise."

"Hard to hide those eyes, though."

He refolded the paper. "I'll need to find a place to copy it."

"I can take it to the library for you and have it scanned and copied."

He smiled and gave it to me. "That's one problem solved."

"You realize you've got a thornier problem than a renegade elf, don't you?"

He shifted uncomfortably. "What's that?"

"While you've been chasing Stumpy, Blaze Whitewreath has been chasing Claire."

His hand froze halfway to his mouth with a fry. "That elf whose picture is on all the sleigh buses? And Claire?"

"They've been spending a lot of time together."

Two streaks of red appeared in his pale cheeks. Interesting. Claire was wrong. Jake was a man who could feel jealousy.

"I can't believe Claire would be attracted to someone like that," he said.

"He's a slick real estate elf. Who might be a murderer."

I filled him in on the details of Blaze's being seen standing outside having a tête-à-tête with Elspeth. Whatever they discussed at that meeting could have given him the motivation to finally kill her—which he could have been doing by degrees while they were more involved. "What do you want to bet that if we searched his home we'd find a mortar and pestle with a residue of arctic wolfwort in it?"

"Why would he have been poisoning Elspeth by degrees?" Jake asked.

"To make it look as if it wasn't murder," I explained. "But something obviously came up recently that made him impatient to get rid of her once and for all."

"And that was?"

"Claire."

"Claire's not that fickle." He pulled out his phone.

"What are you doing?" I asked.

"Some quick research."

"Don't expect Claire to tell you what's going on. She's not even letting me in on the details—and I'm not the one she's mad at for running off to the middle of nowhere after she traveled three thousand miles to be here."

"Then it's lucky I have a plan B."

While he was typing a number into his phone, I looked to up to see Lucia across the restaurant, standing at the cash register counter. "Excuse me," I told Jake, but he was so focused on his phone that he barely heard me.

I went over to join Lucia. "What are you doing here?"

"They make a good egg cream here," she said. "I needed a little jolt of something after standing around all day."

"Were you judging reindeer games?"

Lucia had railroaded me into refereeing reindeer games before, so I knew how standing around in the cold with a stopwatch and waiting for reindeer to thunder by could tire a body out.

She shook her head at how ill-informed I was. "The reindeer games have been halted until after Thanksgiving. Quasar and I have been out collecting reindeer signatures all day. The drawing's tomorrow, you know."

I'd forgotten all about the drawing to decide which reindeer would pull Nick's sleigh in the parade. "Lots of takers?"

"I wouldn't say *lots*. There's a sort of unspoken boycott going on among the elite herds. The most competitive reindeer like the Comets think it's a waste of their time, and the most vain, like the Dashers, feel that it's beneath them to join a lineup of reindeer who will be picked at random."

"That's so messed up."

"Not from their perspective." Lucia couldn't stop being an advocate for *all* reindeer. "They have strict standards, and if they didn't, Nick would be taking off with a bunch of out-of-shape reindeer on Christmas Eve. Would you be okay with that?"

"No, of course not." I could understand the need to pick the fastest and the fittest to pull Nick's sleigh on the big night. But that was a special occasion, and boiled down to only nine reindeer. What about the hundreds of others? Surely they deserved a moment or two in the limelight.

A brainwave brightened Lucia's eyes. "Say—would you like to pick the winners at the name drawing tomorrow?"

"Me?"

"Nick told me that he can't do it—he fears the appearance of Santa playing favorites."

"He would never play favorites," I said.

"You know that, and I know that. But reindeer can get irrational, especially when it comes to who pulls Santa's sleigh. *You* could be seen as impartial, though, and your name would attract a crowd."

I couldn't help but preen a little at that. After the day I'd had, my ego was ready to soak in any compliment. "Because I'm Mrs. Claus?"

"No, because of the poison eggs," she said. "That's bound to bring in a few looky-loos."

"My eggs didn't kill anyone."

"I know that," she said. "No one else does, though, and having someone notorious should reel in a bit more audience."

I wasn't sure I wanted to be used that way.

Before I could say anything, however, Lucia was confirming all the plans as if I'd already answered yes.

"Be at Peppermint Pond at ten o'clock tomorrow," she said, taking her drink-to-go from the counter elf. "There should be a pretty good crowd. You can even take the opportunity to confirm that you're not an egg murderer if you want."

No sooner did Lucia leave than Jake Frost zipped up to take her place at the counter. He had the intensity of a bloodhound who'd just picked up a scent. Either he had news about Blaze Whitewreath, or the diner had supercharged his sandwich.

"Did you track down Stumpy?" I asked.

"No, but I've tracked down Claire."

Chapter 14

"How did you find her?" I asked as I trotted after Jake on the sidewalk. He walked so effortlessly, he almost seemed to be gliding. "Claire wouldn't tell me anything."

"Sometimes if you want a direct answer, you have to choose an indirect path."

I blew out a breath. "I have no idea what that means."

"I talked to Whitewreath Property's secretary and told her I had important business to discuss with Mr. Whitewreath. It only took a few hints that I knew both him and Claire very well to wheedle the information out of the woman."

"You mean you lied."

"Yes."

Why hadn't I thought of that?

The address Jake led me to turned out to be the first floor of an old half-timbered building on Sparkletoe Lane. This surprised me. Aside from Festival Boulevard, Sparkletoe Lane was the most bustling street in Santaland, and the first floor of a building there wouldn't afford much privacy. I'd assumed the address was some kind of Blaze Whitewreath love nest, but when I looked at the butcher paper covering the large plate glass windows of the empty establishment, I began to re-think my assumptions.

Jake walked up to the door.

"What are you doing?" I asked.

We were the same height, so when he turned back to me he looked straight into my eyes. "Knocking?"

Was he a glutton for punishment? No matter how clearly I took in this storefront on a busy street, I couldn't completely banish the idea that we were barging in on something that we shouldn't see.

Jake rapped firmly on the beveled glass of the door, which also had butcher paper taped on the inside. After a few moments, it was pulled open and Claire stood staring up at us in confusion.

Finally, a smile broke across her face. The smile was aimed at me. Jake received only the curtest of glances. "You'd better come in. I was going to surprise you."

When I stepped inside, I was more than surprised. I was amazed.

The whole room was done in eye-popping Santaland colors of green and candy-striped red and white. The old white and black hexagonal tile floor had been newly cleaned so that it sparkled. A long counter was painted red and varnished to a high gloss. Leaning against it was a large sign obviously meant to hang outside. On it, a grinning, anthropomorphic ice cream cone in a red Santa hat leaned cheekily against the curly "T" in *The Santaland Scoop*.

Not a love nest—an ice cream parlor!

I could barely contain my shock. "You're opening a shop here?"

"Great job of sleuthing, April," Claire joked. "I honestly expected you to figure this out days and days ago."

"I was trying not to pry. Why didn't you just tell me?"

"Because I wasn't absolutely sure I'd be able to secure the lease on this place until today. I was worried that it would all fall through and that I would have wasted my time and your time, too."

"But you already have the sign . . ." I glanced around again. "And this paint job is yours, isn't it?"

She smiled. "Blaze talked the owner into letting me do some painting while my bank was shuffling the paperwork. I had the sign cut last week, and finished painting it today." She made a ta-da gesture with her hands. "What do you think?"

What did I think? I could hardly think at all. The prospect of having Claire here in Christmastown permanently made me so happy that my eyes filled with tears. I ran over and hugged her.

"This is so wonderful—beyond my wildest dreams."

"Santaland needed an ice cream store," she said, purposefully misunderstanding me.

"Having my best friend from home is all I needed to make this place perfect." I pulled back, eyeing her seriously. It would be a huge change for her, and she'd spent less than a month here, in total. "But are you sure?"

Her eyes met Jake's. "I'm sure."

Another knock sounded at the door, and Blaze White-wreath strode inside, his Pepsodent smile beaming. He was wearing an orange and blue pattered tunic, and in his arms was the biggest bouquet that I'd seen since leaving Oregon.

"A little housewarming gift," he said, presenting the flowers to Claire.

She took the flowers—not quite as much in awe as I would have been. She was new here, so she didn't understand the value of things like that yet. This time of year, cut flowers in Santaland cost an arm and a leg to import, so the bouquet must have cost him a fortune. Wait till she got a load of the price tag on bananas for her fabulous banana splits . . .

Blaze cast an awkward glance at Jake and me, though he directed his words to Claire. "So your secret is out."

She lifted her arms and dropped them again. "Jake located me soon enough—when he finally decided to."

Uh-oh. "When did you find this place?" I piped up, trying to smooth over that last barb. Jake seemed calm, and clearly admired the shop, but he had yet to say much beyond a murmured congratulations to Claire.

"Early last week," Claire said. She wasn't looking at Jake anymore, although it felt as if there were a force field between them. "It was the first rental property Blaze brought me to after I contacted him."

The Realtor beamed proudly. "The moment she told me she wanted to open an ice cream parlor, I knew the perfect spot." He laughed and backtracked. "Right across from Sparkletoe's Mercantile. Location, location, location."

Sparkletoe's was the biggest hardware and housewares store in town. Everybody went there, which was a big part of why there was so much foot traffic on Sparkletoe Lane. Claire really couldn't have asked for a better site for her ice cream parlor. And if she put her sign out, on Wednesday half the town would see it. Sparkletoe Lane was where all the marchers and floats would muster for the parade.

She paced around the space, mapping out her plans for the shop. "The soft serve machine and the milkshake station will be over here." She sidestepped several feet to her left. "And over here I'm going to put a display case with room enough for sixteen one-gallon tubs. In the back there's another freezer room where I can keep more, although I don't want to make *really* large batches." She grew even more animated as she looked across the open area next to the front glass window. "And over here we'll have about six small tables. I don't want it to feel too crowded."

"This sounds like your store in Cloudberry Bay," Jake pointed out. "With a different color scheme."

"There are bound to be similarities," Claire admitted. "It's going to be my ice cream parlor, only in Santaland."

"With nostalgia for your old life in Cloudberry Bay baked in," he said.

She put her hands on her hips. "There no 'old life'— there's just *my* life continuing. You seem to expect me to regret settling in Christmastown." The tension in Claire's voice ramped up a notch. "As if you *hope* for it, even."

Reflexively, I started edging toward the back room, as did Blaze. Claire and Jake had issues to hash out, and it would probably be better if we weren't standing there while they did.

Blaze seemed just as eager as I was to distance himself from any lovers' spat. I might have misjudged his interest in Claire. Was I wrong about anything else?

After shutting the door behind us to give Jake and Claire privacy, I flipped on the lights. The effect was almost blinding—and chilling. Even the cold room in the back of Claire's shop had been painted in bright red-and-white candy-stripe colors.

Blaze smiled at my reaction. "Newbies to Santaland often go over the top with the Christmas décor."

Claire had certainly done that. I bunched myself up in my coat and buried my hands in my pockets. Ice cream would do very well in this room. I worried I was starting to firm up myself.

For a moment we stood awkwardly trying not to hear the raised voices in the next room, but Blaze wasn't someone who could stay silent for long. "So I take it you were cleared of any part in the dreadful thing that happened yesterday?" he asked me.

"The murder, you mean?"

"It was murder, then? I assumed that if they'd let you go, Doc and his nephew must've concluded that Elspeth died of natural causes after all."

"No, they discovered that she was poisoned, but deduced from testing the eggs that I wasn't the one who had done it."

"Oh." His brow furrowed. "Poor Elspeth. I never thought it would have come to this."

He made it sound as if he had suspicions about her death. "What do you mean?"

"I shouldn't say—" He shrugged. "I don't really have any evidence."

Now I had to know what he was thinking.

"You were one of the last people to have a private conversation with her," I pointed out, "so you could probably shed some light on what was on her mind."

He blinked at me, confused. "I didn't speak to her at all yesterday. I meant to say hello to her at some point, of course, but I assumed we'd cross paths again sometime during the party. And then she was gone."

His voice sounded sincere, but he probably sounded sincere singing the praises of elf shacks with shaky foundations, too, when he was trying to sell one.

"When did you arrive at Kringle Lodge?" I asked him.

"Just after you did, I believe. Claire came with you, and she and I met up right after I got there. We were together until the awful thing with Elspeth happened."

"You didn't arrive early to speak to Elspeth?"

The question puzzled him. "Why would I have done that?"

"Someone said they saw you." But even as the words came out, I realized they weren't true. Balsam had specified that he'd seen a purple coat, and I had drawn my own conclusions because I remembered Blaze wearing that color. But other elves might have been wearing purple. "They saw someone wearing purple."

"It wasn't me," he insisted.

Could Star have been wrong? "Have you ever met the elf who was serving at table yesterday?"

"That funny little thing whose arm wobbled when she was pouring water?"

She probably wobbled mostly when she was around Blaze, the imagined love of her life. And he didn't know her name.

"Her name is Star," I said. "She just saw Elspeth outside talking to someone."

"And for this reason, I'm a suspect?"

"Well, you and Elspeth did have a history."

"We were involved, but it was never serious." He shook his head. "*I* was never serious."

Poor Elspeth. "I think she felt differently about you."

Understanding dawned. "So you think that perhaps I wanted to take extreme measures to get rid of her because I didn't want her texting me."

"Did she text you?"

"No. That is . . . not often." Frazzled, he huffed out a breath. "This is ridiculous. If Constable Crinkles needs a suspect, tell him that he need look no further than that aunt of hers."

Now that he knew he was suspected of Elspeth's murder, his scruples about speaking of his own suspicions against others had apparently evaporated.

But after hearing his implied accusation, it was my turn to be incredulous. "Mildred? She's been so upset over what's happened to Elspeth."

"She might be upset, but back when Elspeth and I spent more time together, half our conversations seemed to be about how much she disliked being Mildred's permanent houseguest. She was always asking me about property inheritance and things like that."

"Why?"

His brows rose. "I gathered that she was Mildred's heir."

That was interesting. "To me that says that they actually did have a good relationship."

He chuckled. "Elspeth was paranoid. She worried that Mildred would disinherit her and leave that hideous old house to the Depression Center, or to Olive. To be honest, I got tired of listening to her whining. An old lady can give her money to whoever she wants, and Elspeth already had a cushy deal being able to live with her aunt rent-free."

"Did she and Mildred ever argue about this?"

"I think the arguments were all in Elspeth's mind." He shook his head. "It got to the point that her living situation was making her sick. She had to pop antacids twenty-four seven just to be able to keep living there. It was pathetic. I told her she'd be better off just getting a place of her own."

"Did she ever give you any specifics about her health complaints?"

"No, just that she felt sick to her stomach a lot." He hesitated. "I know this makes me seem a little callous, but I found her griping about Aunt Mildred and all the psychosomatic whining about her health to be very unattractive. I finally decided that we just weren't compatible." He smiled. "I'm a positive elf."

I remembered the conversation I had with Elspeth the day before she died. "I spoke with her when I saw her at We Three Beans the other day. She was boiling over with a kind of angry optimism."

He laughed. "What does that mean?"

"She intimated that she would be taking a trip. It didn't make sense to me, but she mentioned coming back in a blaze of glory, or something like that."

"Maybe she'd found a better living situation all on her own." Blaze scratched his clean-shaven chin. "*That* might have put Mildred's nose out of joint."

"Mildred wouldn't have begrudged Elspeth her independence."

His square jaw set rigidly. "I'm telling you, there was something not right going on in that house. If you're looking for murder suspects, just hop on your sleigh and investigate those two old ladies."

Mildred and Olive? It seemed so unlikely that those two could be involved in anything like murder. Especially Elspeth's murder.

Although they had both acted strangely this morning . . .

If Blaze was right, maybe there was a reason Olive had been saying that Elspeth tried to kill her.

"This morning Olive was attacked when she was alone in the house," I said. "She mentioned something about Elspeth being at the bottom of it, but we didn't believe her. Mildred suggested that Olive was rattled from the blow to the head she'd taken."

"And you believed Dr. Mildred?" he asked wryly. "Look—properties are my business. I've seen all kinds of crazy family snarls that happen over inheritances. My advice is, go back and ask Mildred a few pointed questions about who'll get the house after she dies. Then see what bubbles to the surface."

I looked at my watch. I was supposed to swing by the library—and wasn't there another errand I'd meant to do? I couldn't remember now. My head was full of speculation about Mildred and Olive. What if Blaze was right, and Olive's accusations against Elspeth weren't as crazy as they'd seemed at first blush?

Of course, it was also entirely possible that Blaze was misdirecting me to deflect suspicion from himself.

I rubbed my gloved hands together to warm them. "I should get out of here before I turn into a human ice cube."

A slow grin spread across his face. "In a hurry to take my advice?"

That smile of his was so disarming. I could see why he was so successful. That handsome face could convince fish to buy desert condos. But there was also something in it I mistrusted.

I ducked my head through the door to the ice cream shop, aware suddenly that the arguing had stopped sometime during my conversation with Blaze. Claire and Jake jumped apart—they'd obviously managed to patch things up.

I lifted my hand as I hurried toward the door. "I have to go." As my hand touched the doorknob, I glanced back at Claire. "Everything okay?"

She smiled. Even Jake was smiling. "Everything's perfect," she said. "See you back at the castle."

Getting back to the castle—to sleep, especially—sounded so good. But I had a few stops yet to make before I could call it a day.

Chapter 15

I swung by the library with an eggnog latte for Juniper. "I nipped into We Three Beans just before it closed," I said, handing it over to her at her post at the front circulation desk.

It was an hour before closing time. Evening was usually a quiet time at the library, unless there was a special event. Tonight was one of the quiet nights. Juniper handed over the copies she'd made of the flyer, and with a wave of her hand batted away my offer to pay for them. "Consider it my contribution to the Gobbles search. Any news today?"

"Not about Gobbles." I told her about Doc and Algid's confirmation that Elspeth was poisoned, and then brought her up-to-date on Claire's opening an ice cream parlor.

"Ice cream." Her voice was filled with wonder. "Right here in Christmastown."

Frozen treats seemed exotic to Santalanders, and even a little bit strange. Their whole world was frozen, so eating cold things didn't appeal to elves as much as it did to people in warmer climates. But most elves hadn't tasted Claire's ice cream. Juniper had, and I could tell the prospect of its being available to her all the time brought her nothing but happiness.

"But the best part is, Claire will be here." She smiled. "Does she need a place to stay? I have a spare room."

"She's always got a place to stay in the castle."

"That won't be very convenient to Sparkletoe Lane, though. My place is only a five-minute walk from there."

It was as if we were having a friend tug-of-war, with Claire as the rope. The truth was, I was excited to be living near my two best friends. That they got along with each other was icing on the cake.

"I'm glad there's finally some good news to cheer you after all the bad news," she said.

Had something else happened that I didn't know about? "What bad news?"

She cast her eyes down. "You know. Band."

I nearly laughed. With all the mayhem going on, band seemed the least of my worries. "I don't care about that."

"You don't? You sure looked upset this afternoon."

It was true. I had been upset. "I think that had more to do with JoJo's taunts about Elspeth than being demoted."

"Repurposed."

"Part of the reason all the stuff with Elspeth has hit me so hard is that the way things ended still bothers me."

"Of course—she was murdered. It must have been horrible."

"Not just that she died, but that she died thinking *I* killed her." Until tonight I hadn't detailed for Juniper the way Elspeth had fingered me as her murderer and tried to call out to the other diners to have them help her—presumably to help her escape from me. I told her about it now.

Juniper's face tensed in concentration as she listened. I could tell she was playing the scene in her mind. "So she pointed and said 'April—help?'"

I nodded. "We weren't close friends, but I don't know what I ever did to make her think I would murder her."

"Maybe she didn't think that," Juniper said. "She pointed at you and called your name, and then said 'help.' Sounds to me like she was asking *you* for help, April."

I shook my head. "Why? There were so many people better able to help her. You should have seen Nick—he leapt out of his seat in nothing flat and tried to do CPR."

"She might not have been thinking of CPR. If she knew she was dying in those last moments, maybe she was thinking longer term. Everyone knows you've helped solve some mysterious deaths before. Maybe she was asking for your help . . ."

"To solve her own murder?" I finished for her, incredulous.

Crossing my arms, I hiked my hip against the edge of the desk and considered her words. Elspeth's asking for my help was less disturbing than her thinking that I was an evil poisoner. But believing that Elspeth had turned to me in her dying moments also brought the burden of responsibility. How could I refuse a dying frenemy's last request?

Hands poised over the keyboard, Juniper asked, "What was the name of that poison?"

"Arctic wolfwort," I said.

She typed on her computer, and then read from a website. "It's a very fast-acting poison." She frowned. "I don't think it would be a choice for someone trying to poison Elspeth over time."

"Maybe it was just what the killer had on hand. Convenience."

Her gaze stayed on her monitor. "But it says here that it has to be carefully prepared. And small amounts can do severe damage, depending on individual susceptibility." Her lips twisted in thought. "So my guess is that there were either two poisoners, or one person using two different poisons."

"Why would they have switched poisons?"

She thought about that. "Because the original one wasn't working?"

I frowned. "I hate what I'm thinking."

She leaned forward. "Who do you suspect?"

I couldn't bring myself to say the name aloud. It grieved me even to think about it.

Juniper leveled a disappointed look on me. "If you won't tell me, you should let Constable Crinkles know the suspect's name. Even if there are two poisoners in Santaland and whoever you're thinking of is only the incompetent first poisoner, you can't be sure that they won't become competent sometime in the future and actually succeed in killing someone." She frowned. "And what if they get wind of your suspicions of them? That someone could be you."

She couldn't have chosen better words to unsettle me. "Thanks, that's just what I needed to worry about."

"Tell Constable Crinkles," she repeated.

I pushed away from the desk. She was right. I'd been putting off telling Constable Crinkles my suspicions for the weakest of reasons—because I personally liked the suspect. But it was doubtful that my liking them would make the villain, whoever it was, hesitant to bump me off if they thought they were about to get caught.

As I turned to go, I looked over at the *Missing* poster of Gobbles on the bulletin board at the front of the library.

"That's a larger size flyer than these, isn't it?" I held up my voluminous purse, where I'd stuck the flyers.

She looked at it proudly. "I enlarged the file you sent and added a border."

"At least no one's snatched this one yet."

"I've kept my eye on it," she said.

"Did you see anyone suspicious come into the library today before the other flyer you'd posted got stolen?"

She scrunched her brow in thought. "No, but I wasn't really paying attention every single minute. Mostly there have just been the usual kids in and out all day, along with regular adult patrons."

Lots of elves coming through meant lots of possibilities for who could have taken that flyer down.

Thinking about the flyers, I suddenly remembered the picture Jake had given me. I took it out of my bag. "I need to use the copier."

She crooked her neck to look at the picture of Stumpy Shivers. "Golly doodle! What a scary-looking face. Who is he?"

"A wild elf Jake is chasing. I told him I'd make copies of the picture that he can post around."

"The wild elf's *here*? In Christmastown?"

"Jake thinks so. Might want to lock your doors." I went to the copier and ran off twenty copies.

"Will I see you tomorrow?" Juniper asked when I was done.

"I hope so. Lucia's appointed me to pick the names at the reindeer's parade sleigh drawing. It's going to be held by Peppermint Pond."

"Wow—that sounds like fun. Of course I'll be there—even if I have to bribe another librarian to cover for me."

The prospect of tomorrow's fun lightened my steps as I headed in the direction of the constabulary. I called ahead to let them know that I was on my way, and why. Ollie answered the phone.

"Is Crinkles around?" I asked.

"No, he's up at the castle."

I stopped in my tracks. "Castle Kringle?" I asked stupidly. As if there were any other castle in Santaland. "What is he doing there?"

My first worry was that something had happened to Nick. Ollie put that fear to rest right away. "It was a knock-down, drag-out in the castle kitchen. Felice attacked Lettuce."

"Was anyone hurt?"

"No, but apparently they're going to have to make another batch of cranberry sauce before Thursday."

That sounded bad.

"Luckily, the sauce was already cooling before Lettuce got her face mashed in it."

"That's terrible."

"And an awful waste of cranberries," Ollie agreed. "Of course, I'd rather wash cranberries off my face than sugar syrup out of my hair, which is probably what Felice is trying to do at this moment."

What had I done? When I'd asked Lettuce to join the kitchen staff, I'd never anticipated so much culinary violence. Jingles was right—two cooks was one too many.

"Don't worry," Ollie said. "Santa stepped in and convinced them both not to press charges. Good thing, too. Uncle Crinkles and I have got a lot of work yet to do on this float. We don't have time to deal with prisoners right now."

Good to know the constabulary had its priorities in order.

"Ollie, could you do me a favor?"

"Sure, what?"

"If Constable Crinkles is still up on Sugarplum Mountain, have him meet me at Mildred's."

"This about the robbery-not-a-robbery thing this morning?" he asked.

"It's about Elspeth."

I turned my steps toward the funicular. The single-cable railcar went from downtown Christmastown straight up Sugarplum Mountain to Kringle Heights. Taking it was a faster way to get to Mildred's than the sleigh bus. While the car ascended,

I taped a few copies of the Gobbles flyer on the wall. It was surprising that Christopher and his gang hadn't already covered the funicular. I knew Christopher used it, and presumably Hal did, too, since the Chao-Clauses lived in Kringle Heights, not too far from Mildred.

Of course, my dream was that Gobbles would be found this evening or at least sometime soon. *Someone* must have seen him. *We should be offering a reward*, I thought.

I probably should have thought of that before Juniper ran off all these new copies of the flyer. How would the bird thief react if I announced a reward? Would he consider that a provocation?

By the time I reached Mildred's, Constable Crinkles was already waiting for me there. In the living room, a cozy fire roared in the massive blackened hearth. The constable stood in front of it, warming himself. After my walk from the funicular stop, I was glad of the warmth, too.

Mildred offered me tea and fruitcake. "People have been so kind," she said. "We've received sixteen of them so far."

Sixteen fruitcakes. That was a lifetime supply. Of course, given the amount of alcohol those cakes soaked in, they probably had the shelf life of about a lifetime.

"No, thank you." I hated to take their fruitcake—even if there were sixteen of them—when I was here to make an accusation.

"Olive is making tea for the constable," Mildred insisted. "She can bring an extra plate for you."

There are only so many times I can be offered a dessert, even fruitcake, before I give in and accept. That night the magic number was two. "Thank you," I said.

"Find Gobbles yet?" Crinkles asked me.

"No, not yet, but I have high hopes. Christopher's been out with some other kids putting flyers all around. They've been great."

"I hate to think of that bird out in the cold, poor thing," Mildred said.

Considering the day she'd had, it was amazing she had any emotion to spare for a missing turkey. Her generosity made me doubt myself. Was I wrong to give credence to the insinuations that Blaze had tossed around?

"Gobbles will turn up," Crinkles assured us.

I just hoped he didn't turn up on someone's dinner table. Before we could get sidetracked by a Gobbles discussion, though, I drew up my courage. "I actually came here to talk about Elspeth. And who was poisoning her."

Mildred gasped. "What?"

Crinkles's lips turned down in a dramatic frown, and he looked solemnly at Mildred. "I'm sorry, Mildred, I should have told you this before. Doc has confirmed that Elspeth was poisoned. With arctic wolfwort."

Mildred must have expected this news, but still she recoiled a little, as if she wished she could flee a discussion of anything so negative.

Crinkles continued, "And now I guess I have to ask, Mildred, do you know anybody who might have wanted to poison Elspeth?"

I was shocked that he hadn't pressed her about this before. He'd had the information about the poison for the better part of the afternoon. But of course there were papier-mâché donut holes to prepare, as well as a chef war at Castle Kringle to mediate.

Mildred fidgeted, straightening some copies of *The Christmas-towner* magazine on the coffee table before her. "I can't think of anyone."

"No one?" I asked.

"Of course not. Elspeth was . . ." Instead of finding the word, she turned and fluffed one of the couch's throw pillows.

This one had a needlepoint Currier and Ives–style print on it. No doubt either Mildred or Olive had done the needlework.

"Elspeth was a difficult person to get along with," I said.

"Not always," Mildred said quickly. "She could be perfectly nice sometimes. And you should have known her when she was a girl. She loved to play cards with me when she was younger. When she first moved here after her parents died, we had lovely times together."

Those times had been over two decades ago, though. "How was your relationship more recently?"

Mildred blinked at me. "Not as good," she admitted. "But Elspeth was very busy. And she'd begun to feel sickly, too. Chronic illness can affect one's personality."

"So can being slowly poisoned."

Mildred gaped at me. "Slowly? But Elspeth died at the dinner very quickly. You saw that as well as I did."

"You told me yourself that Elspeth had been suffering stomach upset. Doc Honeytree confirmed this, and he also agreed that the symptoms she showed could have indicated that she'd been ingesting small doses of poison over a long time."

Her mouth dropped open. "I don't know anything about that."

"Don't you?" I pressed.

At that moment, I could hear the tea trolley pushed by Olive squeaking toward us. Mildred flicked a nervous glance in the direction of the sound, looking as if she wished she could rescind her offer of tea and fruitcake. "No, I don't."

"That makes two of us," Crinkles said, clearly baffled.

I pressed on. "Do you know anyone who could have had the motive and the opportunity to do that to Elspeth?"

"Of course not," Mildred said. "If you're insinuating that *I* could have done it . . ."

"I'm not," I said.

"Then who . . . ?"

The answer came from the other side of the room, where Olive was still half hidden behind the tea trolley. "Me," she announced. "*I* was the one poisoning Elspeth."

Chapter 16

We all swiveled toward Olive. The diminutive elf stepped out from behind the trolley and approached, looking vulnerable in her old gray-and-white tunic over a skirt and booties. Like a mouse in an apron.

"I did it," she confessed. "I'm the one you should be accusing, not Miss Claus."

Miss Claus was always how Olive referred to Mildred.

"No one has accused anybody of anything," Crinkles said.

Olive shot a quick glare at me. "She was insinuating, though. And once you start insinuating, it's just a short sled to an accusation."

Crinkles's brow furrowed. "What exactly are you saying you did, Olive?"

"I poisoned Elspeth." After that shocking declaration, she lifted her chin defiantly. "*Sort of* poisoned her."

Mildred's entire face looked in danger of melting. "Olive!"

"I'm sorry, ma'am," Olive said quickly. "But notice I said *sort of*. Whoever finished her off over at the lodge on Sunday wasn't me."

Crinkles leaned forward, confused. "So what was it that you did?"

Olive drew her shoulders back. "For a few months I laced her food with ice-rat poison."

The matter-of-factness in her confession shocked me. Crinkles, too, looked flabbergasted. The only person in the room who didn't look shocked—aside from Olive herself— was Mildred. Disappointed, yes. Shocked, no.

"Why would you have done something so monstrous?" I asked.

"To deal with monsters, you have to become a little bit of a monster yourself," Olive said. "Otherwise the monsters will win every time."

It was an upsetting philosophy to hear coming from an elf, especially here at Mildred's house. Also, although there had never been any love lost between us, I had a hard time seeing Elspeth as a *monster*.

"What did Elspeth do that was so terrible?"

Olive looked regretfully at Mildred. "I'm sorry, ma'am. I never wanted you to know, but I have to say it now. Elspeth wanted to kill you. She asked me to arrange for you to have a fatal 'accident.'"

Mildred stared at the rug. I expected her to say, "I don't believe it," or something like that. Yet she didn't.

"Why?" I asked. "Why would she approach you with such a—"

I was about to say "with such an outrageous idea," but judging from Olive's confession, it wasn't so outrageous that she'd kill someone. It just had to be the right someone.

"She thought I must be harboring some bitterness—she assumed everyone was as resentful as she was herself. She offered me retirement and an annuity."

"What did you say to her when she came to you with her murderous proposition?"

"I told her I'd do no such thing." She shook visibly at the memory.

Crinkles looked mystified. "I don't understand. Why would Elspeth want to get rid of Mildred?"

I remembered what Blaze had said about Elspeth's complaining, and I turned to Mildred, who looked shaken and smaller than she had even a minute ago. "Elspeth was your heir, am I right?"

"Not my *sole* heir," she said. "I have other nieces and nephews I've left a few items to. And of course Olive will receive a stipend after I die. But Elspeth gets the house." She shook her head. "She would have gotten it, I mean."

"After your death." I looked at Olive, who nodded curtly.

"I think she wanted to set me up," Olive said. "Mildred would be gone, and she could point at me as the culprit. And no one would believe the word of an elf against a Claus."

I wasn't so sure about that. Though I could understand an elf's harboring that fear. Not all the Clauses were as scrupulous as Nick.

Olive looked at Mildred with mournful eyes. "I'm so sorry, ma'am. I know this is terrible to hear. I would have done anything to spare you pain. But I couldn't stand here and listen to you being accused."

"I always knew I wasn't Elspeth's favorite relative," Mildred said shakily. "She thought I was silly and tedious. But I never dreamed she *hated* me."

"Elspeth was a conniving piece of work," Olive said. "I started to worry that she would finally work up the gumption to do her own dirty work. She began practicing on me."

"Practicing?" Crinkles asked.

"Spreading oil on the kitchen floor for me to slip on. Loosening a board on the basement stairs I travel up and down dozens of times a day. She was either trying to hurt me or showing me what she was capable of doing to Mildred. That's when I started slipping the rat poison into her food."

Good heavens. It was like château *Hunger Games*.

Mildred's expression was pure anguish. "Oh, Olive, why didn't you tell me all this?"

"Because you loved Elspeth. And for your sake, I didn't want her dead. I just wanted to let her know that she couldn't mess with you or she'd have me to answer to. Most of all, I wanted her out of the house. She was a hard nut to prize from the shell, but it finally worked. She figured out what was going on with her stomachaches and told me that she'd found a way to raise money and move out."

That must have been when Doc Honeytree's indigestion pills started working. Olive had put the brakes on the rat poison.

But where had this mysterious money come from?

"She told you that she'd found a way out?" I said.

"Yes, but of course that doesn't matter, does it? I poisoned her. I'm not trying to duck out of any punishment. I knew what I was doing was wrong." She drew her shoulders back. "But I'd do all that and more to get rid of someone who's a danger to Miss Claus."

Crinkles looked very disturbed. "I don't know what to say."

I didn't, either. That's why I was texting Nick. **Can you come to Mildred's house? ASAP?**

The reply dots only flashed for a few moments before his message appeared on the screen. **On my way.**

He hadn't even asked why.

When I looked up from my phone, Olive had crossed over to Crinkles. "Constable Crinkles, I think the appropriate words would be, 'You're under arrest.'"

"*Who's* under arrest?" Crinkles asked. "For what?"

"Me, for attempted murder," Olive told him.

"Elspeth was threatening you," I said. "It was almost self-defense."

Now that I'd opened this can of worms, I wanted nothing more than to close it back up again. Olive and Elspeth had been playing cat-and-mouse games, flirting with murder, but I believed Olive when she said she didn't deliver that fatal dose of arctic wolfwort.

"You said yourself that you were just trying to scare her into leaving here," Crinkles said, clearly loath to arrest a septuagenarian elf. "You didn't mean to kill her."

Olive's actions seemed an extreme way to push out an unwanted housemate, but I understood Crinkles's reluctance.

Our moral compasses were tap-dancing all over the place.

Mildred stood up. "Constable, if you're going to arrest Olive, you'll have to arrest me, too. What's the phrase? 'We were in on it together.'"

"No, we were not," Olive said. "I acted on my own. Mildred knew nothing about the rat poison." She looked at me, then the constable. "You both saw that she had no idea."

Crinkles lifted his arms and then let them drop again, hopelessly muddled. "I haven't said I was going to arrest anyone yet. Why should I? Neither of you killed anyone."

"Elspeth is dead," Olive reminded him. "By poison. I didn't deliver the fatal dose on Sunday, but you've only got my word for that."

The constable frowned. "Right, so if you didn't do it, I'd just be wasting my time."

I understood his hesitation. Maybe, technically, arresting Olive and Mildred would be the logical step, but everything about it felt wrong to me. I remembered the picture in my bag and pulled it out to show Mildred and Olive. "Do either of you recognize this elf?"

Crinkles, Olive, and Mildred all gathered around to study the sketch.

Mildred pulled out a lorgnette and peered through it, frowning. "He's very disreputable looking, isn't he?"

I glanced at Olive. "Do you recognize him?"

She shook her head. "Never saw him before."

"He wasn't the one who attacked you this morning?"

She looked at the picture again, but sighed. "I never saw who attacked me."

"Hold on," Crinkles said. "That's the wild elf Jake Frost asked me about. The one who stole the gems."

I nodded. "Stumpy Shivers."

"Why would you think he came here?" Mildred asked.

"I wondered if Elspeth might have known him."

Mildred's voice looped up. "A wild elf? And Elspeth? I don't think so."

She was still protective of Elspeth. Or maybe she simply knew from Elspeth's snobbiness that she never would have had anything to do with the likes of Stumpy Shivers. The more I thought of it, I doubted it, too.

I tucked the picture away. "It was just a thought. Nick is on his way. Maybe he'll be able to help sort this out."

Everyone in the room breathed a collective sigh of relief. "Oh yes, Santa'll know what to do," Crinkles said.

"Nick's always so reasonable," Mildred agreed.

"In the meantime," Olive said, "I'll go pack my jail bag."

"Pack mine, too," Mildred called after her, as if the two of them had frequent use for jail bags.

While we waited for Nick, we drank the tea Olive had brought in and also had a piece of fruitcake. It was really good—moist, sweet, and soaked in spirits—but I could barely taste it. The world seemed so topsy-turvy right now, I might as well have been eating sand. Crinkles downed two pieces.

Nick arrived just as I was taking the tea tray back to the kitchen. He gave me a quick kiss and then looked into my eyes. "You seem tired," he said.

"I'll be okay. You should talk to Mildred and Crinkles." I gave him a thumbnail sketch of Olive's confession, and somehow he was able to follow the twisted tale of poisoning-yet-not-fatally-poisoning.

"Let's sort this out and get you home," he said.

As if my getting home was of any importance compared to Olive possibly taking the blame for Elspeth's death when anyone who knew the details of the case could see that she didn't actually cause her to die, rat poison or no rat poison.

Then again, feeding someone rat poison did tend to make a person look guilty.

I gave myself a reminder never to get on Olive's bad side. She was like one of those *Arsenic and Old Lace* ladies with a hint of Sonny Corleone.

When I returned to the living room, Nick had a supportive arm around Mildred, and Crinkles was straightening his hat in preparation of leaving.

"Mildred and Olive are going to stay at the constabulary for a little while," Nick explained to me.

"Both of them?" I protested. "Mildred didn't do anything."

"I couldn't possibly stay here without Olive," Mildred told me. "It would have been hard to stay here so soon after what happened this morning in any event. We're better off at the constabulary."

I could see her point, but what if Crinkles decided that he had two perfect scapegoats to pin Elspeth's murder on? He might stop looking for the killer.

"Don't worry," Nick told me. He could always read me like a book. "We're going to figure out who really killed Elspeth. But this at least will put Olive and Mildred somewhere out of danger."

I hadn't thought of that. If the home invader hadn't found what he was looking for this morning, what was to stop him from coming by again? And the next blow to the head might prove fatal.

Nick and I loaded Mildred and Olive's suitcases on the constabulary sidecar, and then we gave the two ladies a ride into town.

Deputy Ollie greeted Mildred and Olive like a concierge welcoming guests. "The only hitch is that I'll need to move the turkey fryer out of the prison cell."

"What's it doing in there?" Crinkles asked his nephew.

"I couldn't think of anywhere else to put it," Ollie answered. "The inflatable donuts are already in the interrogation room." Also known as the dining room.

On the way back home, I scooted close to Nick and leaned against him as he drove the team back to the castle. Despite the fact that it was late, we stayed on the ground this time around, and I was grateful for that.

"I know it's a cozy constabulary," I said, "but it still feels wrong to leave Olive and Mildred there."

"They'll be okay," he assured me. "It's not like the two ladies will be doing hard time. Didn't you hear Olive and Ollie talking about deep frying their turkey?"

They'd been discussing the best kind of oil to use.

"Ollie and Olive," I mused. It sounded like a sitcom.

Maybe after this morning it was better that Olive and Mildred were at the constabulary than at Château Mildred. "My trouble is, I just can't feel completely calm when there's any kind of chance that Olive or Mildred could end up getting exiled to the Farthest Frozen Reaches. You should have heard the story Jake was telling me about that place today. Some wild elf slaughtered his brother—allegedly—and now might be hiding out here in Santaland."

Nick frowned. "You saw Jake?"

I told Nick all about Claire's surprise. He looked almost as happy about the ice cream parlor as I felt. He'd been to her shop in Cloudberry Bay, and had gobbled down his fair share of the several gallons she'd given us last Christmas.

"Are they coming back to the castle tonight?"

"I didn't press them. He and Claire looked like they needed a quiet evening to themselves." I blew out a breath. "Before he has to get back on the trail of that crazy jewel robber."

"A quiet evening together sounds wonderful."

He put an arm around me and pulled me closer. I burrowed into his warmth.

By the time we reached the castle, I was so tired that I'd come close to nodding off to sleep during the sleigh ride. As we came in, Pamela was just heading upstairs to bed. She stopped to put her hands squarely on my shoulders so she could look deep into my eyes. From the seriousness in her expression, I expected her to express her concern about Mildred, or for how I was feeling.

Instead, she looked at me directly and asked, "Did you check up on the frozen turkey wait list?"

Chapter 17

For the reindeer draw the next morning, I dressed in my newest, best Mrs. Claus outfit—a green lambswool sweater dress with red trim—and put my hair up in a loose bun. I didn't quite cut the storybook Mrs. Claus figure that Pamela did, but the outfit made me feel prepared to stand on a dais and represent the Claus family.

Even Jingles was impressed. "Rocking the duty day look."

"Thanks." I grabbed Elspeth's baton.

Jingles frowned. "What's that for?"

"Marching band." I held my hand out and performed a simple wrist twirl. Jingles had to duck out of the way.

He wrinkled his nose at it. "Strange accessory for a reindeer event."

"It's not for the drawing. I'm supposed to stop by Tiffany's tea shop so she can give me the rest of my uniform. I'm hoping she can give me a few twirling tips."

"It kind of ruins the slinky effect of the dress, though," he said, giving me another head-to-toe check. "I like the boots."

His furrowed brow undermined the compliment, however.

I looked down at them. The high red suede boots had more of a heel than I was used to.

"You sure you'll be able to stay upright in those?"

"O ye of little faith." I did have a tendency to slide when I wore heels, though. "I think I'll be okay. I'm just picking nine reindeer names from a jar, not running a marathon."

"Actually . . ."

Never had that word had a more ominous ring to it. "What else? Did I sign up for some holiday fun run that I've forgotten about?"

"Nothing like that," he said. "I just meant that the day's already thrown a few curveballs. Or maybe I should say curve eggs."

Oh no.

"There's been another set-to in the kitchen," he said.

"What's happened?"

"The cooks were apparently arguing over dressing."

I frowned. "Didn't we provide Lettuce with a uniform?"

The steward corrected me. "Not clothing dressing—meal dressing."

"Stuffing?" I asked, perplexed.

"Mrs. Claus—the dowager Mrs. Claus—calls it dressing," Jingles said.

Pamela was from the southern United States. They seemed to have their own words for everything down there.

"Something about cornmeal and apples versus bread-crumbs and snailfish . . ." Jingles shook his head. "I didn't hear the entire argument, but it ended with the day's eggs being used as missiles again."

This had to stop. Thanksgiving was two days away. The food needed to be on the table, not the walls.

I followed him down to the breakfast room. Nick was sitting at our long family dining table with what looked like a double helping of toast in front of him.

"Toast? Again?"

He smiled at me. "It's good toast."

Well, toast was always good. Just not for every meal.

Jingles pulled out my chair but I remained standing in case I needed to go straight to the kitchen to sort things out.

"It's okay, April," Nick said. "Sit down and have breakfast—er, toast. It'll be okay."

"Weaponized eggs is not okay. And snailfish? In stuffing?"

Nick raised a questioning brow. "Is that bad?"

His question caused a momentary *can-this-marriage-be-saved?* brain freeze. It was that North Pole divide. Sometimes it came in the form of having to listen to him humming "The Twelve Days of Christmas" all through July; today it was snailfish stuffing.

I collapsed into the chair. "I know Santalanders like to put their own spin on things, but turkey with snailfish stuffing is one revolution too far."

"It's just a soupçon of snailfish," Jingles assured me. "Like anchovies in a sauce."

Anchovies weren't winning me over.

"Snailfish stuffing is Felice's recipe?"

"Lettuce's," Jingles said. "Now Felice is threatening to quit. And since there's an opening up at the lodge . . ."

I try not to be swayed by trivialities, but snailfish in Thanksgiving stuffing wasn't something my brain could overlook. In the battle between Chef Felice and Chef Lettuce, I was now firmly on Team Felice.

Nick lifted his napkin to his lips to cover a smile. "I called up to Kringle Lodge. Midge and Amory are on their way. I'm hoping to broker a peace. From our brief phone conversation, I think Midge, at least, will be persuadable."

Nick was wonderful. I hopped up and gave him a hug. "Thank you so much."

"I know you have a lot on your mind this morning."

I could feel his gaze as I stood and hurried over to the sideboard to load up a plate with toast.

"Is that outfit for the reindeer drawing?" His eyes were dark, and he looked me up and down with a sexy, slightly lopsided smile that was very un-Santalike. "You look better than a mountain of gumdrops."

I laughed. He was suited up as well, in red velvet trimmed with white. "I would say you look like a million bucks, but I'm not sure how that measures up to gumdrops."

"Different currency, same compliment."

It was tempting to forget the toast and plop myself down on Santa's lap, but then Jingles not-so-subtly hitched his throat from the doorway.

"Amory and Midge Claus have arrived," he announced.

Midge marched in first, with Amory skulking in behind her like a teenager being forced to apologize for some wrongdoing.

"We've come for our cook," Midge announced. "Amory let her go without consulting me, and Elfworks Employment Agency was no help. We're in a bad way."

"So are we," I said. "It's been Gettysburg every morning in the kitchen."

"We'll be happy to take Lettuce back," Midge said.

Amory stepped forward. "As long as we can make it known, publicly, that the lodge was in no way responsible for Elspeth's death."

"I'm sure everyone will figure that out when the culprit is finally discovered," I said.

"But by then the lodge's reputation will be tainted."

Midge puffed out a breath. "I told him it's ridiculous to worry about our reputation when we're more likely to develop a notoriety for serving lousy food because we can't keep servants employed because *he* keeps firing them." When pronouncing the word *he*, she jabbed her finger at Amory like a prosecutor pointing to the defendant's table.

And just a few days ago they seemed to be getting along so

well. Amazing what one household staffing crisis could do to a relationship.

"But we need to show that when murders happen at the lodge, there's some accountability," Amory insisted.

I couldn't help laughing. "You should engrave your motto on a plaque for your desk: *The Buck Stops . . . with the Nearest Support Staff.*"

He shot me a withering look. "Easy for you to sneer. *You* were the one who started this whole mess by picking that ridiculous argument with Elspeth."

"She was the one who started an argument with me," I said.

He folded his arms over his chest. "And then you retaliated by giving her those poison eggs."

"They were not poison! Doc Honeytree cleared those eggs of any wrongdoing."

"Putrid, then."

Nick, who had stood when Amory and Midge entered the room, made a *simmer down* gesture with his hands. "Let's try to talk about this calmly. We are one family with two houses and two cooks. There is no problem."

Midge sat down. "Thank you, Nick. It's good to hear someone else being reasonable for once."

I tried not to take that remark personally.

Bristling, Amory sank into a chair opposite me.

Nick turned to Jingles, who'd been observing us in discreet silence. "Would you ask Lettuce to join us, please?"

"Yes, sir." Jingles turned on his heels and pushed through the swinging door to the kitchen corridor.

"We need to ask Lettuce what she would like to do," Nick said.

He was right. We'd been dickering over an elf as if she had no free will. Maybe she wouldn't want to be separated from Butterbean again.

"That's very democratic of you, Nick." Bored, Amory looked at the baton I'd brought down and set on the table. "What is that?"

"A baton."

I held it up. What had Tiffany said? *Extension of my arm.* A very sparkly extension. "It was Elspeth's unintended legacy to me." I frowned. "Along with an accusation of murder."

Amory's brow scrunched. "She willed you a twirling baton?"

I shook my head. "Tiffany retrieved it for me from her things. Elspeth's death left our marching band with a twirler deficit."

Midge's brow raised skeptically. "And you're filling it?"

I guess I wasn't successful in making the baton seem like an extension of my arm.

From the kitchen door, Jingles cleared his throat discreetly. He and Lettuce were standing side by side. Lettuce looked at all our faces while I studied her. I couldn't be sure if the red tint in her cheeks was embarrassment or a result of the cranberry incident. Finally, her gaze fell on Nick.

"I apologize for the limited menu, sir. That was not my doing. That elf in there who calls herself a chef—"

Nick cut her off. "It's all right, Lettuce. You don't have to explain about the toast. We brought you here because the opportunity has come up for you to return to your old position at Kringle Lodge."

The kitchen door swung open, and Butterbean darted through. The small, round elf skidded to a stop next to his sister, drew up proudly, and tossed his head so that his blond cowlick flicked defiantly. "As if Lettuce would ever be so desperate that she would go back there. Nothing on earth would convince her to crawl back up to the lodge after the way she's been treated."

I couldn't say that I would have been able to go back to work at the place that had just scapegoated me for a murder when it was patently obvious that I'd done nothing wrong.

"Five percent raise," Midge said.

Amory thumped his hand on the table. "*What?* Have you lost your hooting senses, Midge?"

Lettuce looked anxiously at her brother.

"Seven percent," Midge said.

Amory gaped at his wife. "*Seven?*"

"I accept," Lettuce said. "I'll get my things."

Butterbean looked bewildered. "You *want* to go back?"

"At least at the lodge I didn't have other elves trying to kill me with cranberry sauce. Besides—" Her mouth closed and she headed for the door.

Butterbean scuttled after her.

Across the table, Amory was fuming about the waste of money.

"Stop firing elves, then," Midge told him, "and we won't have to keep hiring them back at higher salaries."

I let out a long breath. At least I wouldn't have to worry about the stuffing.

Although I still had the turkey problem.

"I don't suppose there's been any word about Gobbles up at the lodge, has there?" I asked, my voice looping up with pathetic hopefulness.

"Why would we have your turkey at the lodge?" Amory asked. "Do you think *we* stole him?"

"No, of course not," I said quickly.

"We're coming here for Thanksgiving dinner," he reminded me. "Although Midge ordered a frozen turkey so the lodge elves can have their own feast. She picked it up yesterday."

I regarded her with envy. "You must've had a really good spot on the frozen turkey wait list. We haven't gotten ours yet."

Her gaze narrowed. "Are you on Wait List B or Wait List C?"

I blinked. "I just assumed there was just the one."

"Oh no—I was at the top of B." She shook her head pityingly. "If you haven't been called yet, you're definitely a C-lister." As the crushing news hit home, she added, "I'm sorry."

The ignominy of having a low frozen turkey wait list position made me sink further in my chair. Jingles and Butterbean had proposed this Thanksgiving holiday for my benefit. I was supposed to be showing how it was done, but I couldn't even procure a turkey.

I couldn't help musing, though, that maybe this week *was* exemplifying a traditional American Thanksgiving. It was that little-discussed flipside of a Norman Rockwell holiday: panic, family tensions, and a mad scramble to bring all the ingredients together.

As if summoned by the mere idea of family tensions, Pamela swept into the breakfast room just as Midge and Amory were getting up to leave. "It's good to see you," she greeted them. "Although I'm assuming you'll be here on Thursday, too. April's confirmed the time everyone's supposed to arrive, I'm sure."

Midge glanced at me awkwardly. "No . . ."

Pamela looked at me with silent impatience, as if I were an actor who'd missed my cue. "Well?" she prompted.

"Sorry—with the murder and everything, it must have slipped my mind." I looked at Midge and Amory. "Arrive around twelve thirty. We're aiming to serve at one."

"Wonderful," Midge said as Nick escorted them out to the castle's foyer. "Good luck with the wait list."

I winced. I was really hoping to make it through an encounter with Pamela without a turkey discussion, but I supposed it was inevitable.

"No word from the Cornucopia this morning?" she asked when we were alone. "Not that I mean to interfere with how you run things . . ."

I managed not to roll my eyes. "I haven't heard from them yet. I was going to go by Soy to the World and pick up the Tofurkey loaf. It's going to be our backstop."

"Oh dear." Pamela shook her head. "You really are just giving up, aren't you."

Was I missing something? Was I supposed to grease some elf's palm at the Cornucopia to get a better spot on the frozen turkey wait list?

"Don't worry—it's all being taken care of," I announced, lying brazenly. "And Lettuce is going back to the lodge, so we've eliminated the risk of snailfish stuffing."

Pamela's face fell. "Snailfish? I never knew about that threat."

"It's like the thermonuclear bomb," I said. "Peace of mind depends on shutting the very possibility of it out of your brain."

"You are a strange one," she said, in that wondering tone she had when referring to me. It was one of life's ironies that in a place as foreign as Santaland, this woman who came from my native country often seemed the most alien to me, and me to her.

I straightened. "Thank you for giving me the nudge that I needed to send out a reminder to all of Thursday's guests about what time to arrive."

"I'm sure you would have remembered," she said, in a voice that made it crystal clear that she knew I would have forgotten.

I pushed my chair in. "I need to drive into Christmas-town. Are you going to be at the reindeer drawing?" She was dressed very nicely in a blue-gray suit of rough silk that set off her silvery-white hair perfectly. She looked like a motherly ice cube.

"I'm afraid I'll have to miss it. I'm going to go over my final preparations for pie baking tomorrow, and then I have a meeting day for the Kringle Heights Ladies Guild."

The mention of the Ladies Guild, though, made me duck my head. After one incident—one involving Elspeth, naturally—I was persona non grata with the guild.

"Well, I should get going," I said to cover any awkwardness. "Busy day."

Purposefully, I headed for the foyer door, but was cut off by a serious-faced Nick coming through it. Now instead of escorting Midge and Amory out, he was leading Doc Honeytree and Constable Crinkles in.

I backed into the breakfast room again.

Seeing the new arrivals, Pamela stood to greet them and then reflexively crossed to the rope pull and gave it a tug. Jingles appeared a moment later.

"Tea for our visitors, Jingles," she said. "And see if there's something in the kitchen to go with it." Under her breath, she added, "Besides toast."

Jingles ducked out with a questioning look at me. I could tell he was reluctant to miss whatever news was causing the constable's and the doctor's long faces.

It was clear Nick had already heard, and he wasted no time letting me know the problem.

"There was a mix-up." Before I could ask for specifics, he confessed, "It was all my fault."

I didn't understand. "Your fault—for what?"

Doc Honeytree shook his head. "Nonsense. I should have double-checked the egg."

My heart sank. Eggs again.

"You see, the egg Nick gave to Algid to test turned out to

be the wrong egg," Doc continued. "It's not quite clear how such a mix-up came to pass."

I could guess. The doctor was half blind; it was amazing there weren't more of these mix-ups.

"We didn't realize we'd tested the wrong egg until we were checking an egg that the kitchen staff at the lodge had bagged up for us."

I thought back. "My platter of eggs was sent to the kitchen."

"That's right," Doc said. "But on Sunday evening we tested the egg that Nick gave us."

Nick eyed me apologetically. "I was eager to prove your innocence, and I saw the eggs on the buffet on a Castle Kringle platter. I assumed they were yours."

"Midge sent my eggs to the kitchen before dinner even started," I said, going through the events in my mind. "But you probably missed that. You were talking to Constable Crinkles, I think."

Crinkles piped up, "I remember it now—we were discussing the parade, Santa, when I heard raised voices coming from the other side of the hall. I recall glancing over thinking to myself, *Well, for whoopee's sake! What's Elspeth Claus on about now.*" He looked into our faces and paled, as if worried he'd said something offensive. "Not that I mean to speak ill of the dead . . ."

He hadn't said anything about Elspeth that everyone else in Santaland hadn't thought already.

"So what is the takeaway here?" I asked. "My egg actually *was* the killer egg? That's not possible."

"It contained the same substance that killed Elspeth," Doc Honeytree explained.

"Arctic wolfwort." I'd never even heard of the stuff before yesterday. Now I was accused of being so familiar with it that

I could harvest it and grind it into a powder and sprinkle it on a deviled egg.

"I'm so sorry, April," Nick said.

"But this is all impossible. Really impossible," I said. "I didn't poison any eggs."

Again, I recalled Elspeth's dying moments. That stare, and the pointed finger. Whether or not she thought I'd poisoned her, I owed it to her—to both of us—to figure out who did.

"The questions we should be asking are, 'Were all my eggs poisoned, and if not, who poisoned the sample egg?'"

Nick frowned. "Midge said they finally threw out most of the food from the potluck, except for the bits they sent over to Algid."

Crinkles's eyes turned sorrowful. "They threw away that whole honey ham?"

Nick shrugged, clearly worried about more than wasted ham.

I bit my lip, worried, too. Everyone saw Elspeth eat that egg, and then they found poison in a sample egg. I couldn't wish those facts away. But I couldn't go to jail now. I had so much to do. *I* wanted to find the killer more than anyone.

"I was telling Jake about the dinner last night," I said. "He thinks it was probably the wine that was poisoned. But there's nothing left of Elspeth's glass to test."

From her seat at the table, Pamela asked, "Isn't the absence of the glass evidence in itself? Someone is covering something up."

"Or the elves just cleared it away by habit and forgot about it."

"Then where is the broken glass?" I asked. "There has to be someone at the lodge, in the kitchen, involved."

"Oh, walnuts!" Crinkles said in frustration. "I don't know what to do. The constabulary's full, and we all know you didn't do this, April. You've been trying as hard as any of us to find out who the poisoner really was."

It was a lucky thing Constable Crinkles had never seen *Columbo* or read an Agatha Christie. He might have had second thoughts about a suspect "helping" an investigator. And then I would be back at the constabulary, along with Ollie, Mildred, and Olive, trying to figure out how to deep fry a turkey in a portable bathtub.

How had Ollie managed to get his hands on a turkey when the castle couldn't?

I sighed. "I can't be arrested now. I've got to be at the reindeer drawing soon." I knew it sounded like a ridiculous excuse for letting a murder suspect run around loose, but it was all I had.

I should have remembered that what would be considered ridiculous in other places was often just business as usual here in Santaland. Especially where the Christmastown Constabulary was involved.

Crinkles's face crunched into a determined frown. "I'm not going to take you in. The constabulary's already crowded, what with Mildred, Olive, and the turkey boiling pot."

I felt a little bad at the reminder of Olive and Mildred. They were being held at the constabulary on suspicion of murder. What if it got out that Mrs. Claus was given more consideration than rank-and-file Clauses, never mind elves.

On the other hand, being locked up in the cozy constabulary would be a huge inconvenience to me at the moment, and a hindrance to finding out who had really killed Elspeth. Since *I* hadn't done it, the murderer was still out running free.

"Are you going to put me under house arrest?"

"That wouldn't serve any purpose, either," Crinkles said. "You seem to notice things."

"We could hire Jake Frost to notice things," Nick suggested. His reluctance to see his wife any more involved in finding a brutal killer was clear in his eyes. And he still didn't know about the note I'd received.

"Jake's got his own headaches right now." Crinkles shook his head. "Stumpy Shivers! We need a murderous wild elf running around Santaland right now like a coat closet needs a woolly bear moth."

"I remember Stumpy Shivers, the father." Doc scratched the gray stubble on his chin. "Heard his family had all died in a snowstorm over in the Reaches after he was exiled."

"All except Stumpy Junior," I said. "Although there's some question about what happened to Stumpy's brother, Stinky. His body was never found."

Doc *tsk*ed. "Bad blood."

I sucked in a breath. "Star and Balsam both said they saw someone talking to Elspeth outside the lodge before all the other guests arrived. I assumed it was Blaze from their description. But neither of them got a good look. What if that was Stumpy?"

"Could it have been Stumpy who laced Elspeth's food or wine with wolfwort, though?" Doc asked. "A stray wild elf would have been noticed in the dining room."

"Unless he had an accomplice," I said.

The idea shook me. Could the renegade elf Jake was searching for be in league with whoever had poisoned Elspeth? And who was now trying to frame me . . .

We all exchanged looks. A muscle worked beneath Nick's jaw.

"It has to be someone in the lodge's kitchen staff," I said, but then I had another memory.

Nick saw my expression change. "What?"

Did I dare mention it? Was I even correct? I tried to sift through the sequence of events at the lodge on Sunday. "Amory left the room after Elspeth was poisoned," I said. "But I can't remember whether it was before or after my eggs were taken away to the kitchen. Either way, he could have had access to that batch."

"Amory?" Nick frowned.

"Was *that* why he fired Lettuce?" Crinkles asked. "Maybe she caught him in the act."

That didn't seem logical—then again, Amory wasn't a logical man. I could almost imagine his fevered brain thinking he should fire the elf who saw him framing me, but then why wouldn't Lettuce have squealed to me the moment she arrived at the castle? At the very least, she would have told Butterbean, and he would have said something. He still resented Amory from his own experience with him.

Pamela frowned. "I can't believe Amory or any Claus would harm Elspeth. It must be this wild elf—Stumpy or Stinky or whatever his name is. It's terrible that his evil deeds are ruining what should have been a perfect week of celebration."

Speaking of which . . .

I flipped open my phone to check the time. "If I'm not under arrest, I really should get downtown. I'm picking the names in the reindeer drawing." Nick, in the interest of Santa impartiality, wasn't going to be there. Just Lucia and I were representing the Clauses there.

Crinkles inhaled a sharp intake of breath. "I don't want to miss that, either. Do you need a ride to town?"

I nodded and thanked him. Walnut's Sleigh Repair had towed my sleigh away from Mildred's, but it still wasn't fixed.

"We'd better hurry," Crinkles said.

I grabbed my purse and my baton and left the castle in the constabulary sidecar. For a person not under arrest, I certainly was hauled around by law enforcement a lot.

Chapter 18

"Snug Brighthearth, *Christmastown Herald*."

The elf journalist showed up bright as a button to the reindeer drawing with his notepad in hand. In case anyone still had doubts about his profession, the brim of his elf cap had a card with the word *Press* on it.

He flagged me down as I was heading through the crowd toward the dais where Lucia was waiting for me with the jar of entry slips. Nearby I could see Quasar, his nose flickering excitedly. A throng was gathered by Peppermint Pond—elves and reindeer, snowmen and a smattering of people. I spied Clement and Carlotta in the crowd, looking amused by it all. Juniper and Claire were waving their arms from the back to catch my attention and say hello. How had I missed them?

Maybe because half of Santaland seemed to be crowding in this area between the banks of the pond and the Christmastown Municipal Hall across the street. Pumblechook was trying to direct all the foot traffic, while Crinkles was arguing that snowmen had no authority to direct anybody. Both had to yell over a group of elves singing "Over the River and Through the Woods." It was happy chaos.

With so many others present, I didn't know why the reporter would want to talk to me. I soon learned.

His hand hovered over his notepad. "Weren't you arrested for the murder of Elspeth Claus?"

"Just held on suspicion," I said, "until—"

I bit off the words. I was going to say *until my eggs were cleared*. But that would be misleading now, since my eggs were implicated all over again. Falsely implicated though, in order to frame me for a crime someone else committed.

"Mrs. Claus?" The reporter was blinking at me expectantly.

"No comment," I said. "At least, no comment about Elspeth Claus's death. This is a day to celebrate the reindeer of Santaland."

"Not all reindeer seem in a celebratory mood."

He was right. A big crowd of reindeer milled around the dais, yet the largest, fittest reindeer had gathered on the periphery, showing that they were there to be witnesses to this abomination against their concept of reindeer meritocracy. Lucia had warned me that many—the famous herds like the Comets and the Dashers, Cupids, Blitzens, and so forth—still objected to the idea of a random drawing.

And then there were the other reindeer. Most of these misfits weren't even identifiable by their herd of birth. Some had odd markings—one black-and-white reindeer looked as if he was a reindeer–milk cow cross. Others' coats were unusual hues: red, black, and albino. Their antlers were all a mess—either absent, or in the process of being shed, or just a messy tangle of horns. One reindeer's antlers grew straight, like upside-down walrus tusks sprouting out of his head. There were also reindeer with obvious challenges: reindeer who were missing ears, lame, or were blind. One reindeer had a sort of peg leg.

One thing they all seemed to have in common today, though, was enthusiasm. A few had decorated their antlers with streamers or flashing lights. One had made a turkey wattle for his long neck, and a few others had little cardboard Pilgrim hats on the tips of their antlers. I'd never seen reindeer bubbling with so much enthusiasm before. Some even wore signs like the old *Let's Make a Deal* audience—*Pick Me!* And *This Reindeer Is No Turkey!* And *Sleigh Me, Santa!*

The sight of them all filled my heart to the brim. Quasar had done his recruiting well. It was laughable to think that a few days ago we hadn't even known if the misfits would want to participate. Their excitement made the Comets and the Dashers and all the others on the sidelines look like the worst kind of killjoys.

"This is an unprecedented event in Santaland," I told Snug as I climbed the steps to the dais and made my way over to where Lucia was standing next to a microphone. "It's an opportunity for all reindeer to have a chance to step up and pull Santa's sleigh. The reindeer are going to make the parade unforgettable."

Snug didn't climb the steps after me. Instead, he sidled along below me at the front of the dais, squeezing himself between reindeer bodies and the platform, which was about five feet off the ground. "But about the murder," he persisted. "We've never seen a Mrs. Claus in jail before. Are you glad to be out?"

"Of course I'm glad, as any innocent person would be," I said sharply. "You think I'm a murderer?"

Unfortunately, I realized too late that the mic in front of me was live. It broadcast the last phrase I spoke over the assembled crowd, followed by a screech of feedback.

In the next moment, the singing, milling, and talking all stopped and a park full of surprised faces were blinking up at me.

Salty, who'd come to help Lucia set up the dais, scurried over to check the mic. The tapping made everyone jump. But at least the feedback stopped.

I cleared my throat. "I really didn't kill anyone," I said. "Otherwise I wouldn't be here"—I let the silence stretch for just a split second—"at the first-ever Santaland Random Reindeer Choosing."

After a moment, the crowd erupted into whoops, claps, and hoof stomping.

Solemnly, Lucia picked up the jar of entry slips and brought it to me. She flipped the mic off. "Nice save."

"Thanks," I said, before flipping the mic switch again.

"We're going to pick nine reindeer," I told the crowd. Lucia and I had debated whether it should be eight or nine. Whether the Rudolph position should be permanent was always a controversial question in Santaland, but we finally agreed that including as many reindeer as possible was the goal here. "The chosen ones will need to present themselves at Castle Kringle tomorrow morning at eight o'clock for the harness fitting."

I had to wait for the excited buzz to die down before asking the reindeer and elves to clear space in front of the dais so the chosen reindeer could gather there after I said their names. "If you could all just move back and to the left to make a path so that the reindeer who are chosen can gather at the front . . ."

It seemed a simple enough direction, but the result was pandemonium. Some of the reindeer weren't clear on the concept of left versus right, which resulted in several collisions and arguments. It didn't help that Pumblechook was off to the side, barking contradictory orders at them. Beyond the crowd, I noticed some of the elite reindeer exchanging smirks at the muddle the misfits were in.

"If everyone could just stop and take a step back—"

Before I could finish, a dark spectre appeared over the crowd and swooped down low, causing the reindeer to freeze. Grimstock landed at the edge of the dais, which so startled everyone that they all stepped back to put space between him and them.

He really was an unattractive bird.

But his sudden appearance inadvertently had created the desired result. It also reminded me about Gobbles. This seemed as good a time as any to make a public service announcement.

"Before we get started . . ." I took a deep breath. Was I authorized to do this? I didn't see why not. I was Mrs. Claus. "Everyone knows by now that our turkey, Gobbles, has been missing for the past two days. Castle Kringle is now offering a reward for any information leading to his return. If you see him, or hear of his whereabouts, please contact me or anyone at the castle."

That was going to be the extent of my appeal to the public, but before I knew what was what, I felt myself being pushed aside as Salty reached for the microphone. He had to tip it down to make it work for his shorter frame, and then he launched into a more emotional appeal.

"I want to add that if you're holding Gobbles and you're watching this, please know that we just want him back." His voice was shaky with nerves and trembling emotion, but he forced himself to continue. "Also, remember that he's a very sensitive turkey and he's not used to the cold weather. He needs at least a cup and a half of grains per day, and he also enjoys sunflower seeds and many kinds of berries. If you sing 'O Christmas Tree' to him, he'll sometimes bob his little head and—"

His voice cracked then and he couldn't go on. Lucia stepped forward and escorted him away.

Solemn eyes gazed up at me expectantly. The appeal to Gobbles's birdnapper had put a damper on the mood in the park.

I cleared my throat. "And now to choose the first name."

Even concern for the turkey couldn't suppress everyone's high spirits for long, and the crowd seemed to vibrate in anticipation as I stuck my hand into the jar. I pulled up the first name and read it aloud. "Flouncer."

A roar went up, and the crowd rippled with excitement as heads and antlers turned, trying to find the lucky Flouncer before she appeared, hopping like a gazelle up to the front. Among the throng, elves cheered and broke into "For she's a jolly good reindeer" until the entire park seemed to be singing and swaying.

When the din finally died out, I picked the second name. "Blunder." I just managed to refrain from yelling *Come on down!*

Another roar, and after Blunder bustled to the front of the dais, managing to bludgeon another reindeer in the side on the way up, the crowd broke into song again.

"This is going to take forever," I whispered to Lucia.

She shook her head, smiling benevolently down on all her reindeer friends. "It's their day. Let them have it."

There were never eight happier beings chosen to do a day's work. After Flouncer and Blunder, the next names chosen were Crawler, Snuffle, Bolter, Huffy, Daisy, and Cannonball. The crowd gave each a hero's reception.

The only hitch occurred on the ninth pick. I pulled the name out and hesitated, angling the paper toward Lucia. She read it and shrugged.

"Quasar," I announced.

The expected cheer went up, and everyone was singing long before Quasar reached the dais. When he stepped forward, though, it wasn't to join the newly picked team. He climbed right on the dais, sending Lucia and me to scurry off of it to make room for him at the microphone.

Nose fizzling with nerves, he lowered his head to the mic and said in his earnest, careful voice, "I'm s-so honored to be chosen, even if it was a random drawing. I put my name into the jar two days ago, back before we knew that anyone would want to participate. But there's been such a great response, and since I was one of the organizers of the event, I don't feel right taking a spot. Th-therefore, I must withdraw." He swung his head toward me. "Mrs. Claus, please pick another name."

The reaction from the crowd was mixed. There was applause, but also beneath it was a murmur of disagreement with his decision. I was torn. Honor Quasar's sportsmanlike impulse, or reward his self-sacrifice by insisting he take the spot.

"It's o-okay," Quasar said, reading the dilemma in my eyes. "I really meant it."

I stepped back to the mic. "For the ninth and final position, the reindeer is"—I stuck my hand in the jar for the last time—"Dasher."

Dasher? He was one of the elite reindeer most vocally opposed to a random drawing involving misfits. Apparently his vanity had won the day and he hadn't been able to resist putting his name in the running.

This time, instead of a roar of approval there was a collected gasp of astonishment, followed by a lone, familiar reindeer voice in the back yelling joyously, "That's me! *I* got picked!" The crowd parted to let Dasher through. He had taken extra care with his appearance today, which stood out all the more as he stood among the misfits. His coat had been brushed and conditioned to a high shine, his antlers looked suspiciously perfect, and his hooves were an unnatural glossy black. He was head and shoulders taller and bulkier than most of the others who'd been picked, except for Cannonball, a dark reindeer who was shaped just like his namesake.

I frowned down at Dasher. "You said you were against the random drawing."

"But I didn't say I wouldn't participate in it," he said.

"Anyway, you called my name. I won fair and square. Is that reporter from the paper going to take our picture now?"

I felt disgruntled, and most of the rest of the crowd did, too. There was no singing "For He's a Jolly Good Fellow" for Dasher, but Snug Brighthearth did step forward and take the picture—in which Dasher was preening front and center.

"And for this Quasar gave up his spot," I grumbled at Lucia.

I'd expected her to be incensed for her friend, but she was very accepting of reindeer foibles by now. "I should have known that old showboater wouldn't be able to resist putting his name in the pot when there was a chance for getting his picture in the paper. And of course he'll love to vogue down Festival Boulevard."

Oh well, maybe Blunder would step on his hoof during the parade.

I looked over the crowd to see how Comet was dealing with his fellow elite reindeer spokesman's defection. But the big names in sleigh pulling were already filing out of the park.

Over the backs of the departing reindeer, I saw a flash of something small and dark in the distance. And just for the briefest of moments, his features looked clear to me: a face with small, beady eyes.

Stumpy Shivers?

With a sharp intake of breath, I yelled in the microphone, "Stop that elf!"

But Salty, under Lucia's directions, had already unplugged the mic. Elves and reindeer close by looked at me curiously, but my voice never reached anyone who was in range to actually catch Stumpy. I leapt off the dais and started running. I made it about fifteen feet before the spike heel of one of my fabulous boots sank into a reindeer hoof rut in the snow and down I went.

Juniper and Claire hurried over to get me back on my feet. "What's going on?" Claire asked me. "You looked like you'd seen a ghost."

It was worse. I'd seen a homicidal elf. Or had I? I studied the crowd, but I definitely couldn't see him now. "Where's Jake?" I asked.

Claire's brows knit. "He said he had to meet Quince and Pocket in Tinkertown to talk to that secondhand seller again."

"Snuffy Greenbottle?" Juniper asked. "I love his place. I can always find treasures there."

I'm sure Jake's fear was that one of the treasures Snuffy was selling was actual treasure: stolen jewels.

"I have to get back to the library," Juniper continued, turning to Claire. "Candy's covering for me. But I'm dying to at least peek into your new shop."

Claire was very happy to oblige with a quick tour of the Santaland Scoop, so we all headed back toward Sparkletoe Lane together.

As we walked, my eyes scanned the familiar streets of Christmastown for the unfamiliar figure of a wild elf. I expected him to be lurking in some doorway or behind a light pole. But he was nowhere to be seen now. He'd just vanished.

Had I actually seen him? Or had I seen another elf in black and let my fears jump to conclusions?

Stumpy wasn't the only thing that had vanished, I realized as I took in the fabulous decorations everywhere. More turkey lights had been strung around plate glass windows, and Pilgrim figures were everywhere—if not full cutouts in store windows, then in the ubiquitous Pilgrim hats everywhere: on the squash display at the grocery store, on a stuffed dog in the pet store window, and sometimes just on newel posts on building stoops. Fresh streamers in autumn golds and reds wound around lampposts.

But there was something I wasn't seeing: *Missing* flyers for Gobbles.

It was eerie. Pole after pole was bare.

I pointed out the absence of the flyers to Juniper and Claire.

"Maybe Christopher and his crew didn't make it to this part of downtown," Claire suggested.

She was probably right.

Except Christmastown's downtown area didn't cover that much territory. And the three of them had been armed with plenty of flyers. On closer inspection, I could tell a few poles had been denuded of the flyer from the little bits of tape and poster that remained.

"Do you think the city of Christmastown took them down?" Juniper asked. "The council can be awfully persnickety about posting bills."

Maybe, but the public service stickers from the Cornucopia about how long to cook a turkey remained on some poles.

"Come to think of it, I don't think I saw any this morning as I walked to the pond, either," Juniper said. "Like, none."

Claire gasped. "That wild elf that Jake's chasing. Maybe he took them."

I leveled a skeptical look on her. "You mean you think Stumpy Shivers traffics in stolen jewels and missing-turkey flyers?"

"Well, when you put it that way . . . probably not."

"What could have happened to them all?" Juniper wondered aloud. "They just didn't walk away on their own."

Oh no, I'm sure they had help with that.

And I was beginning to have a good idea of who had done it . . . and who might have Gobbles. In fact, it was so obvious I wanted to kick myself.

Before we got to Sparkletoe Lane, I stopped. "I need to go see Tiffany at her tea shop. She's supposed to give me a skirt for the parade." I had another reason to want to talk to her, but I did need to pick up the skirt. Hopefully she'd also give me some twirling tips. Every time I thought about marching in front of the band tomorrow, my stomach clenched.

Our trio parted ways at the corner, with Juniper and Claire continuing on to the Santaland Scoop, and me heading to Tea-piphany. I had to gather my courage for this encounter. It was never easy to tell a proud mom that her son was a turkey thief.

Chapter 19

Tea-piphany was a little gem of a place. Usually the decor was Christmas-focused, with beautiful poinsettia-print tablecloths, twinkle lights around the ceiling, and small cedarbough and candle centerpieces on all the tables. Now Tiffany had decorated the whole place with a Thanksgiving theme. Cornucopia arrangements of fake fruit and berries sat on every table, and her usual twinkle lights had been replaced with little lights shaped like acorns. A large ceramic turkey greeted customers from his roost on the counter next to the cash register.

When I spotted Tiffany through the plate glass of the door, she was standing alone at the counter, frowning down at a pie.

When the jingle of the bell over the door alerted her to my entrance, my sister-in-law flashed that million-watt smile that had once earned her high marks from tough skating competition judges in her youth. "Hi, April! How did the reindeer drawing go?"

"It was fun."

"I wish I could've been there. I wanted to keep the tea shop open—although I should have known better. With all that going on at Peppermint Pond, I haven't had a single customer. The reindeer must have drawn a big crowd. I could hear the noise."

A strain I didn't usually see in Tiffany's face showed around her eyes and mouth, and two horizontal tension lines had settled into her forehead. Maybe this wasn't the greatest moment to bring bad news to her.

"Is something wrong?" I asked her.

"No, everything's fine," she said in a clipped, determined voice.

Clearly, she was lying. I hated to see her upset. A couple of years earlier, she'd sunk into a long period of depression after her husband, Nick's older brother, had died. She had since clawed her way back into the light, opening the tea shop and teaching skating to youngsters and taking care of Christopher, our future Santa. Holidays, though, could sometimes bring with them a melancholy nostalgia, a sadness for people no longer with us. I worried the Thanksgiving festivities were dragging her down.

"I can tell that something's bothering you," I said. "If you need to talk . . ."

"No, it's f-f-f-f-f—" She started sniffing, holding back tears.

"Tiffany, I'm so sorry. If there's anything I can do, please tell me."

She slapped her hand on the counter, both in frustration and an effort to pull herself together. "Okay, yes. There is something you can do. Are you hungry?"

That wasn't a question I was expecting. "Yes—all I've had today is toast."

"Great." She reached under the counter and produced a plate. Tea-piphany used nice china, some of it mismatched, from beautiful old sets. This one had a rose pattern on it, and the way she slapped it on the counter, it was a miracle it didn't shatter. "I need you to try this pie."

I looked down at the pie, which appeared to be some kind of custard or sugar pie. "You don't have to twist my arm."

"It's pineapple chess pie . . ." She stopped and wiped a tear off her cheek. "My Grandmimi's recipe." She sniffed again and then hacked an oversized wedge of it and slapped it on the plate.

I nodded. Sadness and nostalgia. They could sneak up on a person.

"It looks fantastic," I said.

"Try it and tell me what you think." She shot me a dead-eyed stare. "Your honest opinion."

I cut off a piece with the fork she pushed across the counter and gave it a taste. It was a kind of pie I'd never had—at least not with this specific flavor. The pineapple was definitely there, but very mellow. It didn't have that citrus snap of a lemon pie, and was more interesting than a plain chess pie. But just as sweet. Achingly, wonderfully sweet.

"I *love* this," I said, forking off another bite as soon as I'd swallowed the first one.

Tiffany looked at me skeptically and poured me a cup of tea. I was going to need something to go with all this sweetness. "You really like it?"

"Who wouldn't?"

"Pamela," she said. "She said I couldn't bring it to Thanksgiving dinner on Thursday."

I almost dropped my fork. "What? That's crazy."

"Tell me about it. She insisted I needed to audition my pie before I could bring it to Thanksgiving dinner. That was kooky enough, but I went ahead and baked this one as a sample. She told me it wasn't right for a formal fall dinner."

"Okay, first, who ever heard of a pie audition? And second, this pie is fabulous. What's not to like?"

"She said it was too weird tasting to be a traditional Thanksgiving pie."

"She's wrong," I said.

Tiffany shook her head. "Part of me thinks she doesn't even deserve my Grandmimi's pie. I'm tempted to boycott the whole event."

"Boycott Thanksgiving?" I asked. "I'd hate it if you did that. Just bring your pie. I love it, and so will everyone else."

"And what will Pamela say?"

"Who cares? She doesn't run the castle." I frowned. "I mean, she sort of does—but she shouldn't. We're two Mrs. Clauses and she's only one. We outnumber her."

Tiffany laughed. "You talk a big game when you're telling someone else to defy Pamela."

God, she was right. "I know. She's had me feeling like a whipped puppy all week because I didn't get to the Cornucopia on time to secure a good place on the frozen turkey wait list. Now we might be having soy turkey and walrus for Thanksgiving, and she's acting like it would be a sacrilege to put them on her perfect table."

"Still no sign of Gobbles?" Tiffany asked.

I tried to keep my smile in place, but Tiffany caught the shift in my expression. "What's the matter?" she asked.

"Nothing."

She tilted her head. "Now who's covering something up?"

I took a deep breath. She'd been truthful with me; I owed her the same honesty. And she would have to find out sometime. "There was a reason I came by."

She sucked in a breath. "Omigod—I completely forgot." She reached under the counter and brought out a paper sack. "I went over to Mildred's yesterday and rummaged through the mess until I found this." She pulled a pleated wool skirt out of the bag. "It's Elspeth's marching-band skirt. Do you think it will fit?"

She came around and held the waistband up to my middle. "Pretty close, I'd say. If it's too small, you can extend the closure with a big safety pin. But I bet you won't have to resort to that. It looks like it will fit you."

"Thanks. I'm not sure about this twirling gig. I never even twirled seriously in school." I frowned. "Does anyone twirl seriously?"

She sputtered. "You obviously never spent much time in rural Texas."

I laughed. "No, I never did."

"Honestly, you just need to do the basic wrist twirl—switch hands, if you're able. That will keep one arm from tiring out. There's not really time to teach much more at this short notice. I'm rusty, but I can do a few easier tricks just for visual interest. It will work."

I nodded. "I'll try to twirl before bed tonight."

Tiffany looked down at the pie and sighed. "I suppose I should keep this out to offer the boys some when they come back." She looked at the clock on the wall. "And they should be back by now. Did you see Christopher, Hal, and Winky at the reindeer event?"

I shifted uncomfortably. "No, were they there?"

"They said they would take a break from putting flyers up by stopping by the pond." She smiled happily. "I just think it's great that Christopher's leading that little group around, doing such a nice thing."

Here goes nothing . . .

"*Mis*-leading might be the more appropriate word," I said.

"What?"

"Christopher and his merry band haven't been putting up flyers. They've been taking them down."

Her smile melted, and a flush rose into her cheeks. "That can't be." A little Mama Bear righteousness crept into her tone. "And frankly, it sounds a little ungrateful. Those boys have been out there for hours a day putting up flyers for you."

"They've been out, but they've been making sure that

there are as few Gobbles posters around as possible." I pointed to her own window, which was bare. "Take a look for yourself—it's the same across the whole town. It's like there's been a flyer rapture."

For a moment, her mouth opened and closed, like a fish. "Why would they do that?"

"So there will be fewer elves and people on the lookout for Gobbles," I said. "Probably because Christopher knows where Gobbles is and doesn't want him found."

I pulled out the threatening letter I'd received with those perfect letters dripping fake blood. Now that I studied it again, the *or else* seemed like an adolescent taunt.

Tiffany saw it right away. She made a sound of disgust. "That's"—I expected her to say *outrageous*, but her face fell midsentence—"probably something Christopher would do." She sighed. "That rascal."

I wandered over and inspected all the scones and cakes she had in the glass case near the register. "At least I'm reasonably certain that Gobbles is somewhere safe. As you said, Christopher loves Gobbles."

"But so do others," she said, growing more outraged now. "Salty was here this morning, completely distraught about that bird. I had to give the poor guy two pieces of cranberry-carrot cake to calm him down."

That must have been after he made his appeal for help at Peppermint Pond. Lucia kind of swept him offstage because he was depressing the reindeer. He'd looked upset even as he was unhooking all the sound equipment.

She sighed. "Honestly, April. Every time I've convinced myself that I've done an okay job at raising my son these past few years, something like this happens to make me second-guess everything."

"You've been a great mother," I said. "And Christopher is a wonderful kid. He's obviously involved in the Gobbles shenanigans, but I can guarantee that everything that he did was out of compassion for that turkey. He's kindhearted."

"And duplicitous."

"If he's going to run around behind your back, isn't it better that he's doing something like this, instead of getting into real trouble?"

Just then the doorbell tinkled. Into the store marched Christopher, Hal, and Winky. The whole crew.

Or was it?

My guess was that there was a mastermind behind this plot of theirs to undermine the search for Gobbles. Clearly it wasn't Salty—his panic about Gobbles couldn't have been feigned. Nobody was that good an actor. But I was willing to bet some other adult had convinced these kids that they could hide Gobbles safely away until after Thanksgiving, when the danger of the ax was passed.

At least until Christmas.

It didn't take long for the three boys to notice the expressions on our faces. Winky, no fool, began backing toward the door they'd just entered through. "I think I need to get home," he said.

"Not so fast," Tiffany said. "I have some questions for you guys."

The boys exchanged glances of pure dread. *Busted.* I remembered that sinking feeling of getting caught, from my own childhood. A little of my anger at them dissipated.

But Tiffany had shifted into full-blown Disappointed Mom mode. She stood before them, arms akimbo. "What have you been doing with the flyers?"

Christopher made a valiant attempt to brazen it out. "We were putting them up around town. Aunt April saw us yesterday."

Thinking back, I could see that the kids had been doing a very obvious performance of putting posters out. As soon as my back was turned, they'd probably ripped them right back off. "There aren't any flyers out now. None."

Christopher struggled for an answer. "Maybe they blew off?"

Tiffany was having none of it. "Don't lie, Christopher. You're setting a very bad example for these other boys. They're younger than you—how could you drag them into this?"

"He didn't!" Hal said loyally. "We wanted to help."

His mom's voice looped up. "By sending your aunt a threat?"

"I really think I oughta go home," Winky said.

"Be quiet." Christopher realized he was trapped. "We were just trying to save Gobbles. I mean, *I* was."

"So you admit that you've known all along where the turkey is?" I asked.

He ducked his head. "He's in the castle. In the Old Keep."

"So I *did* hear gobbling in the night," I said.

At least I knew now that I wasn't going mad.

"He said you did," Christopher said.

"Who's 'he'?" Although. I knew. Of course I knew—it had been obvious from the first.

"Butterbean said you almost caught us that first night. Gobbles was real upset over being moved out of his cage and so he kept making noise. Butterbean moved his sewing machine into the Old Keep to cover the sound."

"Gobbles was in the Old Keep all this time?" Tiffany asked, amazed.

"Sometimes Butterbean moved him up to the tower, and once the turkey even stayed in Butterbean's room. He said Gobbles was really well-behaved." A look of frantic worry came over his expression, which was mirrored in the faces of the other two boys. "You aren't really going to kill Gobbles, are you?"

"Please don't!" Hal said, with tears in his eyes. "Gobbles didn't hurt anybody. Why should he have to die?"

For the crime of being delicious.

"If the turkey's okay, we're not in trouble, are we?" Winky asked. "Can I go home now?"

"I guess." I sighed and looked at Tiffany. "I'd better take Christopher back to the castle." I glanced at Hal. "We can stop in Kringle Heights on the way home and drop you off."

The poor kid's lip trembled. "Is Gobbles really going to die?"

I thought of Salty, and now these kids, and then imagined Felice wheeling a cooked Gobbles into the dining room on Thursday. I didn't feel good about that, either.

"I'm not sure what will happen," I said. "But we need to get him back to his cage."

By the time Christopher and I had delivered Winky to his mother's workplace, Soy to the World, and Hal to Joyce in Kringle Heights, the sun was going down as we returned to the castle. Of course, this all could have been accomplished faster if I'd had my sleigh back. I needed to call Walnut's to see what the holdup was.

"I'm sorry, Aunt April," Christopher said after we dropped off his Claus cousin. "Especially about the note. I didn't mean for it to really scare you."

"It didn't. In fact, it made me more determined to find out where Gobbles was." Never too early for a kid to learn about unintended consequences.

Jingles met Christopher and me at the door and could tell immediately from our faces that something was up.

"What's going on?" he asked.

I could never hide anything from him. And in this case,

since he was the head of staff at the castle, it would have been wrong to keep him in the dark.

"We've located Gobbles," I said. "You'd better come with us."

Jingles's eyes widened in surprise as I indicated that Christopher would lead the way to the bird. Then he seemed to understand what had happened—except, of course, Butterbean's involvement. I wasn't sure how he would take that news. Jingles didn't tolerate insubordination.

I decided to text Salty, too, since he would need to look Gobbles over and escort him back to his cage. He must have been waiting by his phone for news, because within a minute he had joined us. Our foursome moved quickly toward the Old Keep. I didn't bother to take off my coat, since it was always freezing in the old, unused part of the castle.

As Jingles pushed the thick cedar door open, the blast of cold air was notable, as was a strange yet faint sound. It didn't sound like gobbling. It was more like someone gagging.

We exchanged looks of alarm. "Butterbean!" I called out.

Jingles frowned. "Butterbean?"

Ack-ack-ack came the faint reply.

Christopher pointed toward an opening that led to a narrow circular staircase. "Up in the tower." He took off running, and all the rest of us could do was follow. The tower wasn't my favorite place. It had steep stairs and over the centuries had developed a decided tilt. What it was leaning over was Calling Bird Cliff, which the castle backed up on. Being at the top of the tower, with its low crenellations, gave me the queasy feeling that I might just topple off and fall into the valley below.

But this was a rescue mission, and we rushed up the hundred winding stone steps to the tower. Jingles and I were winded when we reached the top, and we'd been bypassed halfway up by Christopher and Salty. By the time Jingles and

I stepped into the round tower area, the other two were staring down at different parts of the tower floor. Salty was focused on a pen that had been set up. Outside the wire frame someone had placed a kerosene space heater. Not that it was working well against the freezing wind blowing around us. Inside the cage, there was straw strewn on top of the stone floor, along with a few stray pieces of oats and other grains. A bowl of water had been partially overturned and had frozen. There were several feathers in the straw—but no turkey.

Opposite the cage, Butterbean lay on the hard stone floor. His feet were bound and his hands were tied behind him. Christopher pulled off the blindfold and was working the cloth gag off his mouth when Butterbean, red-faced from stress and trying to call out, saw us.

"I was attacked by a monster!"

I frowned. "A snow monster?" They were huge. Surely someone would have noticed an abominable coming into the castle.

"No—a ruffian elf. And he took Gobbles!"

Chapter 20

Poor Salty. He looked like he might have a conniption. He'd been so worried these past two days about Gobbles's whereabouts, but Gobbles had actually been in the safekeeping of Butterbean and Christopher. And now, just when he'd been on the verge of getting his turkey friend back, the bird had been taken hostage by a vicious wild elf.

I reached into my bag for a photocopy of the picture Jake had given me and held it up in front of Butterbean. "Is this the elf who attacked you and stole Gobbles?"

He squinted at the picture. Recognition flashed in his big eyes. "Yes! That's him. I thought he was going to kill me. Who is he?"

"He's a wild elf from the Farthest Frozen Reaches." I untied his hands and feet. "Jake Frost is hunting him on suspicion of murder and robbery."

But why would Stumpy Shivers want a turkey? How did he get into the castle?

I glanced around. "Are there ways to get into the Old Keep that aren't through the front of the castle?" I asked Jingles.

He nodded. "A couple. But those entrances are supposed to be locked."

Supposed to be was the key phrase there. Someone must have sneaked around the castle to the back, then sneaked in and attacked Butterbean.

If this crime wave kept up, I was going to have a serious discussion with Nick about castle security.

Still focused on the empty cage, Salty groaned. "Poor Gobbles!"

Butterbean frowned up at him. "Poor *Gobbles*? What about me? I'm traumatized."

"How dare you sit there wallowing in self-pity." Jingles was vibrating with indignation. "For days you were hiding a turkey you knew we were all hunting for!"

"You're right." Contrite, Butterbean forced himself to his bootied feet and shook the circulation back into his legs one at a time. "I'm very sorry about Gobbles, and for lying to you all. I have no real excuse." He sighed. "Little did I know when I sent off for a mail-order turkey that the fat feathered fellow would worm his way into my heart."

Salty nodded as he stared down at the turkey feather in his hand. "I hear you."

So did I. Animals had a way of making us love them. Even Grimstock was starting to grow on me.

"Love makes us all irrational creatures," Butterbean said. "That's what I was scolding Lettuce for this morning, when she couldn't wait to run back to the lodge. I said to her, 'If you think—'"

As he spoke, I was distracted by something fluttering on his back.

"What's that?"

Confused, he twisted. "What?"

I turned him around. A folded note was pinned to the back of his dirty and torn uniform tunic.

I unpinned it. "This letter was attached to your back," I said, studying the envelope. "It's addressed to *mrs c at the castle.*"

Stumpy the gem thief, the birdnapper, the killer, was communicating to *me*? For some reason, I hadn't thought I factored into this series of crimes at all, except accidentally. Now cold dread clenched at my chest.

People needed to stop leaving me notes.

I opened the letter with numb fingers. The others gathered around.

"What does it say?" Jingles asked.

The small printed letters crawling in crooked lines across the wrinkled paper weren't easy to read. "It says, *I want my jewls—drop them at the narwal fountin at midnite or this day mite be gobbles last—ps come alone mrs c and tell no 1.*"

Fear shivered through me. Why? Why would he think *I* had his jewels?

"This is terrible," I said, my voice shaking.

"I'll say." Jingles looked over my shoulder at the note. "His spelling and capitalization are atrocious, and he clearly has no idea how to handle a plural possessive."

I scowled at him.

"Well, it's true," Jingles said. "Obviously, we're dealing with a barbarian."

"It's a ransom," Salty said in despair. "He's holding Gobbles hostage."

Jingles arched a brow at me. "Do you know what jewels he's talking about?"

"I know what he's referring to, but I haven't the foggiest idea where they are."

Events were starting to slot into place, though. Stumpy Shivers had stolen the miner's gemstones and come to Christmastown, probably because he had an accomplice who could fence the rocks in a place where they would fetch a higher price and wouldn't be recognized as stolen merchandise. Elspeth had been preparing to leave on a trip and insinuated to me that she was going to come back rich. She had obviously been the fence—until her accomplice decided she was expendable.

The only thing that didn't fit was how she ever met up with an elf like Stumpy Shivers to begin with. As Mildred said, Elspeth wasn't one to want to take a walk on the wild elf side. There had to be someone else involved. But who? Her ex-beau, Blaze Whitewreath? I couldn't see how he figured into this scheme. He seemed to love brokering real estate deals, but that was a far cry from flat-out murder and stealing.

Also, I had a hard time imagining Blaze running around with a stolen turkey.

I tried to piece other details in. Whoever had written the note knew that the turkey was valuable to us. That could be a lot of people, since we'd been putting up posters all over town. Thanks to Christopher and his crew, the flyers hadn't stayed up for long, but Gobbles's kidnapper might have seen one of them. And today I'd announced that there would be a reward for Gobbles's return . . . right before I thought I'd caught a glimpse of Stumpy Shivers.

But how would Stumpy have found out that the turkey was being kept here, in the Old Keep of the castle?

I looked around suspiciously.

"What?" Jingles asked, noting my expression.

"How could the birdnapper have known that Butterbean and Christopher were keeping Gobbles here?"

The two seemed to cringe in wide-eyed innocence. "We didn't tell anybody," Christopher said.

"You never spoke about it to Winky or Hal?"

He shook his head. "Honest."

"You never let drop some elaborate hint about why you were so sure they didn't have to worry about Gobbles being in the hands of evil birdnappers?"

"All I said was that he was in a safe place."

Could the kids have guessed from that hint that the bird was somewhere on the castle grounds?

"I swear," Christopher insisted. "I didn't give any details, no matter how many questions they asked me. And Winky asked *a lot* of questions."

"You're sure he didn't know that Gobbles was in the castle?"

He shook his head again.

I turned my attention to Butterbean. "What about you?"

The elf blinked his big blue eyes innocently. "My lips were sealed. I give you my word."

That answer didn't satisfy Jingles. "The word of an elf who's been lying to us for days. Is this how you show your gratitude to someone who helped you when you'd hit rock bottom?" He pointed to me. "She took you in. And this week she took in your sister, too."

His sister. "Did Lettuce know about all of this?" I asked, pointing to the turkey pen.

"No—I never said anything," Butterbean protested. "Of course, she might have *suspected* . . ."

Of course she might have. Christopher had told me that Gobbles spent one night in Butterbean's room. Lettuce could have found a stray turkey feather and guessed.

I put the ransom note in front of Butterbean again. "Could she have written that note?"

"Oh no—Lettuce is a very good writer."

Did that matter? Whoever penned the letter could have been trying to make it seem as if it had been written by a barely literate wild elf.

Butterbean was practically trembling. "Are you going to have to tell Santa about this?"

Telling Santa one's iniquities was always seen as a terrible thing by elves. They took their Santa lore seriously, and being condemned to the naughty list was something to be dreaded.

"Of course she's going to tell Santa," Jingles said, fists planted on his hips. "Do you think she's going to lie to her husband, Santa Claus himself, for your pathetic sake? You might as well come clean about everything you know. Maybe then you can beg for your job. Although don't expect Mrs. Claus to take you back, like Amory Claus took that sister of yours back to the lodge. Your sister at least is a cook. You're expendable."

"Jingles, that's enough." Once he got wound up about something, he was like a terrier with a chew toy. I looked down at Butterbean. "I can't say what will happen. Right now my focus is on finding Gobbles."

Butterbean shook his head. "I wish I could help you. All I saw was a flash of black—that elf must move like a cat."

That jibed with what Olive said.

I pulled out my phone to take a picture of the note.

"You're not going to fire me today, are you?" Butterbean asked, panicked.

"She should," Jingles said.

My finger hovered over the camera button. I hadn't really thought about firing Butterbean, to be honest. Handling staff problems had always been my least favorite thing about running the Coast Inn. One thing I liked about life at Castle Kringle was that I had Jingles as a buffer to deal with the host of elves who kept the castle ticking along. But Jingles could be overemotional at dealing with staffing problems. Like now.

On the other hand, Butterbean *had* stolen our turkey.

"I should be the one getting in trouble," Christopher said. "I was the one who asked Butterbean to steal the turkey."

I laughed. "You think you aren't in trouble?"

Christopher flushed red. "Oh."

I doubted Tiffany would be too hard on him, but it wouldn't hurt to let him sweat it out a little.

His actions hadn't been malicious. I needed to remind

Tiffany of that. Likewise, Butterbean's actions were wrong, but done out of softheartedness. I needed to figure out a way to get Jingles to simmer down, too.

"We can think about this tomorrow. Right now, Jingles and I have work to do."

Jingles blinked. "We do?" He shook his head. "I mean, of course we do." He glared down his nose at Butterbean. "We'll deal with you tomorrow."

Butterbean bobbed on his feet. "Can it be after the parade? Please let me redeem myself. I've worked so hard to make my turkey balloon. I want to represent the castle and make you all proud."

Everybody deserved a shot at redemption. I put my hand on his shoulder. "Of course you should take part in the parade."

He beamed. "Thank you, Mrs. Claus! My balloon will be a tribute to Gobbles."

With a last, worried glance at Jingles, he scurried away.

"Can I go, too?" Christopher asked.

"Of course—but don't leave the castle. We all need to be very careful until this lunatic is caught."

Christopher was about to head back down the winding steps when I stopped him. "Oh, and do you have any marbles?"

His eyes filled with confusion. "Marbles? Like *playing* marbles?"

"I need a bag of them," I said.

He looked doubtful, but he wasn't about to refuse me anything now. "Sure, I can loan you some."

I doubted I'd be giving them back, but I could always buy Christopher more marbles.

"Bring them down to the salon," I said. "I'll be there in a little bit."

"Marbles?" Jingles asked when Christopher was gone.

I nodded, distracted by Salty, who was sitting on one of the tower's crenellations in a daze. I was glad it was dark outside and I couldn't actually see how far the drop was from the tower to the cliff below. Otherwise his being on the edge like that would have made me even more nervous.

As it was, I wanted to get him away from there. He was too distraught to be that close to a ledge. "You can go too, Salty. But you also need to be careful."

He looked up at me, almost as if he'd forgotten there was anyone else in the tower with him.

"You're going to pay the ransom, right?" he asked. "You're going to get Gobbles back."

Jingles sputtered. "How can she do that? You heard her say she didn't have the jewels. She can't ransom Gobbles back."

"Oh yes I can." I put a hand on Salty's arm and tugged him up to his feet and away from the edge of the tower. "That's exactly what I'm going to do."

I sent a picture of the note to Jake Frost, with a message. **Come to the castle. I'm hatching a plan to catch your wild elf.**

"Absolutely not," Nick said.

The family had gathered in the salon to be updated on what had occurred in the Old Keep today, as well as the plans for tonight.

Nick was adamantly against going along with the elf's ransom demand. Especially since I intended to deliver the ransom myself. "You can't go out in the middle of the night to meet a crazed elf."

"It's Christmastown, Nick. Hardly a hotbed of danger. The Narwhal Fountain is well lit all night."

"Great—you'll have excellent visibility when he attacks you like he attacked Butterbean this afternoon."

"The elf just wants his jewels," I said.

"Which you don't have."

"He doesn't know that."

"It's insane," Nick said. He appealed to his mother, who sat knitting in her usual spot as the discussion raged around her, like a benevolent Madame Defarge. Lucia was standing not far away, cracking walnuts in front of the fire. "Please tell her that it's insane."

"I think she sees the dangers, Nicholas," Pamela said on a sigh.

"And how else are we going to get Gobbles back?" Lucia asked.

Nick rolled his eyes. "Gobbles is a turkey. I'm not willing to risk my wife's life for a bird who's scheduled to be killed the next day anyway."

"Don't let Salty hear you say that," Lucia warned him.

Pamela *tsk*ed. "Such a kindhearted elf. I sent a hot toddy out to him earlier this evening."

Poor Nick. He looked like a man trapped in the middle of a nightmare.

Jake Frost had been mostly silent during the family gathering, but he and I had discussed the plan at length before presenting it to the Clauses. Now he spoke up. "It's not just Gobbles," he reminded Nick. "This elf killed a miner, and maybe his own brother, and he probably had something to do with Elspeth Claus's death, too."

"How?" Claire said. "We'd have noticed him at the lodge, surely."

"He's working with someone there."

Lettuce, I thought. It had to be. Hours after she went back to the lodge, someone snuck into Castle Kringle, knowing exactly where to go to find Butterbean and Gobbles. When I thought back on Elspeth's murder, Lettuce's involvement made even more sense. Much as it hurt me to admit that

Amory's hunch was correct, Lettuce could easily have slipped a little powder into the wineglass by Elspeth's place. And she could have framed me by slapping some leftover poison in the eggs that had been taken to the kitchen.

Not to mention, this morning Lettuce had seemed eager to get back to the lodge. I'd assumed it was to get away from Felice. Now I assumed she was in a hurry to pass information along to Stumpy.

The trouble was, I didn't have concrete proof. Just a bunch of hunches that all seemed to fit.

Jake continued, "I wouldn't want to be Stumpy Shivers's accomplice now. My guess is that he or she won't have long to live after Stumpy has the jewels back. So that will be another murder." He looked at Nick and reported, "It's not just about a turkey."

Nick shook his head. "The person I care most about is April."

Claire sighed. "That's so sweet."

It was. "But I'm going to be fine. Jake will be nearby when I make the drop."

"And who will be there when Stumpy Whosit figures out that the jewels are actually a bag of Christopher's crushed up marbles?" Nick asked.

"Jake and Constable Crinkles. I'm going to grab Gobbles and get away before Stumpy realizes he's been cheated. And then Crinkles, who'll be hiding nearby, will pounce."

We hadn't told Crinkles about his part yet, but we assumed he'd be eager to get on board.

It was at this point that Nick finally broke down. Having Santaland's principal lawman involved apparently gave him no confidence in the plan. "Forget Crinkles. *I'll* chase Stumpy after the swap."

Jake crooked his head. "No offense, but you're sort of conspicuous."

Nick rolled his eyes. "I'm not going to be wearing my Santa suit. I can be incognito, too."

Jake considered this. It took mere seconds for him to see the benefit of having Nick, not Crinkles, at his back. "Okay."

I took a deep breath. It was still several hours till midnight, but we needed to do a lot more planning to get everyone in place on time.

After we'd hammered out a few specifics, I hurried up to my room to change clothes. I was still wearing my sweater dress and boots from this morning. My whole objective when I met Stumpy Shivers was to drop off the marbles, grab the turkey, and run. I needed to be dressed for maximum agility.

I pulled out flannel-lined jeans, shearling boots with grippy soles, a thermal shirt, and a wool sweater Pamela had made for me. Yes, it had a polar bear wearing a Santa hat on it, but it was the warmest sweater I owned. As I was pulling it on, Claire knocked at the door and slipped inside.

I expected her to make a joke about my goofy sweater, but instead she sank onto the edge of the bed and admonished, "You'd better not let Jake get hurt."

I was taken aback. Downstairs, during all the discussions of our plans, Claire had seemed perfectly calm, almost cool about it all. Certainly cooler than Nick.

"Jake's had more experience with these matters than I've had."

"With homicidal wild elves?" She shook her head. "Does this happen a lot around here?"

"Not too often . . ."

She glared at the carpet. "It would be just my luck to finally take the plunge and decide to spend the rest of my life with a guy, and then have him be killed trying to rescue a turkey."

"You heard Jake earlier. It's not just about Gobbles."

"Oh sure. It's also about . . . what did he say? Saving some elf who may be Stumpy's accomplice." She puffed out a breath. "*That's* worth getting killed over."

"We can't just let gangster elves go on crime sprees."

"Okay, but promise me that you guys will do your best not to take any dumb chances." She shook her head. "No, scratch that. The whole plan is one dumb risk."

"I don't want Jake to die, either. I also don't want *me* to die." I bent to lace up my boots and watched Claire twisting her hands in worry. "If you're so afraid for Jake," I asked, "why aren't you having this conversation with him?"

"Because if I told him I was nervous, he would use that as another excuse to say we aren't suited for each other. It took my setting up an ice cream parlor to convince him that I was serious about living here. If I start flaking out about his profession, he'll probably go running right back to the Farthest Frozen back of beyond." She sighed. "Maybe he was right all along. Maybe I *don't* fit in here."

"Don't say that. If you fell in love with a detective in the United States, there would be the same risks. More of them, in fact."

"True . . ."

I sat down next to her. "I'm assuming that Jake plans on staying a detective." I couldn't imagine him as anything else.

She nodded. "He's talking about opening an office in Santaland and leaving Quince and Pocket up north. They like it up there."

"So this worry about his being a detective, it's not something that's going to go away."

She nodded. "I know. I've got to get over it. The trouble is, I don't know how not to be nervous. Why did I have to fall in love with the only guy in Santaland into living dangerously?"

"This really isn't typical," I said. "Most of the time he'll probably be investigating lost reindeer and missing snowman hats."

"Good," she said.

I frowned. "Did you ever wonder why snowmen wear hats?"

She shrugged, barely seeming to hear the question. "Probably because their heads are cold."

Wow—she got it in one. And she'd only been here a fraction of the time I had.

"Don't worry," I assured her. "I think you're going to get along really well in Santaland."

Chapter 21

My sleigh was back from Walnut's Sleigh Repair, and it looked as sleek as new, with white and blue paint that had been waxed until it gleamed. As I stepped into it to drive into Christmastown, I felt as if I were in a spy thriller.

Jake and Nick had left a half hour earlier to give themselves plenty of time to get into position before Stumpy showed up. We didn't want to risk his seeing them and aborting the entire gemstone-turkey swap.

I texted Nick that I was leaving. Jingles saw me off, giving me a bag with a thermos in it. "Hot chocolate," he said.

"I'm just driving into town and back."

He sent me a stern look. "Please. You whine about the cold even in the hallways inside the castle."

He was right. "Thank you," I said.

I tucked the thermos on the seat next to the drawstring bag that contained the marbles. I had no idea how long Stumpy would be fooled by that trick. Hopefully long enough for me to grab Gobbles and speed away and for Jake and Nick to collar him.

I started down the mountain with my headlights on bright. I wasn't the strongest driver on snow. My sleigh was fairly steady, but there were still moments when it would skid, especially on a downhill path. I wanted to give myself as much time to steer clear of obstacles as I could, in order to avoid making any jerky movements or trying to brake suddenly. The night was cloudy and dim, so I needed the lights.

Driving all alone so late gave me an eerie feeling. This was the downside of an electric sleigh. It might have been nice to have a reindeer to talk to during this long, dark ride. The cheery jangling of reindeer harnesses would also have been welcome.

Halfway to town, as the path wound through Kringle Heights, I spied something next to a holly bush. For a moment I thought I was seeing things. The bird standing in the snow was big, dark, and round. *Could it be Gobbles?* Heart racing, I braked the sleigh and skidded over to the shoulder—not that anyone else was on the path tonight.

Trapped in the headlights' beam, the bird turned. Disappointment washed over me.

"Grimstock."

He had the disarming habit of popping up at odd moments. I had no idea what he was doing out here in the middle of the night—I doubted buzzards had regular bedtimes—but he certainly seemed intent on something by that bush. I left the lights shining as I got out to take a look.

As I picked my way through unplowed snow up to midcalf, I noticed other heavy foot tracks in the snow, and then something more unsettling: feathers on the ground. My heart started beating faster. Were they Grimstock's? They were too large to be feathers from a sparrow or a crow. These feathers were long . . . like a turkey's. And there were several of them on the snow, as if there had been some sort of altercation. Then I caught sight of another darkness glistening on the snow, too.

Blood.

I swallowed back dread. What had happened here?

I looked around, half expecting Gobbles to limp out to me from behind a tree trunk or a bush.

Then I crept closer to Grimstock. It wasn't just the feathers on the ground that had brought the vulture here. Something was in the holly bush. No—something was sticking out from under it. A bootied foot.

My stomach lurched. I wished I could back away and not look—but of course I had to see who it was.

The boot was attached to a leg with unadorned wool stockings. An elf, of course. The body had clearly been shoved under the holly bush in a hurried, haphazard effort to hide it. The snow was smashed around the area from the trip some elf had made between the holly bush and the road. When I pulled a branch back to see the elf's face, I knew immediately who the victim was.

In shock, I fell back on my butt. Of course it didn't hurt because I landed in over a foot of snow. But I doubt I would have felt it even if I'd landed on concrete. I was in shock.

With shaking hands, I pulled out my phone, removed my right glove, and called Nick. "I'm halfway down the mountain in the Kringle Heights area, not far from Carlotta and Clement's house. We need to get Crinkles up here."

"Now?" he asked with a hint of impatience. "I thought you wanted to do this drop."

"I don't think our wild elf will be there to receive it."

"Why not?"

"Because Stumpy Shivers is here on the side of the snow path, dead."

"What was Stumpy Shivers doing here?" Crinkles asked.

Nick looked at me. This is what came of keeping your local lawman in the dark. Now we were both hesitant to launch into the whole saga of what had been going on while the constabulary had been preoccupied with inflatable donuts and parade floats.

Jake stepped forward. "He was probably on this road for the same purpose that April was—to meet up at the Narwhal Fountain."

Calmly, and as logically as the situation would allow, he proceeded to fill Crinkles in on the events of the day.

The constable listened patiently. Fortunately, he didn't seem too upset about having been kept out of the loop this evening. On television shows, if people attempt to pay ransoms on their own, there's usually a cop around to tell them how foolhardy that is.

Not Constable Crinkles.

"Good plan," he said. "Too bad he got killed before we could bring him to justice."

Nick nodded. "Another kind of justice caught up with him first."

Crinkles tugged at his chin strap, as though it was cutting off circulation to his brain. Who knows? Maybe it was.

"This is a big mess though," he said. "Now I've got a dead wild elf." He looked at me. "And you all mixed up in it again."

"I'd never spoken to Stumpy before, but he left me this note." I flashed the ransom message from the picture I'd taken on my phone.

Crinkles read it and frowned. "Looks to me like he gave you a motive for murder."

I froze. "What? No—I didn't kill him."

Maybe he regretted not hauling me back to the constabulary this morning, when the deviled egg confusion had resurfaced.

"I never said you did," Crinkles replied. "But an elf is dead, and here you are with your ransom note, and no alibi except that you were driving into town and meet with this self-same elf."

"I only stopped because I saw Grimstock. I thought he was Gobbles."

"What's happened to Gobbles?" Crinkles wondered aloud.

That was a good question. He'd clearly been here. Had he made a dash for freedom? Or had someone else picked him up on the road? Worse yet—and more likely—maybe Stumpy's killer now had Gobbles.

I never should have said anything about offering a reward.

"Are you going to take me in?" I asked.

Crinkles's eyes flashed wide. "Golly gumdrops, no. We've got the parade tomorrow. It'd be pretty dumb to have done all this preparation and then have the entire plan flop on account of everyone's distracted because Mrs. Claus is in jail."

I doubted my absence from the parade would make that much of a difference. Still, it was gratifying to hear that someone else thought I would be missed. Even if that someone was Constable Crinkles.

"Wait till you see the constabulary float now," he went on. "Mildred and Olive have done an amazing job helping to decorate it. The donut holes, especially, turned out well."

Headlights came up the sleigh path, accompanied by the sound of a jangling reindeer harness. Doc Honeytree nearly bypassed us, but his reindeer stopped.

The doctor seemed unfazed by Nick's distillation of all the crimes we thought Stumpy Shivers was involved in. In fact he barely seemed to be listening. He sank down into the snow by the victim, and I held my breath as he studied Stumpy's body. Truth be told, I'd been a little nervous that he'd discovered the body had been pecked at. It would've been hard to look at Grimstock after that. I mean, I knew buzzards fed on carrion, which was gross enough. I just didn't want to think about who the carrion once had been.

Doc stood up again. "Blow to the head killed him, I'd say, but Algid will take a closer look back at the office."

Nick sent me home while he and Jake helped carry Stumpy's body to the doctor's sleigh.

Crinkles's last admonition to me was to get some sleep so I'd be in good shape for twirling in the parade tomorrow. Twirling was about the last thing on my mind at the moment.

When I arrived home, Lucia, Pamela, and Claire had gathered in the salon again to find out details of what happened. Some of the servants slipped in, too, including Salty and Jingles. Sleep would have to wait.

"Well, that didn't work out very well," Pamela said, once I'd explained why the drop hadn't taken place.

I could feel my lips twisting into a smile. "No."

"Now we've got a dead elf and still no bird," Lucia said.

Poor Salty was so pale he looked like a negative of himself. "Where could Gobbles be?"

"He either escaped, or he's with whoever killed Stumpy."

"What about the ransom, though?" Salty asked. "Wouldn't the accomplice still be expecting you to make the ransom exchange?"

"I don't see how. We're not even sure Stumpy's murderer knew anything about the ransom note."

"You don't know that the murderer didn't write the note, either," Claire said.

I thought about that. "But if he did, he would have known that I would be traveling down that path at approximately that time. And then he would have known that I would need to call someone to deal with a dead body on the road."

"Unless he thought he hid the body real well," Lucia said.

Another point I hadn't considered. It was only the sight of Grimstock that had made me stop on the sleigh path. If the buzzard hadn't been there, and if it had just been me zooming down the mountain, would I have noticed that foot under the holly bush? Probably not.

Maybe we made a mistake by not going through with the swap at the Narwhal Fountain. Although I didn't see how I could have gone into town; that would have meant leaving Stumpy's body by the side of the road.

When Nick came home, he had no fresh news to add. Everyone filtered back to their bedrooms. When Nick and I were behind our closed door, I collapsed in relief onto the bed, clothes and all. I'd barely slept for the past two nights, and exhaustion was finally catching up with me. I did manage to strip down to my thermals before crawling under the covers. My last memory before conking out was Nick kissing my forehead.

I was woken up in the dark by my phone, muted, vibrating on my nightstand like a restless beetle. Reflexively, I reached for it. Through half-opened, bleary eyes, I tapped my password in and saw that someone had sent me a video. I stared at it until what was on the screen came into focus.

The grainy video's setting was the Narwhal Fountain. The plaza around the fountain was empty, with a shimmering film of snow blowing in the wind across the pavers. A queerly altered voice rasped, "I was here. Where were you?" And then, to my horror, the sound of Gobbles gobbling very loudly sounded. The fact that he wasn't on screen chilled me. I sat up, shaking. When the gobbling stopped, the altered voice returned. *"You have one more chance, Mrs. Claus. Tomorrow night. Be there, or Gobbles gets it."* The video ended with the voice shouting *"Halt!"* as if telling himself to shut off the recording.

I reached over and nudged Nick. He groaned.

"You'd better see this." I reached for the light switch.

Nick sat up, eyes red with fatigue. Playing the video woke him up. As soon as the video finished, he watched it again.

"Lucia was right," I said. "Tonight she was saying that Stumpy's accomplice would have shown up for the turkey-gem swap because he would have assumed I'd never find Stumpy's body."

Nick nodded, his expression thoughtful. "At least he's giving us the opportunity for a do-over."

"Not till tomorrow night, though." That seemed a million years away. "If only we could figure out who Stumpy's accomplice—and now murderer—is. This voice is so altered, it's impossible to tell if it's male or female, even."

Together, Nick and I watched the video again. The gobbling shook me. What kind of psycho elf would involve an innocent turkey in their sinister scheme?

"Whoever this is," I said, "they're a real sicko."

Nick crooked his head. "But they change their voice at the end. Why?"

"'Halt'?" I frowned. He was right. The voice seemed slightly lower . . . and real.

"Why would a guy making a video tell himself to halt?" Nick wondered aloud. "Who even says halt?"

Realization dawned on me. I barked out a laugh, then flopped against the pillows. "No one says that—except crazy snowmen who think they're keeping the peace. It's Pumble-chook's voice on the end of that tape."

Nick scrolled to the end of the video and listened to that one word three times. "You're right. It's Pumblechook."

"And he's a witness," I said.

Nick frowned. "If he's still alive."

Chapter 22

Nick was up and in his best Santa finery by the time I was struggling into my marching band getup. I hadn't felt so self-conscious about my appearance when I'd thought I was going to be hidden behind a bass drum, but now I would be front and center. I pulled on warm woolen tights, shrugged into my red band jacket with gold braiding, and then pulled on the skirt Tiffany had given me. The outfit was topped off with my uniform shako hat with plumes coming out the top. I looked like something out of a crack-brained production of *The Music Man*.

Nick came up behind me. "You'll be great."

One good thing about my hearing that video last night—it had knocked angst about the march today right out of my mind. I had weightier things to worry about than how well I could twirl an aluminium tube with two rubber stoppers at the ends. I wanted to get to the constabulary ASAP to talk to Pumblechook. Nick, of course, would be busy with the reindeer this morning.

"I'm heading to Christmastown soon," I told him.

"I'll see you at the march." He picked imperceptible lint off his velvet Santa hat. He might be leading a team of mostly misfit reindeer, but he wanted to look his best.

"I'm sorry I was so restless last night. All I could think about was getting to Christmastown and tracking down Pumblechook to ask him about that video." I thought about how long this day was going to be—culminating in another midnight attempt to get Gobbles back and catch Elspeth's killer. "I'll be so grateful when this day is over."

"Maybe that's why they call tomorrow Thanksgiving."

I gave him a hug. "I'll see you in Christmastown when you make your grand entrance."

He bent down and kissed me. "Do you ever dream of moving to Oregon and running a cozy inn?"

"Sometimes I think you only married me for my hotel."

"Wrong." He sent me a mock lascivious look. "It was for your twirling."

I laughed. "I almost forgot the stupid baton." It was leaning near my nightstand.

I picked it up, gave Nick a mock salute, and headed out to face the day.

"Where is everybody?" I asked when I passed through the breakfast room. Pamela was sitting alone there. For a moment I thought maybe we were being served in the bigger dining room—but of course that was off-limits since the Thanksgiving tablecloth was already in place.

"It's all hands on deck outside," she explained. "Most of the misfit reindeer got here early. They're eager."

This I had to see. I was heading for the door when she waylaid me with a hitch of her throat.

"I don't suppose you ever heard from the Cornucopia about the frozen turkeys," she said.

Really? With everything going on, she was still going to needle me about the frozen turkey wait list?

"I've been sort of busy," I said. "I'll check again this afternoon."

"You do realize a frozen turkey has to thaw, don't you?"

"Of course."

"The window of thawability will soon close."

I don't know what it was—maybe the fact that I didn't get enough sleep, or that I felt I was letting everyone down, including Pamela and Elspeth, or I was just plain balking at being judged by my mother-in-law all the time, but my irritation reached its limit.

"You're incredible," I said. "A few days ago you were saying that you weren't going to interfere, and you've done nothing all week but nag me about frozen turkeys. Worse, you also made Tiffany feel inadequate—*Tiffany*, who does more than any of us."

She looked genuinely shocked. "I just didn't think a pineapple pie was appropriate for a traditional Thanksgiving."

"It was her grandmother's pie! Making your grandmother's food is important on Thanksgiving—as important as using your family's heirloom tablecloth."

She drew up proudly. "When I was young, Thanksgiving pies were pumpkin, apple, or pecan. She should have known that in making something flaky, she'd be taking a risk."

"Risk of what? It's not as if Michelin's going to be rating our Thanksgiving dinner. What kind of lunatic makes her own family audition pies for holiday meals? It's bonkers. *You're* bonkers."

As the words slipped out of my mouth, I was kicking myself. I couldn't believe I'd just called my mother-in-law bonkers. She was Mrs. Claus.

Of course, I was Mrs. Claus, too.

From the doorway, Nick cleared his throat. His gaze was darting between Pamela and me.

My heart sank. Nick *would* catch us in this moment. An open argument between me and his mother was probably what he'd been dreading for years.

"I thought you'd gone already," he said to me.

I flicked a quick look at Pamela, who was red-faced but remained stubbornly unapologetic.

"I'm just leaving."

He fell into step beside me.

"She started it," I told him under my breath before he could say anything.

"What happened?"

"She made Tiffany audition a pie—and rejected it."

"What?" His brows scrunched. "That's bonkers."

"The pie was delicious, too—not that that should matter."

"More pie is never a bad thing," he said solemnly. "I'll have a talk with her."

"I think I just did," I said.

Nevertheless, I was happy that he'd seen my point of view.

The castle driveway was filled with reindeer, and also elves trying to marshal the reindeer into some kind of order. Salty was busily providing feed and water—which they would probably need to tank up on, since they were going to have a long morning. The great ceremonial sleigh had been pulled out and now two elves were giving it a last-minute polishing. Several stable elves were trying to arrange the team in terms of size and abilities. Cannonball's harness didn't fit, and Salty was scrambling to rig up a girth extension.

Throwing a wrench into the proceedings was Dasher, who insisted that the only place for him to be amongst the group was at the very front, in what was traditionally the Rudolph position.

"Since there was no reindeer of the Rudolph herd picked, there's no reason why *I* shouldn't lead," he said. "I'm the only reindeer here with ceremonial sleigh experience. Shouldn't we put our best hoof forward?"

Clearly, he had come expecting that he would be the marquee reindeer on the team. There never was a more coiffed caribou: his hooves were polished, his coat was as dazzlingly shiny as a thoroughbred's at the Kentucky Derby, and his antlers looked as if someone had put the tips through a giant pencil sharpener. The ends came to sharp points, and they were coated in what appeared to be lacquer.

The crowning touch was that he had doused himself in some kind of reindeer cologne that stank up the whole yard.

"What *is* that?" I couldn't help asking. The odor was strong enough to gag a walrus.

"Mushroom spruce reindeer cologne," Dasher said, preening.

"It's very . . . distinctive."

He twitched with false modesty. "Yes, well. *Distinctive* is a word I've heard to describe me once or twice. If that reporter from the *Christmastown Herald* writes a story about us, I should probably remind him of that."

The other reindeer weren't thrilled. Snuffle shook his head. "I'm not getting harnessed behind *that.*"

I could sympathize. My eyes were starting to water.

"What's the matter with it?" Dasher asked.

"It's too strong," Snuffle said. "The odor sets off my allergies."

"*Everything* sets off your allergies," he sneered. "You're a mucus factory."

"*You* smell like rotting leaves," Cannonball said, standing up for Snuffle.

Dasher drew back in offense. "At least I'm not going to drag the entire sleigh down, Butterball!"

"You can't call him names," Daisy said.

In parting, I sent Nick a sympathetic look. He had quite a morning ahead of him.

At my sleigh, I found Claire loading a couple of large tubs in the cargo area in the back. "Do you mind hauling me and a few gallons of ice cream down the mountain?" she asked.

My mood picked up immediately—both at the prospect of her company and the ice cream. "Of course not. When did you make ice cream?"

"Last night, waiting for you all to get back. I had to do *something*, and Butterbean had this great idea. He suggested that giving away ice cream cones outside my store would be a good way to generate some great advance publicity for the Santaland Scoop."

That was a good idea.

"Butterbean's a genius, isn't he?" Claire said. "I can't wait to see his balloon. Do you really think it'll be as big as the ones in the Macy's parade?"

"He says so."

"Amazing."

She hopped into the passenger seat and we took off. It felt suddenly like one of our Oregon road trips, except of course in Oregon we were almost never on a snow-packed mountain, catching glimpses through the trees of what looked like a picturesque Bavarian fantasy village in the valley below.

Claire was in a state of euphoria as she looked over it all. "Maybe I'm part elf. I love it here!"

I wondered if at least part of her joyful mood had to do with the fact that the killer Jake was hunting had been killed. The fact that we now had to hunt down *his* killer hadn't quite sunk in, even after I slowed down and pointed out the spot where I'd found Stumpy last night. Claire hadn't seen the video, so she couldn't know that Stumpy's accomplice seemed to be, if anything, more ruthless than Stumpy himself.

Could that ruthless accomplice actually be Butterbean's sister? Lettuce had to be involved somehow. But despite her willingness to give as good as she got from Felice, I couldn't imagine Lettuce bludgeoning another elf and shoving his body under a holly bush.

As soon as we passed through the great arched metal gate

into Christmastown, it became clear that Thanksgiving parade fever had taken hold of the town. I'd intended to drop Claire by her store, but the crowds around Sparkletoe Lane didn't allow for easy access. The fact that Sparkletoe Lane was the mustering point for the parade was causing a huge snarl of elves, floats, and sleighs. Up ahead, Bella Sparkletoe was attempting to direct sleigh traffic away from her street to clear room for the parade participants. No telling where the constable and Ollie were this morning.

Maybe Butterbean really was a genius.

"Pull over," Claire suggested when we passed a side street that was not so clogged. "I can walk from here."

It was probably the closest I could get to Claire's store anyway. I needed to go to the constabulary to talk to Pumblechook, who I hoped was still alive and getting ready to be part of the constabulary float. But first I needed to help Claire carry her ice cream to her shop. Of course, we were slowed down by needing to pick our way through the crowd. Luckily, the biggest logjam was even farther up the street from the Santaland Scoop, where Butterbean was inflating his turkey Pilgrim balloon with helium. The balloon was anchored beak-down to the snowy road as a helium tank slowly filled it. The process was mesmerizing. If I hadn't been in a hurry, I could have stayed and watched till the parade started.

"Do you think you'll be able to handle all this business today?" I asked Claire after we deposited all the ice cream in her cold room.

"I hope so. Jake promised to help me."

That was good. Curious elves were already pressing their noses against the parlor's plate glass windows. I had a feeling Claire's shop would bring about a frozen treat revolution here in Santaland.

When Jake showed up, he looked at Claire and smiled like a man who'd won the lottery. I almost hated to inject the subject of the Stumpy Shivers investigation into the conversation, but I was impatient to get to the constabulary and back before the parade started. I'd sent Jake the video last night before I realized that Pumblechook was on it, so now I got out my phone and showed him the video.

It made strange viewing among all the revelry. Outside, a group of elves were singing "Winter Wonderland" so loudly that Jake could barely hear Pumblechook yelling "Halt!"

His expression was disturbed. "Have you checked on Pumblechook?"

"Not yet—I messaged Crinkles this morning, but I haven't received a reply. They're probably busy with their float."

He nodded, as if it were perfectly normal to have the law of a town distracted by parade float décor. "Maybe I should go—"

I stopped him. He'd promised Claire to help out with the ice cream during the parade, and she'd never forgive me if I dragged him away to do a snowman wellness check. "That's okay," I said. "I'll just dash over there—I have my sleigh."

I left them and made my way back to where I'd parked. When I turned the key, however, the engine remained stubbornly dead.

Today of all days. And in the middle of downtown. I could have asked one of the many reindeer in town for the parade for a tow, but Claire and I had removed the emergency harness from the sleigh's storage area to make room for ice cream.

Growling in frustration, I climbed down and hurried on foot toward the constabulary. Not that it was possible to go really fast when the sidewalks were so clogged. Could all these elves be in the parade? Everyone seemed to be in some kind of costume: elves in Pilgrim costumes; square-dancing elves in flared skirts or checked shirts and ten-gallon hats; elves in motley on unicycles; tiny elves in foam turkey costumes and tap shoes. And Pilgrims: full Pilgrim outfits were on display, but for those with no costume, a paper Pilgrim hat was enough to show their Thanksgiving spirit. One enterprising elf had a cart set up, selling the hats. I was tempted to buy one myself as a souvenir. Maybe later.

Music was everywhere. Christmas music poured out of speakers set up by store fronts, some competing side by side. Elves would sing a verse of one song and then switch to another half a block away. A barbershop quartet offered a rendition of "Over the River and Through the Woods" near the constabulary, while a one-elf band played "Santa Claus Is Coming to Town" on the opposite corner.

I crossed a street clogged with reindeer revelers having an impromptu hopping contest. Reindeer just couldn't suppress that competitive spirit even for a morning. Then, near the constabulary, I was nearly run over by Puffy in his donut delivery wagon.

Puffy's reindeer apologized to me. "These rabble reindeer think just because there's a parade today they DON'T HAVE TO FOLLOW THE LAW." That last bit was addressed more to the hoppers than to me.

"It's okay," I told him. I glanced up at Puffy in the driver's seat. "Did you just come from the constabulary?"

Puffy, who looked as much like his name as physically possible without being an actual marshmallow, nodded. "Crinkles thinks we need more polar bear claws."

"Can't have too many," I agreed. "Your polar bear claws are the best."

The compliment managed to puff him up even more.

"Did you see Pumblechook at the constabulary?" I asked him.

"Oh yes." The donuteer's face sagged. "Very sad."

Fear stopped my heart. Had the killer gotten to him? "Is he gone?"

"No—but he's a re-roll job. The paramedics are with him now."

I called my thanks to him and ran the rest of the way toward the constabulary, almost falling twice. Luckily I was able to use Elspeth's baton once as a makeshift cane to keep me from spilling all the way to the ground.

All the time, I scolded myself. Why had I waited? I shouldn't have bothered with sleep last night. As soon as I figured out that it was Pumblechook on the video I should have rushed into Christmastown to try to warn him of the danger he was in.

But Nick had argued that if the psychopath who'd made the video had wanted to hurt Pumblechook, he would have done it right away. And if he had, the crazy elf was sick enough that he wouldn't have been able to resist sending photographic evidence to us as a threat.

I'd been dead tired, so it hadn't been difficult to convince me to wait till morning to check on Pumblechook. Big mistake. I hoped it wasn't a fatal mistake. If the snowman paramedics were attempting a re-roll, they must believe he was salvageable.

Ollie and Crinkles were on their float, which had been transformed into something amazing. The donut hole border looked great—I wasn't sure I would have known what the blobs were if I hadn't made some of them myself, but Puffy's logo was a clear giveaway. The inflatable smiling donuts flanked the constable, who was busy stacking his donut boxes as Ollie staple-gunned crepe paper streamers to the blue wool backdrop.

"Hello, Mrs. Claus," Ollie said. "Ready to twirl?"

The two of them seemed pretty unconcerned about an assassination attempt. "Can he speak?" I blurted out in greeting. "Did he tell you who did this?"

The constable's chin disappeared into his chins. "Who did what?"

"Who attacked Pumblechook."

They exchanged frowns. Crinkles said, "Nobody attacked Pumblechook. He fell off the float."

"He got too close to the edge," Ollie explained. "We'd arranged to hydraulic lift him onto the platform, but then one of the inflatable donuts caught a gust of wind, hit him, and off he went."

"Where is he now?"

They pointed to a spot just up the street, closer to the constabulary entrance. "We moved the float to give the paramedics more room."

I hurried over to where a couple of elves in white coats were re-rolling the base of the snowman. His torso was powder, too. Miraculously, though, the top segment of his body seemed to have fared better. His nose had fallen off, but he was still recognizable. Someone had haphazardly put his constable hat on his head, and I straightened it for him.

"Pumblechook," I said. "Are you feeling all right?"

"Are you from internal affairs?"

One of the paramedics looked up at me and said in a low voice, "Sometimes accidents can scramble their brains."

I nodded and said more slowly, "No, I'm not from internal affairs. I'm Mrs. Claus."

"I'll be filing a report against that donut," Pumblechook declared. "Assaulting a police officer."

I bent down further so that we were almost eye to eye. "It's very important that I speak to you about last night. You saw someone by the Narwhal Fountain."

"Who?" he asked.

"That's what I need to know. It was late. You yelled at him to stop."

"What did I say?"

"'Halt!'"

The word jolted his memory. "I remember! The one with the big bag."

I nodded eagerly. The criminal must have had Gobbles in a sack. "Yes."

"Like he was carrying a present gift bag," he said.

"You're sure it was a he, then?"

"Oh yes. I remember thinking that he looked like Santa with that big bag."

My face fell. "My Santa? Nick?"

He chuckled. "No, this fellow looked more like a story-book Santa Claus than the current Santa. He wasn't as tall, either, but I only saw him from a distance. He was wearing a big coat and a red Santa hat, and he had a long white beard."

A disguise. Of course Stumpy's killer wouldn't want us to see what he really looked like. "Why did you call out after him?" I asked. "Did you see the turkey?"

If it was possible for a snowman to look perplexed, Pumble-chook did in that moment. "A turkey? No. I was going to arrest him for littering. He tossed down a candy wrapper, but by the time I reached the evidence, the suspect had fled. The wrapper didn't have a turkey on it. It had a snowman in a Pilgrim hat."

That knocked me back on my heels. I'd seen the candy wrapper he described—when Flake the elf was showing it to Nick—but who else had seen it?

Ollie came up to me. "How's he doing?"

"He'll be back together in no time," one of the paramedics said.

"We have to get in place for the parade, Mrs. Claus. Can we give you a ride?"

"That's okay. I'll walk."

I would probably make it faster on foot than maneuvering through the packed streets on the constabulary float.

"Thank you, Pumblechook," I said. "You've been very helpful."

"That's *my* line," he joked.

I thanked the snowman paramedics, too, and made my way back through the throng of elves and reindeer who were starting to line up in a slightly more orderly fashion along Festival Boulevard in anticipation of the parade beginning. As soon as Santa's sleigh was spotted flying down from the mountaintop in the distance, the marching would start. Nick would stop short of the intersection of Sparkletoe Lane and wait as the rest of the marchers turned onto Festival Boulevard. The other marchers would come down Sparkletoe Lane and parade past Santa's sleigh as they turned onto the boulevard. Finally Santa would bring up the rear of the parade, tossing candy and ho-ho-hoing to everyone. The crowd seemed impatient for the show to get on the road.

Pumblechook's information disturbed me. The candy that Santa would be tossing from his sleigh would be the candy I'd first seen Flake showing to Nick several nights ago. That Thanksgiving candy had not been in circulation yet: it was just for today. The only other place I'd seen it had been at Kringle Lodge, on Amory's desk. Select elves at the Candy Cane Factory no doubt had access to the candy, but Amory had said that they would keep it "under wraps."

But he also had left a bowl of it there on his desk. Anyone at the lodge could have taken a piece.

"Anybody" seemed preferable to the unhappy suspicion percolating in my brain.

He looked more like a storybook Santa Claus than the current Santa. In Claus family lingo, Amory looked as if he were "born to don the suit." In other words, he had the build of storybook Santa Clauses; Nick always had to work hard to make himself appear jolly and roundish. Amory, despite his toxic personality, looked the part of Kris Kringle.

How much did that gall him? To have spent all his life

looking like Santa Claus, the natural leader of Santaland, and yet to always be relegated to the lodge at the top of the mountain and be thought of as one of the lesser Clauses? That had to sting.

But how would his resentment tie in with murdering Elspeth, and stolen jewels? The lodge had undergone extensive repairs this year. Was he so desperate for money that he and Elspeth had gone in league with a wild elf jewel thief? She'd appealed to him for a loan. Maybe her request had led to commiseration over money woes.

I frowned. Could Amory have been the mystery man both Star and Balsam had seen outside talking to Elspeth? After all, Amory had seemed to ridicule the idea of looking further into the man in purple's identity. It could have been his clumsy way of putting me off the scent.

"April!"

I looked over to see Jake carrying two to-go coffees from We Three Beans. I wished I had time to nip in for a coffee.

I waved my baton at him as if it were a fairy wand. He smiled.

"I'm taking coffee to Claire. What with the parade lineup on Sparkletoe Lane, it's mayhem outside her shop. She's been mobbed. Juniper was helping her, but now Juniper has to march—" He looked at me, puzzled. "Shouldn't you be with the band, too?"

"I talked to Pumblechook," I said, and proceeded to relate what the snowman had told me. "Do you think it could be Amory?"

"Maybe we'll find out tonight. Our weird-voiced guy on the tape wants a do-over."

I nodded. "At least now we know he'll probably be dressed in a Santa suit."

Jake nodded. "And he doesn't know we know it. That's good."

"We just have to get through this nerve-racking day."

He was about to say something, but whatever it was got swallowed up by a great roar as Santa's sleigh was spotted way off in the distance, beginning its flight down the mountain. Blocks away, the band struck up its first song.

"Oh God," I muttered. "I've got to go."

Jake looked amused. "Break a leg—isn't that what they say?"

"Not to musicians, and not to women who are apt to fall on the ice three times per day anyway."

I took off running, but it was a hard slog. The crowds on the sidewalk surged toward the intersection of Festival Boulevard and Sparkletoe Lane. When the Santaland Marching Band launched into its first chorus of "Over the River and Through the Woods," I was still two blocks away. As it turned onto Festival Boulevard, the first float of the parade received an excited ovation from the crowd: on a rolling platform of cotton wool cloud fluff, tiny elves dressed like turkeys were all doing the time step. The sidewalk became a forest of arms holding phone cameras up, trying to capture all the magic.

I felt a tug on my arm—on my baton, actually. I held fast to it, remembering Tiffany's admonition to make the baton part of my arm. I was in the middle of a surge of people, and I turned in confusion to see who was jostling me. But before I could glance behind me, I was given a shove. My foot twisted, threatening to take me down. Someone behind me was trying to yank the baton out of my hand. I twisted around, pulling it free and then swinging it like a bat against whoever was trying to steal it.

It was an elf. Balsam. I don't think I'd ever seen him away from Kringle Lodge. He looked smaller here, yet strangely malevolent, and angry that I wouldn't relinquish the baton.

What the blazes was wrong with him? I yanked the baton

again, and the stopper at the end of the aluminum tube made a popping sound as it came out, sending Balsam stumbling backward. Suddenly the baton was like a champagne bottle that had just been uncorked. But instead of liquid, jewels poured out of my baton. Gemstones the color of pale rubies showered through the air and landed on the sidewalk and the edge of the boulevard.

Chapter 23

Shock was my first reaction. I wasn't alone. It took a moment for the elves around me to realize what they were seeing. Everyone had been so focused on the parade, they hadn't quite registered what the tiny things pelting them were until they blinked at the glittering red against the snow for a few moments. And then, like a swarm of bees changing direction, they dove for jewels.

Balsam, too, scrambled to scoop them up. Even though it had seemed like a spray of them had shot out of my baton, when they landed on the ground they were spread out on the well-trodden snow. Those trying to pick them up had to search and pluck them up individually, like chickens pecking at grain.

My stunned gaze focused on Balsam. I could tell he was torn between fleeing and grabbing jewels. He plucked up what he could, tossing them in his elf cap as he skittered along the ground.

Adding to the confusion, a group of square-dancing elves was passing, their western-style elf booties threatening to crush gems further into the packed snow. And then another roar went up—not for the square-dancing elves, but for something spotted in the distance.

"Santa's almost here!"

High in the air, Nick was steering the sleigh into position, squaring his team up with lower Festival Boulevard. Dasher might have been the right choice for lead reindeer after all, because he looked fantastic—powerful and majestic. The other reindeer were doing themselves proud, too. Yes, Flouncer was a little erratic, but Nick's steady handling seemed to compensate for her erratic movements. Only Cannonball seemed to be giving real trouble. He was lower than the others, which created a lopsided effect. Nick was still managing to drive them all very expertly.

I looked away, trying to focus. My reflexes felt sluggish. Why had Elspeth hidden jewels in her baton? And how had Balsam found out about those jewels?

To know about those gems, Balsam must have killed Elspeth. I was staring at a murderer. A handsome, dimple-chinned fiend. Then, belatedly, it hit me. His face was like the handsome flipside of Stumpy's: the appearance of the slain elf last night hadn't shared much in common with Balsam, except that both elves had a distinctive indentation on their chin. They were family.

Maybe even long-lost brothers.

"Stinky."

Balsam halted his scramble for jewels and looked up, handsome eyes wide with surprise for a moment before they narrowed to angry slits. Just how Stumpy's had appeared in Jake's sketch.

"Stop him!" I pointed at Balsam. "He's a murderer!"

Elves looked up. Some seemed ready to do as I said and hurl themselves at Balsam. Then the most extraordinary thing happened. Up ahead, Butterbean's giant turkey Pilgrim turned onto Festival Boulevard. A collective gasp rose from the crowd. No one had ever seen anything like it. I had never seen anything like it, except on television. Its hat was higher than the tallest buildings along the boulevard. Butterbean proudly held a rope keeping his creation from floating away. Several reindeer were also helping to wrangle the giant balloon, including Quasar.

The sounds of awe from the audience soon became sounds of dread. At first I didn't see the problem. Then I noticed what was going on. Nick's sleigh was squared up and coming in for a landing on Festival Boulevard, but the reindeer hadn't been prepped to see a building-sized turkey floating in front of them. Dasher, the lead reindeer, looked terrified. The rest of the team was trying to descend, but Dasher was like a deer in the headlights, heading straight for the helium turkey.

Startled spectators called out directions. "Down! Down!"

Dasher, for all his sleigh experience, suddenly didn't seem to have any brakes. I could see that Nick realized they were in for trouble. He did the only thing he could to avoid a total collision. He pulled the reindeer back up and steered them sharply right.

It almost worked. Dasher, though, nicked the wattle of Butterbean's turkey with his antlers, which were like sword points. A pop sounded, and a hiss, and for a moment the reindeer team looked as if it might go careening down to the street.

All around me, elves were scrambling toward the buildings, trying to get out of the crash path. They needn't have worried. With a sharp crack of his whip in the air, Nick pulled the team together and landed them farther down the street, near Municipal Hall. It was a miraculous recovery, which earned applause and cheers from the elves, people, and reindeer lining the street. My heart, which had been in my throat the whole time, finally stopped hammering, and I remembered the jewels and Balsam.

The distraction had given him a crucial chance to escape. He was half a block away now. I scrambled after him until someone yelled, "Watch out!"

Now what? I flicked a glance behind me to make sure that Nick was still okay. But it wasn't behind me that I should have been worried about. It was up ahead. The punctured helium turkey was losing air, and as it went lopsided it was veering out of control of the reindeer and Butterbean, who were supposed to be holding it down. Butterbean was lifted off the ground by the force of the balloon's death throes. The whole pile of heavy polyurethane fabric looked like it was about to crash on all of our heads; no telling how many would all be smothered by a flaccid turkey Pilgrim.

Parade participants still queued on Sparkletoe Lane couldn't see the pandemonium. The marching band was already playing its third repetition of "Over the River and Through the Woods." I did not want to die suffocated by a giant polyurethane turkey while listening to that song. More important, I didn't want Balsam/Stinky to get away.

Just then, Balsam flicked a glance back at me. Our eyes met, and I could tell by the gleam in his eyes that he'd decided I would be too concerned about saving myself to capture him. And maybe he would have been right.

But when I saw him grin, rage surged through me. Not just at the insult that grin implied, taunting me as a self-interested coward. It angered me on behalf of the people and elves who'd lost their lives so this slimy jerk could enrich himself. His brother had killed an old miner whom he probably barely knew. Then Balsam must have poisoned Elspeth at the lodge dinner, just after she'd spoken to him outside. He'd killed her, and then he'd put poison in an egg to frame me for her murder. And when that didn't work, he'd told me about an elf in a purple tunic to make Blaze a suspect.

Finally, he'd offed his own brother when it looked like they were on the verge of finally ransoming the jewels. I couldn't think of who else could have been responsible for Stumpy's death on the snow path into Christmastown. The two brothers must have had a fatal falling-out in the clutch. A fortune in jewels had broken whatever brotherly bond they had.

There was no one Balsam wouldn't use and then turn on. He was a smug, arrogant murderer, not to mention a cold-hearted birdnapper. I wasn't about to let him get away.

Fueled by anger, I rushed after him. Eyes widening, he turned and fled, knocking over several elves whom I then had to hurdle over. We ran half crouched underneath the flagellating turkey feet like two people ducking helicopter blades. Balsam came within inches of getting smacked in the head with a boot by Butterbean, who was partially airborne. For my part, I collided with a reindeer. Quasar.

"W-what's happening?" he called out to me.

Breathing heavily, I pointed ahead of me, to Balsam. The snowman had knocked down a fruit stand, and Balsam was running an obstacle course of oranges and pears. I was hoping he'd slip on a banana peel, but no such luck. I had to run through those obstacles now, and I doubted I'd pass the agility test as well as he had.

But soon I realized I wasn't running alone. Quasar had let go of the balloon and was fast-trotting alongside me. "G-get on my back, Mrs. Claus." His voice was so high and spacey sounding—he must have inhaled helium—that I almost laughed.

But I couldn't laugh at his offer. We stopped long enough for me to jump on. With his crooked gait, he hopped and lurched over the sidewalk, nose blazing as he fluted out "Excuse us!" to the elves diving for dear life out of our path.

Quasar was a game changer.

"We're gaining on him," I said excitedly, although of course the reindeer was doing most of the gaining.

No fool, Balsam turned off the boulevard. Quasar and I followed. Understanding that Quasar could only do long hops when there was plenty of open space on a straightaway, Balsam hooked a left, and then turned again at the next intersection, so that he was now running again *toward* Festival Boulevard. There was still mayhem that way—even more than before, if possible. Without Quasar, the group holding the turkey was having an even harder time managing the turkey balloon, which was in the whiplash throes of deflation. If we fell too far behind, Balsam could easily get lost in the chaos and escape forever. And then there would be no justice for the murders, and no finding Gobbles.

"Step on the gas, Quasar."

"Ok-kay!" He sped up. Ahead, Balsam was passing Greenie the fishmonger's. With lightning speed, he overturned a table of herring on ice.

I cried out, as did Quasar. It was too late for him to hop over the avalanche of fish and ice that spilled onto the street. We were going down, and we both knew it. Quasar's hoof hit the fish and ice and we skidded and skated as Quasar struggled to keep his legs under him. I felt myself dropping even as I saw Balsam taking his last strides toward Festival Boulevard.

"Stop him!" I bellowed, hopelessly, right before Quasar and I crashed and spilled down in the frozen river of herring.

It took us a moment to stop sliding, and all the while I had my eye on Balsam.

As he reached the corner of the last building on the street, he turned to the right and made as if to run. Instead, it looked as if he hit a brick wall. A hard *smack* echoed down the block. Balsam squealed in pain and grabbed his nose. Then he fell backward.

In the next moment, Pamela stepped over him, a large frozen turkey in a string bag in her hand.

I gaped at her. Had my mother-in-law really just taken out Santaland's most wanted criminal with a frozen turkey?

Pamela eyed the whimpering wreck bleeding profusely on the sidewalk, then stared down at Quasar and me sprawled among the fish. "Didn't you get my texts, April?" she asked. "The Cornucopia called the castle. Your frozen turkey was ready for pickup."

"You must think I'm an idiot," I told Jake as we followed Crinkles and the prisoner to the constabulary. "Before the parade started, I tried to convince you it was Amory who was behind the whole crime spree."

We had to pick our way through the debris from the parade. The elves who'd volunteered for the litter cleanup crew wouldn't start their work until more of the crowd filtered away. Right now, everyone was still too interested in all that had happened to go back to their homes. Those not watching Crinkles frog-march Balsam down the street were standing over the carcass of the giant turkey Pilgrim balloon deflated in the middle of Festival Boulevard. Doc Honeytree, who'd been called to take a look at Balsam's broken nose, had set up an impromptu sidewalk infirmary to tend to various parade mayhem bumps and scrapes.

"Suspecting Amory made sense," Jake said.

"I should have known it was Balsam, though. He had access to Elspeth's wineglass, and he knew where she would be sitting because he probably put out the place cards himself. When Elspeth dropped dead, he wasn't even in the room, yet the next minute he was telling us he'd already called the doctor and had brought a shroud to cover her up with."

Jake shrugged. "None of those clues was definitive."

"Jingles even told me Balsam was a phoney," I confessed.

"As soon as I heard about the Shivers family, I should have realized that Tremblay is a rough French translation of Shivers."

Inside the constabulary, at the long table where just a few nights ago we'd all been making papier-mâché donut holes, Balsam spilled the whole story of the Shivers brothers and their crimes. According to his confession, he—Stinky—used the blizzard that killed his parents to escape the Farthest Frozen Reaches and try to better himself. He gave himself a more fragrant first name and landed a good job at Kringle Lodge. He might have continued on this path of self-betterment if his brother hadn't found him and tempted him over to the dark side with the gemstone theft scheme.

After Stumpy had talked Stinky/Balsam into helping find a fence for the gems he planned to steal, Balsam heard Elspeth begging Amory for money. He knew he could bring her in on the scheme and that she would be able to smuggle the gems out of the country more readily than either of the elf brothers, to a place where an unsuspecting buyer wouldn't recognize the gems as stolen and would give her top dollar for them.

"But then Elspeth got greedy and wanted more," Balsam informed us, holding a package of frozen peas, which Ollie had retrieved for him, over his nose. "She said that if we didn't give her a bigger cut, she wouldn't help us at all. We'd already handed over the gems to sell and she had them hidden, so she thought she was holding all the cards. At that point, Stumpy said we needed to do away with her. He threatened to kill me if I didn't help him. Stumpy was always vicious—you can't imagine how he tormented me when we were young. He terrified me."

And yet Balsam was the only one of the confederates still alive. I wasn't buying his efforts to rationalize his actions.

"Elspeth told me she had the gems hidden in a very personal place at Mildred Claus's château," he continued. "After Elspeth was out of the way, Stumpy thought all we had to do was search the house to find them. But when he tore the place apart, the gems weren't there. All he managed to do was frighten two old ladies."

The jewels weren't there because Tiffany had taken the baton that evening Elspeth died, when she went to Mildred's house.

"We were at a loss to figure out where Elspeth had hidden all those rocks," Balsam said, "until yesterday, when Lettuce mentioned the baton you were carrying around that was your legacy from Elspeth. We figured you had them and knew all about it."

Lettuce had also told him about Gobbles, all in a misguided attempt to curry favor with the lodge's handsome butler. Balsam gladly listened to all the gossip she cared to spill, but he wasn't interested in anyone but himself. He even had the mendacity to say that his saving the very bird he'd stolen should be a reason to show him leniency.

"Stumpy wanted to kill that turkey just as soon as we got our hands on the money." He looked up at me then. "Said he had no intention of actually giving it back to you at the fountain. He said we should have our own feast to celebrate our newfound wealth."

Jake crossed his arms. "Are you trying to tell us that you killed your brother to save a turkey?"

Balsam's mouth tightened. "Call it the last straw. I never wanted Stumpy around—I left the Farthest Frozen Reaches to get away from him. I'd made a good life here, and he wanted to drag me back into his murky world. The whole plan was his idea—killing Elspeth, stealing the turkey . . . all of it. I just went along because he said he'd expose me—and maybe worse—if I didn't."

"So you killed a woman to protect your new identity," Jake said skeptically. "The money had nothing to do with it."

He shook his head. "I'd have given him all the jewels if he just would've promised to leave me alone."

I couldn't stop a derisive laugh. I would never believe that self-protection and not greed was his motive. "And who were you going to give those jewels that you were scooping off the street today?"

His face reddened. "Naturally, after all that had happened, I needed money to leave Santaland and start over somewhere else."

"You'll be starting over somewhere else, all right," Crinkles said. "You'll be spending the rest of your life mining lumps of coal in the Farthest Frozen Reaches."

Balsam nearly dropped his frozen peas, and his handsome face melted into a mask of horror. "You can't send me there. I've worked so hard to get away. And Stumpy killed a miner—his fellow miners will take their anger about that out on me."

"You killed Elspeth," I reminded him, "and your brother. All your hard work at making a new life for yourself apparently didn't do much for your morality."

"Please—I'll do anything." He looked frantic. "If you promise not to send me back there, I'll tell you where the turkey is."

Balsam was a very successful criminal, but a poor bargainer. He gave up the location of the shed where Gobbles was being held before being informed that he was still going to be sent to the Farthest Frozen Reaches. I wasted no time texting the information to Nick.

"He'll spend the rest of his life freezing in a coal mine," Jake said to me after we watched Crinkles haul Balsam away to the bedroom-cell that Mildred and Olive had just vacated. After consulting with Judge Merrybutton, it had been decided that sending Olive to the Farthest Frozen Reaches for putting ice-rat poison in Elspeth's oatmeal was unwarranted. Especially since Olive had fended off a few attacks from Elspeth—

and Elspeth's criminal confederates—and had acted to protect Mildred. Olive was released to Mildred's recognizance.

It seemed a just sentence. Just as, given Balsam's pride and fastidiousness, exile back to that frozen wilderness would be a well-deserved life sentence for him.

Outside the constabulary, the *Christmastown Herald* was having a field day with Pamela's story. Snug Brighthearth was photographing her with the frozen turkey that had helped capture a killer. The reporter asked to be allowed to go to Castle Kringle and get another picture of her with the bird after it was cooked, and of course Pamela agreed. Although she protested that all she did to take down Stumpy was react on instinct, I could tell she was enjoying her moment in the limelight.

I joined Tiffany, who stood to the side watching in amazement as our mother-in-law vogued for the cameras. Tiffany had come to the constabulary to swear to the fact that she'd found the baton in Elspeth's room after her death and had had no idea what was in that aluminium tube. But I doubted Constable Crinkles held any erroneous suspicions about her involvement.

"I was wondering where you were this morning," Tiffany told me. "Pamela found me before the parade started and apologized for rejecting my pie. Did you say something to her?"

I shrugged. "I think maybe Pamela's been feeling like her influence is shrinking, and she was taking out her frustration on us."

Tiffany looked thoughtful as we watched our mother-in-law reenacting her turkey triumph, including that lethal turkey swing. Clearly, she wasn't feeling overlooked now that she was the hero of the hour.

"I'll probably feel the same way when Christopher gets married," Tiffany said, folding her arms in front of her. "Fortunately, right now he can't get married until he's thirty, since he's grounded until then."

I laughed. "That's a little harsh."

"He lied to us all."

"He was trying to protect Gobbles."

Tiffany snorted. "And look how that turned out."

I left the constabulary and was pitching in to help the clean-up crew clear out the parade route when Nick came through to pick me up. He, Salty, and Christopher had gone looking for Gobbles just as soon as I'd sent the bird's alleged location, and now the turkey perched on the front seat of the sleigh between Salty and Santa.

I didn't know whether to punch my fist in triumph or weep with relief. I'd never been so happy to see a bird.

"Do you know if Doc's still around?" Salty asked fretfully. "I want him to give Gobbles a physical to make sure he's okay."

Gobbles gobbled.

Nick laughed. "He seems fine to me."

As I climbed into the sleigh, Christopher was grinning ear-to-ear.

"You seem in a good mood," I said.

"I've been reading more about Thanksgiving and its customs—at least the ones in the United States."

I couldn't think of any Thanksgiving customs that would make me smile like an idiot if I were grounded for the next seventeen years. "Which one specifically are you interested in?"

"The pardoning of the turkey."

Chapter 24

"I hereby declare you a free bird."

Nick pronounced his benediction over Gobbles in front of the entire table of guests to make it official. Applause broke out—joy mixed with relief. Holding his twenty-four-pound friend, Salty bowed his appreciation and made his exit. Gobbles was returned to his turkey condo, where he and Grimstock were treated to a Thanksgiving feast of acorns, berries, and worms specially prepared for the occasion.

The Claus family and our many invited guests sat down to a lavish feast of roast turkey—not turducken—cornbread stuffing, cranberry sauce, sweet potato casserole, green beans, and mashed potatoes. Salty was given a double helping of the soy turkey option, which he ate with his bird friends.

The castle dining room had never looked better. Jingles and his staff had worked overtime so that all the crystal, silver, and china gleamed. Pamela's gourd centerpieces really were magnificent: multicolored pumpkins from Salty's greenhouse, which had been hollowed out and had sprays of mums, holly leaves, and other greenery cascading from their centers, with apples, pears, and branches of berries.

Jake and Claire were with us, as were Midge and Amory,

Smudge, Juniper, and Constable Crinkles. Notably missing were Mildred and Olive, but their absence wasn't because they hadn't been invited.

I had urged them to take part in the castle's feast, but Mildred had demurred. "We would just be a reminder of all the bad things that have happened this week," she'd said, adding, "Ollie has to stay at the constabulary, so it seems only right that we celebrate with him. He's been so kind to us, and he and Olive are deep frying the turkey together."

I suspected Mildred didn't want to put on a party face so soon after Elspeth's death and all the revelations surrounding it.

"Next year," I said.

She'd given me a hug. "You and Nick must come have dinner with us sometime. Once we've finished cleaning and fixing up the château, it'll be time to make new memories."

I agreed. Although I wondered if I'd ever be able to eat a meal at Château Mildred without lingering thoughts of ice-rat poison.

Dinner at the castle went off without a hitch. The turkey was tender and roasted to perfection by Felice, who outdid herself with every dish.

For dessert, there were four kinds of pie: apple, pecan, pumpkin, and pineapple chess. We were all offered our choice of pie, including the tantalizing option of a little sampler of all four. A dollop of either classic vanilla or salted caramel ice cream from the Santaland Scoop to go along with the pie was also offered, which no one could resist.

"Next year, you'll all probably be tired of my ice cream," Claire said, when the last scoop was served. "I'll be old hat by then."

I laughed. "Ice cream never gets old."

Contemplating having my two best friends in Christmastown as well as Nick and my Claus family around me gave me the same glowing feeling that Pamela experienced looking at all her family treasures.

Juniper, who was sitting two down from Claire, bent forward to address her. "When will the Scoop open?"

"In about a month, if I can get all the equipment in place."

"You'll need to hire someone," Constable Crinkles said. "My cousin's always looking for a job."

"Send him over," Claire told him. "We'll interview him."

"We?" Lucia looked with some amusement at Jake. "Are you hanging up your trench coat to become a cone wrangler?"

He lifted his hands. "Not me. Claire's already hired a manager."

This was the first I'd heard of it. "Who?"

Claire's gaze darted uncomfortably around the room. "Well . . . it's Butterbean."

The room echoed with the clanging sound of a silver platter dropping. Butterbean scooped it up.

"Butterbean!"

The exclamation came from Jingles, who turned, as we all did, to the red-faced footman standing by the coffee urn.

"I'm sorry, Butterbean," Claire said. "I'd assumed you'd given notice."

"Outrageous!" Jingles tossed his head so that the jingle bell on this cap echoed his emotion. "And after Christopher *begged* us not to fire you for hiding that turkey. And after the castle paid for the damages to Festival Boulevard merchants for your giant renegade turkey balloon."

Lucia nodded. "Doc had to patch up several elves and three reindeer injured in the turkey balloon disaster."

Seeing the confused embarrassment on Butterbean's face, I took pity on him. "He's not an indentured servant, you know." Besides, all the reasons they were giving also made excellent

arguments for *not* having Butterbean stay at the castle. His genius would be someone else's problem now.

Unfortunately, that someone was my friend.

Before more argument could break out over Butterbean's
future employment, Pamela tapped her fork against her wineglass. The table quieted, and Pamela's gaze locked on me.
Dread instinctively kicked in, but the verbal barbs I expected
didn't come.

"I wouldn't want this celebration to end without mentioning how thankful I feel to be with my family and our
friends," she announced.

A murmur of agreement rose, as did glasses.

"Hear, hear," Amory said over the sound of clinking crystal.

Pamela cleared her throat to indicate that she wasn't yet
finished. "Most of all, I'm thankful for Tiffany and April, who
did so much to make this week special. Any Thanksgiving is
perfect when you're with people you love. Friends and family
are the real joy of life."

Close to tears, I raised my glass to her. Not trusting my
voice in that moment, I looked to Nick.

"I couldn't agree more," he said, standing. "What's
more, I—"

Whatever else he was going to say was swallowed by my
piercing scream. In a split second, I'd gone from emotional
wooziness to agonizing pain. I pushed back from the table and
hopped up on my chair. At that moment, a large gray cat tore
out from under the table and dashed out the hallway door.

"Lynxie!" I shrieked, grabbing my leg.

Lucia smiled beatifically toward the door. "Aw—it's his
way of thanking you."

"*Thanking* me?" I squeaked. "He's taken a chunk out of
my calf."

"Lynxie's just thankful that you found Gobbles so he can
have free run of the castle again."

I couldn't help myself. I laughed. Almost deliriously.

For a split second, I saw worried faces looking up at me, until Nick also began to laugh. Soon everyone joined in. Maybe we were all still on a sugar high from those four-pie sampler plates.

Or, as Pamela had said, perhaps there was just no joy like having family and friends all together.

My hunch was that it was a little bit of both.

Recipe

Pineapple Chess Pie

Tiffany's grandmother's pie is a very real recipe that came to me from Myrtle Nowotny of New Braunfels, Texas, who was the mother of one of my dearest friends, Linda. It's a slightly unexpected spin on the traditional Southern chess pie, and I loved it immediately. It's a great choice if you're looking for something slightly different from the traditional apple-pumpkin-pecan triumvirate—or in addition to it. As Nick says, more pie is never a bad thing!

Ingredients
2 cups sugar
½ cup butter, softened
4 eggs
3 tablespoons all-purpose flour
1 8-ounce can of crushed pineapple, well drained
1 teaspoon vanilla extract
1 unbaked 9-inch pie shell

Directions
In an electric mixer, cream butter and sugar. Add eggs and flour, beating well. Stir in pineapple and vanilla. Pour mixture into pastry shell. Bake at 350 degrees F for 45 minutes or until a knife or toothpick inserted halfway between the center and the edge comes out clean. Cool before serving.

Acknowledgments

I have so much to be thankful for as a writer, starting with Annelise Robey and all the wonderful people at the Jane Rotrosen Agency. John Scognamiglio is the most supportive editor a writer could hope for, and his brilliant brainstorming is what got the Mrs. Claus series rolling. I also owe so much thanks to Larissa Ackerman at Kensington for helping spread the word about the series, and to illustrator Olivia Holmes and cover designer Kristine Mills, who created the distinctive, magical look of the covers.

I belong to several writers' organizations, but I'm especially grateful to all my fellow authors at Sisters in Crime—Canada West, and Crime Writers of Canada for their support and camaraderie.

The Mrs. Claus series has been lucky to have received favorable response from many wonderful bloggers and podcasters, including Art Kilmer at *A Cozy Christmas Podcast* (www.cozy christmaspodcast.com), and Mark Carstairs of *Carstairs Considers* (carstairsconsiders.blogspot.com). Thanks also to the incredible Angela Maria Hart of the Cozy Mystery Book Club for being a tireless cozy champion.

Most of all, I'm so grateful to the many readers who have read and embraced my slightly odd, cozy mystery twist on Santaland. Thank you, all!

Visit our website at
KensingtonBooks.com
to sign up for our newsletters, read
more from your favorite authors, see
books by series, view reading group
guides, and more!

BOOK /// CLUB
BETWEEN THE CHAPTERS

Become a Part of Our
Between the Chapters Book Club
Community and Join the Conversation

Betweenthechapters.net